# THE HOOK-UP

# THE HOOK-UP

## PAT TUCKER

**URBAN SOUL**
**URBAN BOOKS**
www.urbanbooks.net

URBAN SOUL is published by

Urban Books
10 Brennan Pl.
Deer Park, NY 11729

ISBN 1-59983-006-X

First Printing: August 2006
10  9  8  7  6  5  4  3  2  1

Printed in the United States of America

This is a work of fiction. Any references or similarities to
actual events, real people, living or dead, or to real locales
are intended to give the novel a sense of reality. Any similar-
ity in other names, characters, places, and incidents is entirely
coincidental.

Submit wholesale orders to: Kensington Publishing Corp,
c/o Penguin Group (USA), Inc. Attention: Order Processing
405 Murray Hill Parkway East Rutherford, NJ 07073-2316
Phone: 1-800-526-0275 Fax: 1-800-227-9604

*My sweet Payton . . . your existence mystifies me,*
*Your smile inspires me,*
*Until you . . .*
*I never knew I could love so much.*

# Acknowledgments

Thank God Almighty first and foremost. I'd like to thank my patient and wonderful mother, Deborah Tucker Bodden, for teaching her daughters, Denise and me, that everything worth having requires hard work. Then, my stepfather, Herbert, for keeping my mom happy, and Lydell R. Wilson, thanks for loving and supporting me in ways I cannot fathom.

I have a list of Sheros I'd like to thank for their constant support in my work and in my life . . . Monica Hodge, Shanell Cavil of Impressions.com, Marilyn Glaizer, LaShawanda Moore, and Lee Lee Baines.

Reshonda Tate Billingsley, my sister in publishing . . . I hope these words attempt to express my appreciation for all of your unwavering support. Thanks for the advice, the nod when something worked, and the "hmmm" when it just didn't click. *I Know I've Been Changed* is a gem!

I'd like to thank my handsome little brother, Irvin Kelvin Seguro, my nephews, nieces, and the rest of my supportive family.

Finally, how do you thank someone who has taken you from dreams to a world surreal? It is not easy, but I will try . . . Roy Glenn, mere words can't begin to express my gratitude for your guidance, encouragement, and constant support . . . Thanks to Carl Weber for your vision and the voice it has given so many talented writers.

# YVETTE

The shit was about to hit the fan. Yvette Madison stood there fuming, trying her best to not act a straight ghetto fool, especially since she was decked out in a sterling-silver-sequined gown and matching Manolo pumps. But oh, hell no. No, this nigga was not standing here at the door, damn near naked, when they were supposed to be at the birthday party an hour ago. But that wasn't what was about to set Yvette off. The five-inch Corvette-red fingernails that had found their way around Trevor's waist were about to send Yvette teetering over the edge.

"Trev, why aren't you ready?" Yvette asked through gritted teeth. By anyone's definition, Trevor Gray was a baller; as a matter of fact, he was larger than life. He had graduated from being a street hustler years ago. He lived large and wasn't tight with his money, so that meant he was popular all the way around. Trevor claimed he was a music producer, but people who knew him well knew he was none other than the notorious Highway-T, one of the biggest moneymakers in South Central Los Angeles.

He operated several drug spots on LA's east side, and according to legend, he even had several in the valley and a few out-of-state spots too. No doubt he was moving major shit and doing big things.

Trevor had agreed weeks ago to attend the fiftieth-birthday celebration for Yvette's mother, Peaches. The family had gone all out and rented a luxury yacht, and they were set to cruise the waters off Marina del Rey.

Yvette was hyped when he said he'd go, because even though they had been kicking it for several months, he rarely made public appearances with her. They were always either holed up in one of his many apartments or at her place. She didn't mind, though, she enjoyed spending time with him. But now, finding him tucked away in his Hollywood apartment as if he had no plans was beyond disappointing. It was downright heartbreaking.

"Tray-Tray, baby, who is it?" The sexy voice attached to the fingernails snapped Yvette out of her daze.

Trevor cleared his throat and tried to move the woman's hand. He stood at the cracked door with nothing draping his six-feet-five-inch frame but a wrinkled T-shirt and boxers. His attempts to move the woman's hand seemed useless. The minute he swatted it away, it would reappear until finally she just squeezed her way in front of him.

It was as if she wanted to make sure Yvette could see she was wearing nothing but a red thong. Her long two-tone weave was the only thing covering her 38 double-Ds. She wore a huge, vindictive grin.

Yvette was just about to convert to her South Central ways when another woman came stomping down the hall of Trevor's apartment building. She wore a look of fury, and the two small children she was dragging behind her looked scared beyond belief.

"Trevor, I'm sick of this shit," the woman announced, totally ignoring Yvette and the other woman. "Here go your kids." She pushed the children forward. They looked to be about two and four years old. "I keep callin' and callin' and you keep bullshittin' me."

Trevor, who looked like he would rather be anywhere else but there, spoke for the first time. "Cynthia, what the fuck are you doin'?" Both of the children started crying. Trevor took their hands. "Why the hell you got my kids out here like this? I told you not to be trying to drop them off on me like this! Why you got these kids out here like this, huh?"

"'Cause you got it twisted if you think I'ma hang around while you keep doin' dirt. I still have love for you, but I ain't 'bout to keep being your motherfuckin' fool," Cynthia snapped. With her hands flaring as she spoke she said, "Besides, I told you when I had these kids, if you think I'm gonna sit around by my damn self while you run the streets with every hoochie you can find, you got another thing coming. I wasn't playing when I said I'd drop 'em off! I meant it, and here they are! You deal with them!"

Cynthia looked like she could be a runway model. She was tall, very thin, and strikingly pretty. She was sporting a long sleek black ponytail and big gold and diamond jewelry. She wore black capri pants and a Polo sweater. Yvette had to do a double take. No, that wasn't *the* Polo sweater Yvette had bought for Trevor's birthday.

"Ah, Trevor, what the fuck is going on here?" Yvette asked, finally finding her voice.

Cynthia stood with her hands on her hips and rolled her eyes at Yvette. "Who the fuck are you?" she asked. Just as Yvette was about to respond, Cynthia put up her hand as if to say, don't even bother. She turned her attention back to Trevor. "I'm about to roll out. I *may* be back to get the kids in the morning."

"So, Cyn, you can't speak?" the other woman finally said.

"LaKesha, you know what, I ain't even got time to be dealing with your stupid ass. Fuck you!" Cynthia flipped her middle finger up at LaKesha.

LaKesha swung her fake hair back. "Trevor just did, and real good if I must say so myself."

Yvette could not believe that Trevor was still messing around with his baby's momma, and another woman too. She felt like a fool. She shook her head trying to wean off the hot tears that stung her eyes. She thought her time with Trevor meant something to him, but it was obvious he was only going through the motions.

It was just last night that *she* was wrapped up tightly in his arms. At that moment, when they shared Chinese takeout and Hypnotic, he gazed deeply into her eyes and said, "Girl, you 'bout to make a nigga fall in love."

Yvette had been so thrilled, she didn't know what to say. The first thing she wanted to do was ask him to repeat himself, but she knew that would've been tacky. So she looked at him then and, in the sexiest voice she could muster, cooed, "Baby, I'm already in love."

After that, he took her into his arms and they lay there basking in the afterglow of some wonderful sex. For the first time in their relationship, she had finally felt like she was making real progress with Trevor. She was finally able to think about a future, a serious future with him.

The more Yvette thought about all of the lies and false promises he had made, the more disgusted she became. She was beyond brokenhearted, here she thought she had finally found her knight in shining armor, and come to find out, to him, she was just another piece of ass.

"I thought you wasn't kicking it with LaKesha no more, Trevor," Cynthia huffed.

"Yo, I never told you that," Trevor said.

Trevor's voice brought Yvette back to the current drama.

"It don't matter whether he did or not, Cynthia. You see who's here and who's draggin' her kids all over town trying to drop them off, right?" LaKesha stated. A smirk found its way back to her face. "Besides, are you even sure both those kids are Tee's?" she taunted Cynthia.

"You dumb bitch. You ain't even got your kids. Remember, they were taken away, so I don't even wanna hear shit from you!" Cynthia hollered back at LaKesha.

"I'm just saying what everybody's thinking—them kids don't even look like Tee," LaKesha said innocently.

"Why you trippin', LaKesha? That's so uncalled for. It ain't no reason for you to be trying to clown out here," Trevor warned.

Cynthia looked at Trevor. "So that's what's up?" she asked, infuriated.

Trevor never even looked at Yvette, who stood watching the situation unfold. She wasn't sure what to do. She had already bragged to her entire family that she was bringing Highway-T to the party, and now she had to show up alone. Not only that, but he had been lying all along about still kicking it with his babies' crazy momma.

"So, Trevor, you still screwin' this trick? Even after what we talked about? Why you playin' with my emotions?" Cynthia snarled.

"Don't be such a drama queen, Cynthia," LaKesha said. "Everybody knows how you keep jockin' Trev after he told you it was over."

"All you bitches 'bout to get on my nerves!" Trevor screamed. All three of them turned to stare at Trevor. He pushed his kids into the apartment, then turned and pushed a naked LaKesha completely out. "All you get the fuck out!" He slammed and locked the door.

Yvette was absolutely stunned. She felt the mascara running down her cheeks, but she didn't even care. Cynthia and LaKesha had started banging and kicking on Trevor's door. But Yvette just wanted to get away from the madness. She made her way down the hall to the elevator; she was thoroughly outdone, and disgusted. Once downstairs, she used her cell phone to call a cab. She was so glad she had her cousin Debbie drop her off instead of waiting.

It was one thing to be embarrassed in front of Trevor and his two hos, but it would've been a different story with her family there. Still, she wondered why she and Trevor weren't on their way to the Marina. She couldn't understand how he could've been seeing two other females while he was seeing her.

Yvette was confused and distraught about why she wasn't good enough, despite how hard she had tried. It made no sense that after being in four so-called serious relationships in less than two years, she was no closer to having a man of her own than the day she had started dating.

# CARMEN

Carmen had no love for Compton, and she damn sure wasn't shy about letting her feelings be known. When she agreed to tag along with Gina to a baby shower, in Compton she figured they'd go there, get their eat on, and run up outta there as soon as her man, Don-Juan, called on her chirp phone.

Carmen suspected that Gina was probably just hoping they could chill without any drama. Carmen also knew most people thought she was stuck on herself, but she didn't see anything wrong with knowing just how fine she really was and never letting those around her forget it.

Carmen didn't need anybody to tell her she was cute. She wasn't a natural beauty like Gina, but she kept her honey-colored skin clear and blemish-free. People used to say they looked like each other, with Gina being a few shades darker. They were thick girls with voluptuous figures. While Carmen had to pile on the foundation, eye make-up, and lip gloss, Gina used minimal make-up to enhance her well-defined features.

"So who's her baby's daddy again?" Carmen asked as Gina guided her Range Rover next to the curb.

"Girl, I don't know, some banger from the jungle."

"What?" Carmen cried. "Gangbangers? Girl, that's so tired. You know damn well I ain't down with no bangers, always shooting each other up over some colors and shit. What kind of people you kicking it with?" Carmen checked her lip gloss again. "Besides, I can't stand being around females who ain't gon' do nothing but get jealous of me. You know that wherever there are bangers, there are those thuggish-looking wannabe gangster girls, and you know those kind hate me the most." Carmen puckered her lips and kissed at her reflection in the mirror.

Gina rolled her eyes and flipped down her visor mirror. She quickly touched up her own make-up, then looked at Carmen. "You ready or what?"

Carmen looked toward the small crowd that had gathered near the yard where the baby shower was being held. The little house was no bigger than Carmen's apartment, and she wondered if all of the people would fit comfortably in such cramped quarters. After thinking about being packed into some sleazy little shack of a house with a bunch of ghetto girls, she frowned and asked, "Emp, look what that one is wearing. She didn't know she was coming to a shower today?" As they made their way across the street, Carmen huffed. "How long we gotta stay?"

Gina sucked her teeth. "Why you tripping? I mean, you said you didn't have nothing to do this evening. Besides, I want you to peep these Compton broads anyway."

"See, that's why I don't like venturing out too far. It is quite obvious that these chicks around here come from the projects. You know I gotta be careful who I'm seen with." Carmen noticed Gina's sigh. She knew Gina probably felt like she wouldn't be able to really enjoy herself with Carmen at Wanda's shower. They hadn't even gotten out of the truck and Carmen could sense that Gina already regretted bringing her along. Carmen would be the first to admit she had judged the house all wrong from the outside. Once she stepped onto the plush royal-blue carpet and looked around at the custom-made, top-of-the-line Italian leather furniture and the wall-to-ceiling entertainment system that housed a large flat-screen TV, she couldn't do anything but raise a carefully arched eyebrow.

Nearly an hour after they arrived, Gina and Carmen were getting ready for the stripper. It was one of the main reasons Carmen had suddenly agreed to go to the shower. She had always been down for watching a man shake his ass. Chocolate Crème was known for his baby-smooth skin, his extra-long tongue, his six-pack, and his rock-hard ass.

When the music started blasting, even pregnant-ass Wanda was on the floor shaking her moneymaker. Soon the music faded, and his deep baritone rang through the speakers.

"Ladies, do you know why they call me Chocolate Crème?" he asked over cheering voices.

"Tell us!" someone shouted.

"'Cause I'm dark and sweet like chocolate." He shook his tight ass and let his chest muscles dance up and down. "And I make the ladies . . . creeeme." The music started back up to thunderous laughter and cheers.

"Ooooh weeee, it's getting hot in heerre!" someone yelled.

Carmen had never been to a baby shower where they had a stripper. The Alizé was flowing, and the seafood platters were replenished before the last shrimp or piece of crabmeat vanished. This baby shower was tha bomb! With her fourth glass of Alizé, Carmen looked over at Gina and was glad she had come.

"This is the shit for real!" Carmen cried. "I'm especially digging Mister Chocolate."

Chocolate Crème started walking around the room. Every female in there was eager to see who he was about to pick. With the music still playing, he approached each woman, staring deeply into her eyes, but to the dismay of many, he kept moving. Suddenly he stopped and pulled someone from the crowd.

"Who's she?" Carmen leaned over and asked Gina.

Gina sighed before saying, "Sha-Sha. She's Wanda's cousin."

As Chocolate Crème led Sha-Sha out to the middle of the living room floor, the crowd broke into a chant.

"Go Sha-Sha, go Sha-Sha, it's yo birthday . . ." they sang.

Once in the middle of the floor, the girl stood with her hands cupping her opened mouth. Everybody knew what was coming up next. It was part of Chocolate's signature performance. But to watch it was like imagining themselves on center stage.

Sha-Sha could hardly stand still, and her girlfriends were going berserk. When Chocolate Crème pulled off Sha-Sha's denim throwback miniskirt and tank top, one girl damn near passed out. He produced a blindfold and draped it around Sha-Sha's eyes. The crowd went wild. Soon he started guiding her body to the floor. It was as if Sha-Sha just allowed him to take over. Once she was spread out like an eagle on her back, he hovered over her and started at the tip of her head.

With his infamous tongue, he began a moist trail from her forehead down to her cheek, her neck, then stopped at her lace bra cups. Carmen noticed Sha-Sha's body shaking beneath his touch.

"Oh, my God!" someone screamed.

"Please take me, Crème. Take me!" another woman cried.

He fingered Sha-Sha's nipples through the flimsy material and Sha-Sha squealed, moving her legs up and down in a rapid manner on the floor.

With his free hand he pulled out a can of whipped cream and held it as if he was showing it to the crowd. Once he got their approval, he moved to the lower part of her body and began shaking the can. When she heard him shaking the can, Sha-Sha stopped moving. She lay there motionless with a huge grin plastered across her face.

When Chocolate Crème sprayed the whipped cream on top of her bra and that triangle spot on her panties, the women started fighting for a front-row spot. He got up and looked back down at his masterpiece. Before the crowd knew what was coming, he dove into his infamous centipede-like move and angled his head between Sha-Sha's legs. But he used his massive tongue to swipe the mountain of whipped cream up in one smooth move.

Before the crowd could settle back down, he moved Sha-Sha's panties to one side and slopped up the wetness.

Sha-Sha squealed, clawing at his head, her girlfriends cheered and high-fived each other, and Carmen sat back in shock.

At the end of Chocolate Crème's performance, his sidekick passed out colored business cards with the stripper's picture and pager number on it. Carmen had so much fun she didn't want the shower to end. Although Wanda and her girls weren't the clique Carmen liked to associate with, she had to admit they damn sure knew how to throw a party.

"You having a good time?" Gina asked.

"Guurrrl. Chocolate Crème was off the chain! We gotta call him for a private show real quick like," Carmen said, draining her glass. "Then all this damn

Alizé, seafood—who did you say is her baby's daddy? They must've spent a grip on this shower." Carmen looked around the room. Just outside the large picture window, a familiar-looking Navigator caught her eye as it pulled up across the street. Her heart started racing.

"Gina, I need to bounce. Don-Juan's here. But wait, he didn't know I was gonna be here in Compton."

Carmen ignored the look of confusion on Gina's face. She wasn't the least bit tipsy, even though she had been throwing back glasses of Alizé like it was water since they hit the front door.

"Don-Juan?" Gina looked toward the window Carmen was gazing out of. "It must just be a truck like his."

"Oh, shit . . . Wanda, your baby's daddy is here!" a girl yelled.

"His sorry ass. You know this is his eighth child, right?" an older woman whispered to her friend.

*Eighth child, dayyum. That's foul.* Carmen might've been feeling kind of nice from the Alizé, but the comment once again reminded her of why she couldn't stand Compton girls—because they did stupid shit like that. Who in their right mind would have a baby for a fool who already had seven other children?

"C'mon, let's move this party outside," another woman hollered. The drunken bash spilled out to the front yard. Carmen was slow to move because she wanted a refill of her drink and a bit more crabmeat and shrimp.

As she walked out of the house, Gina suddenly came rushing at her, nearly pushing her back toward the door.

"Wwww-hat?"

"Um, I think we should leave. I don't want you to get fired up out here," Gina said nervously.

"I'm feeling real nice right about now. What the hell would I get mad about?"

Gina looked across the street to the group of men walking away from the Navigator. They were coming toward Wanda's yard. When Carmen followed her stare, she still didn't make the connection until she saw for certain that it was Don-Juan making his way up to the yard.

"Ah, I don't think you understand. That's Wanda's baby's daddy."

"Who?" Carmen struggled to look over Gina's shoulder.

When she followed Gina's stare to Don-Juan, her stomach churned. She didn't want to believe he was there. *I'm through with this nigga and this shit for sure. I need my own fuckin' man. There's gotta be a better way.* Carmen was disappointed, but more importantly, she felt defeated. Don-Juan had been playing her all along.

"Wait, are you trying to tell me that Don is supposed to be Wanda's baby's daddy? I mean, Gina, please, look at me and look at her," Carmen said. "Why would he even want to fuck around with a hood rat like that when he could have me?" Carmen didn't wait for an answer. "Well, I'm about to get to the bottom of this shit right here and now!" Carmen stood with her arms crossed at her chest, waiting to confront Don-Juan's cheating ass. But before he could make it across the street, things started moving like someone pushed a fast-forward button.

A little dirty bucket careened around the corner with its tires peeling and kicking up smoke. The noise pulled everyone's attention toward the street, where the car slowed; a body lunged out of the passenger's window and sprayed a blanket of bullets toward the yard.

# VICKI

Everything about thugs turned Vicki Michaels the fuck on. She had always had a weakness for rough-necks, and she loved everything about them, especially the way they typically walked with some kind of sexy swagger 'cause they were usually hung. The slang they used when they talked: "Yo, baby girl," "Whassup, shorty," "Lemme holla at'chu . . ." Just thinking about the way words rolled off of Peanut's tongue made her hot.

Peanut was the last thug she kicked it with. It was all good until the crazy-ass mother of his baby went all ballistic on Vicki and came hunting her down with a pistol. It didn't take long for Vicki to realize Peanut wasn't worth half the trouble she had encountered with the crazy-ass woman. And when he refused to claim her in front of the woman, Vicki decided it was best if she moved on.

Still, that experience, as wild and crazy as it was, did very little to change her mind about what kind of man she wanted. She loved thugs, and she wasn't ashamed to admit it. Her plans first included finding a baller, but she soon realized most ballers had too much baggage and other women vying for their money and attention. So she figured she'd regroup and get herself exactly what she wanted.

It had been nearly two years since she began her search; unfortunately, she had yet to seriously come up with the type of men she preferred. After all that time, she was left feeling like if she ran into another wannabe baller, she'd die. But true to her passion, Vicki was more than a little excited about her new foolproof plan for landing Mr. Right.

She unlocked the door to her apartment in Carson and pulled the flyer out of her bag when she stepped inside. Vicki could hardly believe the ad that was sure to change her life.

"Pamela, are you home?" Vicki waited for a response from her roommate. "Pam?" she shouted again as she kicked off her shoes and looked around the living room.

When she didn't hear anything, she assumed she was alone. Vicki didn't want to seem desperate to Pam, so, since she was alone, she figured she'd do some research of her own. She turned on her favorite Busta Rhymes CD and fired up the computer she and Pam shared.

Vicki went to the Web sites she had frequented for years. She typed "jailbirds.com" and waited for the site to spring to life. She pointed her curser to the inmate ads and started reading.

Back when she first began surfing the Web for inmates, it was all a big rush. Every day was like a serious cliff-hanger. Was he guilty? Was he falsely accused? Would he call? Albeit collect, she still looked forward to those nightly phone calls. Everything about her day was a source of interest for him; it seemed he was never bored with the little tidbits she had to share. And some of those phone calls could get pretty hot. She'd get all worked up, then be just as eager for the next day so she could experience it all over again.

Then there was the excitement around thoughts of his life in prison. Was there a fight? Maybe a riot? Would he be on lockdown? It was a roller-coaster ride that kept her pulse pumping and her coochie wet.

Vicki had run into some problems with her fetish, but none serious enough to change her mind. As she waited for the ad she had just selected to open, she thought back to some of the more eventful connections she had made. It all started when she read two inmate e-mails. One was from Calvin Campbell and the other from Raymond Roberts. She still remembered exactly what their ads looked like.

### Calvin Campbell

*BIRTH DATE: September 20, 1972*
*RELEASE DATE: December 7, 2005*
*WANTS TO WRITE TO: Women (straight, bisexual)*
*SEEKS: Friendship*

*BadBoy with a Heart of Gold*

*While sitting here in this man-made hell, dreaming of nature's beauty, I decided to compose this ad in an attempt to catch the eyes of a compassionate woman who will bring life and joy to this lonely soul of mine. So, with this thought in mind, let me start by saying my name is Calvin. I'm 32 years old, 5'10", 180 lbs (bedroom physique . . . built to tease and please). I'm a professional photographer and aspiring filmmaker from Hollywood, California. My passions are independent films, music, and making love.*

*Those that know me might say a lot of shit . . . but the truth be told, I'm a cool guy, a little mischievous but overall a good person.*

*I'm looking for a cool lady friend to correspond with; share ideas, opinions, curiosity, and secrets.*

*Calvin Campbell*
*#CJ03419*
*High Desert State Prison*
*PO Box 2090 E5 134U*
*Susanville, CA 96127*

Then there was the e-mail from Raymond. Vicki felt as if he was reaching out specifically to her:

*BIRTH DATE: March 2, 1969*
*RELEASE DATE: Life*
*WANTS TO WRITE TO: Anyone*
*SEEKS: Correspondence, Friendship, Possible Romance*

*Lonely prisoner seeks correspondence from a lonely but free heart. I am a 6'5", 240 lb, light-complected, muscular black man. I made some mistakes and bad choices that I'm being held accountable for.*
    *You are one with unique insights, which is evident by your willingness to correspond with a man that many in society would feel is unworthy of their companionship, just by virtue of his social status. Stay the course; in time you'll find that this decision has led to a most fulfilling facet of your life. And you'll discover the decent and considerate man that I am.*

*Although physically incarcerated, I am quite lib-
erated and nonjudgmental in thought. I would
love to read and write about any and all that interests you. Mutual openness and honesty is my
only request.*

Raymond Roberts
#R-13415
PO Box 5204
Coalinga, CA 93210
P.V.S.R. A-2-124-M

While Vicki was intrigued by both e-mails, something about Raymond's words touched her. The fact
that he wasn't afraid to admit his mistakes, and that he
was paying for them, just made him even more irre-
sistible. So their romance began.

Two months into their correspondence, he wrote a
letter asking for twenty dollars. Along with the care
package she sent, Vicki included the information indicating she had put money on his books. Shortly there-
after, she began sending money on a regular basis. Vicki
didn't mind helping; besides, she thought, he was helping her in many ways.

She and Raymond would still be friends had it not
been for a major slipup on his part. Vicki remembered
it like it was yesterday. The day Raymond broke her
heart with the stroke of his pen. She received his letter
and had settled in to read it. The thickness of the envelope made her even more excited. It was no surprise
that over time, their relationship had grown, so natu-
rally there would be more to write about.

But unlike many times before, when Vicki opened
this particular letter, she nearly lost it. There, jammed
inside the thick envelope, was a total of seven pages of
paper, each with words on both sides. There were

pages addressed to Kim, Samantha, Tamela, Keisha, Tyra, Lauren, and herself. Soon she realized Raymond had been writing letters to six other women at the same time!

When she closely examined the letters, she saw that each was identical. Each letter began with *Dearest . . .* It went on to say, *I hope this letter finds you in great health and even better spirits*. He asked questions about their days, thanked the writer for recent care packages, and ended by asking for two hundred dollars! Each letter closed with *Lovingly, Raymond*.

Vicki quickly ended her correspondence with Raymond and moved on. But she told herself it would take more than one unscrupulous inmate to deter this thug lover. She knew she was on to something and wasn't about to give up on her newfound treasure.

That's why she was so hyped about the flyer she had found. It had information about a new company called The Hook-Up. The flyer's first lines caught her attention and held her. *Think all the good men are married, gay, or in jail? Well, you're not alone . . . bad things happen to good people.* It went on. And since Vicki agreed, she held on to the flyer. It explained that there was an abundance of eligible men behind bars who were eagerly waiting to make a love connection. The flyer said they only dealt with soon-to-be released convicts, and all of the inmates went through a rigorous screening process. She was looking forward to talking to this Frankie person. Vicki had a strong feeling Frankie held the key to her future with the man of her dreams.

# FRANKIE & ERICA

Erica Johnson never thought looking at a vehicle could make her cum. But the tingling sensation between her thighs confirmed that that was exactly what was about to happen as she stared at LadyRae's tight-ass Benz. As she stood near the phone booth Erica noticed the custom Gucci interior and the mahogany Mirage four-spoke steering wheel. Just thinking about the car and all its expensive features had her juices flowing. The steering wheel alone started at five hundred dollars. Oh, how she wanted a ride like that, and the things she wouldn't mind doing to get one.

Erica and Frankie were at the nail shop on Vermont and Martin Luther King Jr. Boulevards. The parking lot was full, and the Benz was parked at an angle, taking up three spaces. But this was where they got their very first up-close-and-personal look at the legendary whip. They had heard about it but hadn't actually laid eyes on the ride that had been the talk of the Eastside and everywhere in between. As usual, the urban legend had done the car no justice.

"Daayum, look at that whip, girl. It's an S500 too. You know that ride cost about eighty Gs, right? Now you know; we need to be down with LadyRae and her crew," Erica remarked.

Although Erica was laughing out loud when she said it, Frankie had a feeling Erica was all too serious and was just throwing the idea out there to see if Frankie would be down. Frankie knew Erica was hurting for money; hell, she was, too, but she was hoping her half sister could hang in there without doing anything drastic. And working for LadyRae would be a drastic, desperate, and deadly move.

LadyRae was serious about her money, and she did some ruthless things when she felt her money was being fucked with, fucked off, or fucked over.

"I already told you, Erica, we can do our own thing," Frankie warned.

"You keep saying that Frankie, but the bills keep stacking up, and we ain't got no cash coming in," Erica retorted.

Before going into the already packed Man-trap nail salon, Erica walked a few doors down to the dollar store just so she could see the Benz up close. It was tricked out, a 2004 model painted in a bright metallic gold with dark gold specks shining throughout. It was sitting on dubs with spinners and daring anything to try and pull up within three feet of it. Everybody knew it was LadyRae's ride, and everybody knew not to come too close. Next to her money and her girls, that ride was more important than the many lives LadyRae came in contact with.

"C'mon, Erica, snap out of it, bitch! You droolin' all over yourself." Frankie tugged at Erica's arm, but the car mesmerized her. "You just lost ten cool points for that one," Frankie joked.

Erica now remembered the day a little more than six

months ago; LadyRae had stepped to them about being a part of her crew. It happened at this exact nail shop. LadyRae was always smooth, thanks to Sunshine, the neighborhood booster. LadyRae's curvy size 14 figure stayed draped in the finest name-brand clothes. She blinged from her ears to her neck, fingers, and even her toes.

She dripped money everywhere she went. Her skin was the color of caramel, and her hair was a light sandy brown. Kids would run up to her in the streets and would damn near chase her car wherever she showed up.

She was known for being the most feared female hustler, and she could rival any big-time drug dealer on the streets of LA. Business was good for LadyRae. Not only was she moving major heroin, but she had some prime locations and was making money hand over fist.

Rumor had it she saved up money she made on the streets in her early days to jump-start her business. Things had taken off, leaving her living lovely with tons of money to go around. Rumor also had it that LadyRae was so large because she had a strong stable of fierce females working for her. LadyRae never got her hands dirty; whatever had to be done was handled by her all-female crew. Every girl she hired had to go through an intense initiation to prove she'd be down for whatever. Word on the street was that LadyRae's initiation involved personally licking each of her hand-picked street soldiers. While Erica didn't know if that was true, Frankie had always said it was best they never had to find out.

All Erica knew was LadyRae's girls always had their shine on blast, were treated well, and never had to worry about cash. It was all champagne wishes and caviar dreams come true for LadyRae's squad.

It was Frankie who convinced Erica they didn't need

to work *for* LadyRae because they could go into business for themselves. Frankie also told Erica to give her six months and she'd come up with a plan to help save her grandmother's house and put them both on easy street. It was a house they shared with three of Erica's uncles, one of whom had a wife and four kids to boot. To say the house was cramped was an understatement.

Well, that six-month deadline had come and gone, and the taxes on her grandmother's house were still overdue and unpaid, and Frankie and Erica were still driving around in the old beat-up '95 Honda Accord that was in desperate need of a tune-up and a new muffler. Erica had decided that she'd borrow the money from LadyRae if she had to. She had done it before and would do it again if push came to shove. But she wanted to at least give Frankie a chance to work her hustle.

As usual, when they walked into the shop, the buzz was all about LadyRae. She was having her feet done in one of the massaging chairs. In addition to the person working on her feet, two technicians were working on her nails, one for each hand. Her right hand sported three-inch fingernails and enough gold and diamond jewelry to buy Erica's grandmother's house two times over.

"Oooh, girl, is that real money they cutting up for LadyRae's nails?" Erica hollered.

Frankie shrugged like she wasn't fazed by the fact that the workers were carefully cutting up hundred-dollar bills to glue onto the tips of LadyRae's incredibly long fingernails.

Against Frankie's protest, Erica stepped in closer to get a better look.

"Whassup?" LadyRae asked as she eyed Erica up and down. She took in Erica's thin but curvy frame. Erica and Frankie had similar shapes, but Erica was prettier. Her almond-shaped eyes and slender nose made her face real inviting. She and Frankie both had dimples, but Erica's were deep. Frankie, although lighter than Erica, had a harder look about her.

Erica wore her shoulder-length hair bone straight; Frankie always kept hers pulled back in a tight ponytail that swayed down her back with each step she took.

"Just peepin' your nails. Damn, that's tight!" Erica squealed.

LadyRae smiled and looked over at Frankie. "Say, Frankie, what's poppin'?" she asked.

"Waiting on a fill," Frankie replied. She scowled when she looked around the crowded nail shop. She knew it would be hours before she and Erica would get some help. It was always like that when LadyRae came to the shop. The workers dropped everything and everyone to wait on LadyRae and her girls hand and foot. And she couldn't really blame them. If LadyRae was cutting up hundred-dollar bills, she could just imagine what the tips were like. And needless to say, the rest of the customers knew not to utter a word of complaint.

"You said you and your girl didn't want to roll with my crew 'cause you had something brewin', but I ain't seen nothing jump off yet. Whassup? You need some seed money?" LadyRae asked.

"Nah, we straight. You know how it is. It takes time to get things off the ground, but I'm still working it out," Frankie said.

"Okay, then, it's all good. Ping, won't you hook my girls up so they don't have to wait?" LadyRae said to the Vietnamese lady working on her left hand.

"Yes, for you, LadyRae, yes, right away." The woman ushered Frankie over to her worktable, then shouted orders in her native language to another woman. That woman escorted Erica to her table and started working on refilling her sculptured nails.

"Can I get a whoop-whoop? What's crackin', y'all,

what's crackin'? I got the outfits for summer fest. Size two on up to twenty-two. You name it, I got it!" Frankie could hear Sunshine before she could see her.

Sunshine was darker than midnight but got her nickname from her smile, which lit up a room. She often came around the hair and nail shops peddling her stolen wares. And taking orders, of course.

"LadyRae, I got that suede halter-top dress you ordered last week," she said, looking toward the back of the shop. "And, Erica, girl, I been looking for you. That Calvin Klein slip dress you wanted came in, too, the size four you needed." Sunshine walked through the nail shop running her mouth and discussing orders with her customers. She had everything from the latest bootleg movies to some of the best designer clothes available in some of the Beverly Center's most expensive stores. Most of the best-dressed women in south central Los Angeles owed their fashion sense to Sunshine, who kept them all laced in the latest trends.

Frankie's head snapped toward Erica, who was now standing next to Sunshine and going through her large plastic bin full of designer knockoff purses.

"Erica, come here!" she yelled.

At first Erica didn't move. She wanted several of the purses she saw in the bin, but she also knew Frankie would have something to say about it.

By the time they left the nail salon, Erica was toting two Prada bags and had gotten her nails, toes, and eyebrows done, all thanks to LadyRae. When Frankie had insisted she had the money to pay for their services, LadyRae looked insulted and told her she should learn how to accept a gift.

It wasn't the accepting part Frankie had issues with; it was what LadyRae might want in return for her act of kindness.

After leaving the nail shop, they headed up Martin

Luther King Jr. Boulevard to Crenshaw for dinner at M and M's Soul Food Restaurant.

"So, Frankie, what's up with this business plan?" Erica said over her piping-hot oxtails. "You ain't said nothing about it lately, and I gotta admit, I'm getting tired of struggling to make ends meet."

Frankie knew where this conversation was going. She hated when they had the misfortune of running into LadyRae. The encounters usually left Erica feeling broke, desperate for more money, and it was Frankie's mission to change that. And Frankie had a plan to do just that. She was just waiting on a call from her jail-guard cousin, Bobbi Maxwell, to put that plan into action.

Three years earlier, Frankie and Erica had made a pact. They would take turns coming up with ideas on how to get rich and get out of the hood. If they couldn't get out, they'd live real good, because both decided being "hood rich" was better than being ghetto poor.

But each time they executed a plan, their ideas had turned into more trouble than they were worth. Besides nearly going to prison, dodging LadyRae after numerous loans, and sweating the next up-and-coming baller, they developed only an even stronger desire to get rich or die trying.

Their last get-rich scheme had been Erica's idea, and it nearly got them killed. Thinking about it, Frankie didn't know what possessed her to go along with Erica and her crazy-ass idea, but at the time, they were short on funds and living in fear of the sheriff showing up to lock them out of the house.

"So if you do your part and I do mine, we get a cut of whatever they bring in," Erica had said.

Frankie shook her head in disbelief. "So lemme get this straight. All we have to do is roll with these nuccas and drop the four-one-one, then get paid? That shit seems too easy to me."

"Trust me, Frankie, it'll work," Erica pleaded. "Look at us. You think there's a motherfucka out there who wouldn't want a taste?"

"Damn, Erica, we might as well go on the stroll if we plan to do that. I don't get it. How do we find these so-called hot boys anyway?"

"Frankie, trust someone for once in your life. Jerome got it all worked out. All we gotta do is look sexy."

Erica had met Jerome, a small-time drug dealer and hustler, one day nearly a year before when she walked out of the nail shop alone. While Frankie thought they were done with Jerome after the stickup game, Erica kept him on the side for future use.

Two weeks into the game, Jerome gave them all the information they needed for the targets. It was a double date with two dudes from the Valley.

Frankie and Erica went out with them three times. On the third date, their targets, Gee-Mack and Big Man, rented posh suites at the Radisson Hotel in San Bernardino and had them filled with exotic wines and expensive liquor. A couple of hours into the party, there was a knock at the door.

"Big! Yo, son, you order room service?" Gee-Mack asked.

Before Big could answer, the door was unlocked from the outside, and four masked gunmen bum-rushed the room.

"Get the fuck down, and shut the fuck up!"

Frankie was so nervous she stood longer than they liked, only to have a sawed-off shotgun pointed at her chest. Her heart nearly stopped as she felt her body being shoved to the floor. She was livid.

When it was all said and done, Frankie and Erica got

five grand each for their work. Frankie wondered just how much Jerome and his squad got, but she wasn't about to ask. She never asked what happened to the ballers they had set up.

Shortly after that, she told Erica they needed a better hustle. They had yet to find one, but Frankie knew she couldn't go back to having anybody set up. All she thought about were those fools coming back for revenge once they put two and two together.

As Erica stood in front of her having a natural fit about still being broke, Frankie remembered the day she vowed to her mother, Samantha, that she'd always look out for her younger sister.

Their mother had died of AIDS. But before she died, on her deathbed she used her last breath to beg Frankie to look after Erica. Erica was nineteen years old, but sometimes her sister acted like she had the mentality of a ten-year-old. She had been born a crack baby, and Frankie felt like she often played the dumb role even though she was far from it. Frankie kept an eye on Erica because sometimes her passion for money was so fierce, she often didn't take time to think about the consequences of her actions, especially if she saw dollar signs.

Their mother, Samantha, had Frankie when she was thirteen. She had spent her entire life as a small-time hustler's girlfriend. She moved from one man to the next, looking for that big baller but never found him. Frankie never called Samantha Mom, Mama, or anything close. She called Samantha by her first name. She told Frankie it was best that way; since she had her so young, she didn't feel like being bogged down and feeling all old by being called somebody's mama.

They had rough times. Frankie remembered having

to sleep in the park many a nights because Samantha fucked up and shot up or snorted what little money they had at any given time. Frankie had been with Samantha until she was eight years old. One day they went to visit a woman Samantha referred to as her auntie in Riverside.

When Frankie woke up the next day, Samantha was gone. She didn't see her mother for the next ten years. On her eighteenth birthday, Frankie left to find Samantha. By then, Samantha's HIV had turned into full-blown AIDS. Erica was thirteen when she met her older sister for the first time.

Frankie and Erica had different fathers. Frankie's father, who was much older than Samantha, split the moment Samantha came up pregnant. While Erica's father didn't hang around, his family did try to step up to the plate.

Erica's father was one of the biggest drug dealers back in the day, and while he hung around longer than Frankie's father, he still had other women all over the city. Most of those women he had turned on to drugs, just as he had done with Samantha.

When their mother died, Erica's ailing grandmother on her father's side gave them a place to stay. But make no mistake, it had always been Frankie's job to look after Erica; other people in the house, some her relatives, couldn't care less. Many of them lived for the day and for themselves; they were all like strangers in a boardinghouse. When Erica's grandmother, who merely tolerated Frankie, died in her sleep, they were really on their own. Frankie vowed to pay off the taxes because no one was shy about discussing how Samantha had taken out a loan against the house and failed to pay it back. That forced Erica's grandmother to scrape and struggle in order to save the house. It was a debt Frankie felt hung over them so much that Erica's other family members only spoke when they absolutely had to. No one believed they'd pay it off, but Frankie was determined, and she knew the moment she did, she and Erica were out of there so the others could fend for themselves.

The call from Frankie's cousin Bobbi came a week after her last conversation with Erica. Frankie was relieved when she saw Bobbi's name pop up on the caller ID. She got up and closed the door to her room.

"Bobbi, what's up? Damn, I'm glad to hear from you. So what about my idea—you think we can make it happen? 'Cause I need some change real fast like."

"This may be just the shit to put us over the top. Not only can we make it happen, but I already have a list of roughnecks itching to make a connection. I think this is your best idea so far. I mean, the stripping thing didn't work out, neither did copying movies or CDs, but I think we may really be on to something here," Bobbi said.

Frankie was glad Bobbi ended her tirade. She was sick and tired of having her failures thrown back up in her face.

"Okay, cool. Well, I've already got a couple of people who are interested on my end. I wasn't sure what to charge them at first, but at least one is willing to pay five hundred."

"Whoa, hold up!" Bobbi giggled. "I know damn well you ain't trying to tell me you got somebody who is willing to pay five hundred dollars for the possibility of some dick they can't even get their hands on right away."

"Girl, do I?" Frankie retorted. "But trust me, it's gonna be a lot of work. 'Cause once you give me your list, I have to find information about them and try to hook this up differently than those sites already out there. Have you had a chance to look at the ones I told you about?"

"Yes, and I can't believe some of the stuff those people write. I can't believe we didn't think of this a long time ago."

Before Frankie could say another word, her door flew open and Erica came in.

"Frankie, are we going to that party tonight?"

"Hold up," Frankie said, trying to end her conversation with Bobbi.

"Bobbi, I need to call you back. When do you go back to work?"

"I'm on four days off now. So I think we need to hook up. You want to come to me? Or I could come out there to you."

"Yeah, let me holla back at you on that." Frankie hung up the phone and turned to Erica. "I hope you're ready to get rich."

Erica's eyes lit up, her face broke into a huge grin, and she threw her slender arms around Frankie's neck. Erica stepped back.

"Don't even come at me like that unless you serious, Frankie. Are you serious?"

Frankie nodded. "As a motherfuckin' heart attack!" she yelled.

"Okay, okay, so whassup? What do we have to do? How much are we talking here?"

"Girl, peep this. You know how we always talking about how a good man is so hard to find?"

"Yeah, 'cause the good ones are all either married, gay, or in jail," Erica said jokingly.

"Well, that's our hustle," Frankie said.

Erica's smile faded. "What's our hustle?"

"We are now in the business of helping these horny bitches find their fix: men, real men. Most of these nuccas ain't had sex in years. Hard bodies with all that pent-up sexual frustration just waiting to be released."

"What the fuck? How the hell are we gonna find men for somebody else when we ain't got none our damn selves?" Erica asked with a perplexed look on her face.

"Erica, that's what I'm trying to explain to you. I know of a place with a shitload of single, hard-bodied thugs just waiting for the right hookup."

"Shiiit, how can I be down?" Erica snickered. "You know how much I love me a thug. Why you been holdin' out?" She started licking her lips.

"Well," Frankie began, "they in prison."

"What?" The excitement started draining from Erica's voice. "Prison? As in the pen? Lockdown?" Frankie could tell Erica wasn't sure if she was serious. Then Erica asked, "Are we so desperate that we now have to find men in the pen?"

"Think of all the desperate broads you know, fed up with man-sharing, baby-momma drama, and the endless games. Now combine that with all the desperate broads I know. Now, *we* gonna offer them the ultimate hookup. Whatever they looking for, I'm sure we can find him behind bars." Frankie's smile resurfaced.

"Besides, you know and I know that you and me and everybody else is willing to go wherever we have to to find a good man with a real good dick."

"You ain't never lied about that," Erica agreed.

In the following weeks, things had moved quickly. In that time, Bobbi had set up their first flock of eligible but incarcerated bachelors. Word about the new dating service had spread like tear gas during a riot around the minimum-security unit at CSP, the California State Prison in Los Angeles County. And every innocent man who had been wrongfully convicted and confined was lining up in hopes of finding a new friend on the outside who would listen to his plight.

When those men realized no one cared about their guilt or innocence, the number of inmates interested in signing up quadrupled. More than half of them decided there wasn't any shame in admitting they were looking for more than just a pen pal. And since the select few who had been chosen to participate in the dating service went back and told other inmates how they were honest about hoping to find romance and desperately needed a sponsor with a generous heart, it was all the inmates talked about in the recreation room, in the cafeteria, and in the yard.

It didn't take long for information about the service to make it through the prison grapevine and straight up to the warden. But he wasn't worried. As long as there weren't any disruptions, he had no complaints.

Frankie was doing her part as well. While she had a list of eager women dying to pay for a shot at Mr. Right, she had hand-selected only three to start out with. Frankie's flyers had garnered tons of inquiries. Women were coming out of the woodwork, and to Frankie's surprise, most of the inquiries came from successful women, women Frankie would've never guessed had the same problems as girls from around the way.

It just went to show that it didn't matter if you lived on Central and Vernon Avenues or in the heart of Brentwood, some issues affected women all the same. The women who contacted Frankie all had something in common: they were tired of being dogged out by men who played them for straight fools.

At first Frankie wasn't quite sure if her business would take off. She asked herself time and time again why anyone would pay for a man behind bars. But Frankie soon learned that most of the women who came to her had a thirst for adventure. They were lured in by the bad-boy image. Or at least that's what most of her clients said. Frankie also felt that if the on-line dating services could make a quick buck, she could too. She just happened to put a whole new twist on it.

When Frankie walked into the house, she noticed it was unusually dark. She and Bobbi had been out at the prison for hours. And while CSP was only about an hour and a half away, they ran into heavy traffic on the 110 Freeway on their way back.

"Erica?" Frankie called as she walked to the back of the house, where her and Erica's room was located.

"Yes, she will call you as soon as she gets in. Yes, Frankie is a *she*. Okay, cool. I'll tell her. Yes, Vicki, got it," Erica said into the phone.

She turned and looked at Frankie. "I didn't hear you come in. What's up?" Erica hung up the phone.

"Nothing much. Things are rolling right along. Who was that on the phone?" Frankie asked.

"Oh, my bad. That was some chick named Vicki. Damn, she's on one, huh?"

"Trust me, she ain't the only one. These females are calling like we got the winning lotto numbers. What's Vicki talking about?" Frankie asked.

"She wanted to make sure you guys were still meeting tomorrow. She wanted to meet earlier, but I told her you already had a few appointments before her, so she was like, 'Okay, cool.' Oh, I almost forgot—she wanted to know if she could bring her roommate. I told her it was all good."

Frankie sat on the twin bed on her side of the room. "Whew! Traffic was a bitch on the one-ten."

"Ain't it always?" Erica closed the notebook she had been using to log the names of the women who called for information about The Hook-Up. "Okay, so fill me in on our newest hustle."

Frankie moved to the edge of the bed. "I really think we're on to something big here Erica. I mean, this ain't like all that other shit we tried. If all goes as planned, we'll have at least three grand by the end of the day Saturday."

"What? Three grand?" Erica's eyes lit up.

"Yes, let me tell you how it works. Okay, first off, Bobbi picks the men based on what our customers request. Once she adds a new name to the list, I go to the library and look up information on their crime."

"We are still going to limit it to only the ones who are getting out soon, right?"

"Yeah, we will take someone with a maximum of twelve months left on his sentence, but honestly, as desperate as these hussies are, we really don't want to go past three or four months. These heifers are eager to get their hands on those bodies." Frankie stopped talking when the phone rang. They both looked in its direction. "Let the machine get it," she said.

After about four rings, Frankie's voice filled the room. "Whassssup! You've reached The Hook-Up. You know what to do when you hear the beep and we'll holla back! Peace!"

"Ah, this is Lisa. Um . . . I mean, my name is Lisa and . . . um . . . Well, my friend gave me this number. I was just looking for more information on what y'all do. Um . . . so, anyway, again, my name is Lisa. I'd rather not leave my last name if that's okay. But if someone could call me back on my cell, I'd appreciate it. Oh, by the way, I think it's a good thing what you guys are doing. Bye."

Frankie and Erica looked at each other when Lisa's voice stopped. The machine clicked and they heard the tape move forward; then the little red light started blinking. Seconds later, the phone rang again. Frankie held up her finger to stop Erica from answering. After Frankie's greeting filled the room, the machine beeped.

"Um . . . I'm sorry. My name is Lisa. I called just a few minutes ago. Well, I forgot to leave my cell number. So here it is." The girl rattled off the number. "If someone could call me back, I'd really, really appreciate it. I hope to hear from you soon, Mr. Frankie. Thank you and good-bye." There was a long pause, and before she hung up, Lisa rattled off her number again.

Erica shook her head. "Girl, there were at least seven other messages just like hers. That's deep. I can't believe these broads are really willing to pay to play."

"You damn straight they are, and we're gonna be right here to take their money." Frankie got comfortable. "Okay, now where were we?"

"Umm, you said we want three months, but we're willing to go with a year left of their sentences."

"Oh, yeah, that's right. Okay, it's real good we got Bobbi on the inside, because she is, of course, able to tell us where these guys are coming from. Even though we say they must provide a clean HIV record, when I checked what she gave me, two of the names from the list came out of the HIV ward, so we gotta be careful. The sweet part about this is, we don't make any promises of anything. The females understand the chance they're taking. All we do is take their order, then go through our list and see who best matches what they're looking for. We basically do all the legwork for them and make the connection. Once we make the connection, it's up to them to figure out how they're going to correspond."

"Damn, that sounds way too easy." Erica laughed.

"I know, but trust me, there's a lot of work that goes into this on Bobbi's end and on mine. You can imagine the number of down-and-out nuccas who are eager to sign up. And not that Bobbi's doin' anything illegal, but we don't want the warden to think this is going to affect her work. So we gotta try to keep things under control."

"I can't wait to get started. How are we gonna decide which women to take on?"

"I think that part will be easy in the beginning. We should only deal with those who can afford to pay. We ain't trying to work with a payment plan or do anything on credit. It's straight-up cold cash or nothing at all."

"Cool," Erica said. "Besides, that'll cut down on the confusion."

"You know it." Frankie got up from the bed. "Okay, so if all goes well Saturday, we'll head down to the county clerk's office first thing Monday morning."

Words could hardly describe the smile that crept across Erica's face. "You mean we're gonna pay the taxes?"

"We'll at least be able to make a down payment," Frankie said.

"Hey, that's better than we've been able to do, so that'll work." Erica didn't want to ruin the good mood with the other money woes. Especially behind something she promised Frankie she'd never do again. She figured once they really started rolling she'd be able to take care of that without Frankie ever finding out.

# YVETTE

By the end of July, Yvette was too through and about ready to climb the walls. So far, it had been an incredibly hot and depressing summer. What had made it even more unbearable was the fact that she had to spend the majority of it alone. Since the fiasco at Trevor's apartment, she'd been lying low and licking her wounds.

But that heartbreaking experience did lead her to a new prospect: sexy Roshawn Carson. He was creamy brown with a set of big brown eyes that begged to be noticed. He wore his khakis sagging with heavy starch and wore the standard long-sleeved white shirt over a short-sleeved white T-shirt and a wife-beater underneath that.

Roshawn sported two thick platinum ropes around his neck—one with a huge diamond-encrusted BMW emblem. He topped off his look with the latest pair of Jordan's, a platinum Rolex, and a matching Rolex ring. His shit was fierce, and Yvette could hardly keep her mind off fucking him.

The fact that he drove a tight-ass candy-apple-red

ragged-top BMW, pimped out with a kit and sitting on
spinners, helped put him very high on her list of things
to do. Though Roshawn probably didn't have half the
cash Highway-T had, Yvette still figured she'd give him
a try. Besides, she'd told herself, her kitty kat hadn't
purred the way it should in a long-ass time.

So, on a humid July evening, she was chillin' in the
passenger seat of Roshawn's Beamer; he said he needed
to make a couple of quick stops before they headed out
to the Cheesecake Factory in Redondo Beach. When
he had called earlier, she wanted to bypass dinner and
all the other shit he wanted to do and get straight to the
fucking, but she wanted this to work, so she decided
they should try to take it slow. Yvette had to admit, it
was good to be back out again. Although she would
never give up on men, she had needed a break after the
fallout with Trevor.

She and Roshawn were now rolling down Imperial
toward Central Avenue. He had the top down, and it
felt good to be with a man, actually going on a date.
She just wished they'd go straight to their destination
and not make a bunch of pit stops. If Lil Jon and the
East Side Boyz weren't blasting through Roshawn's custom stereo system, she might've been able to tell him
that much, but since it was, she eased back into the soft
leather bucket seat and figured she'd enjoy the trip,
'cause later she planned to ride the fuck out of his dick.

Their first stop was at a small motel near the
Normandy Casino. She wanted to wait in the car, but he
insisted she come in, saying it would take only a second.

Roshawn parked right in front of room 3 and jumped
out of the car. He knocked on the door four times, then
looked around, waiting for the door to open.

"Bug, it's me. Open up, dawg!"

The dude who opened the door looked shocked to
see Yvette. His eyes nervously darted toward her, then

back toward Roshawn. When he sucked his teeth like he had food caught between them, her skin crawled. She tried not to look at the massive dragon tattoo along the side of his neck and shoulder, but she had never seen anything like it. When she noticed the gun on the bed, she stood near the door and tried her best not to overhear their conversation. Yvette didn't want to know shit. She just wanted to go on their date, get full, then definitely get her freak on, forget about taking it slow, she told herself.

"Okay, here's the loot. Gee said you can bounce any time after nine tomorrow night, not a minute before," Roshawn warned.

"When you bringing the passport?" Bug asked. He shot Yvette a look of death and sucked his teeth again.

"It won't be ready until five tomorrow evening. You'll be straight. Your flight leaves at ten-fifty, dawg."

"Man, why didn't you bring your homey some grub? Ain't like I can order room service and shit." He grabbed his crotch. "Can't get no ass either," he said as he looked over at Yvette again.

*There goes that sucking sound again.* Yvette just wanted out; she didn't like being around Bug.

Roshawn laughed at his comment but stepped in front of Yvette. "My bad, dawg. I'll shoot through on our way back. I'll hook you up with some food then. Just lie low, and we'll ride this thing out big, homey."

When they left the little motel, Yvette was sure she didn't want to stop anywhere else. She especially knew she didn't want to stop back at the motel after dinner. A little while later, Roshawn brought his Beamer to a stop near the back of Nickerson Gardens. At first, Yvette felt a little uncomfortable being in the projects, especially at dusk, but she figured she would be safe with Roshawn, so she wasn't trippin'.

"Yo, I'll be right back," Roshawn shouted to Yvette,

who was trying her best to put on her brave face. He didn't bother telling her to tag along. She didn't think it was cool being left like a sitting duck but again told herself they'd only be there for a hot minute.

When Roshawn walked away and disappeared around a corner, she took the opportunity to lower the music. It was one thing to be sitting in a nice car in one of the most dangerous housing projects in Watts, but nobody said she had to have the music blasting. As Yvette raised her head back up, she thought she saw two men running toward the small park located in the center of the housing projects. She looked in the direction in which she saw Roshawn disappear, then eased back in the seat.

She hoped he wouldn't be too long, because she didn't feel like being jacked for a car that wasn't even hers. Before she could get comfortable, Yvette nearly bolted up out of her seat when she heard crashing noises all around her. She wasn't sure if a car had run into one of the buildings or what was going on.

Her first instinct was to duck, until she heard the word "Police!" All around the housing project, officers, dressed in black from head to toe and with guns pointed, attacked the doors of several units.

Soon after, the ghetto bird started humming up above. The chopper cast a bright light on several people in a nearby parking lot who found themselves surrounded by police. With her heart beating faster than she could think, Yvette didn't know what the fuck to do.

When officers finished breaking down doors and dragging people, mostly men, out of apartments, Yvette climbed over to the driver's seat and looked to see if anyone was watching her.

The courtyard was swarming with officers; there was no doubt—they were several hundred deep. Yvette had never in her life seen so many officers. It didn't take long for residents to start filing out of their apartments with hands on top of their heads. Yvette threw the car into gear and slowly pulled away from the curb.

Once she left the parking lot, she quickly turned onto Imperial, then made a quick right onto one of the side streets. As she fled Nickerson Gardens, she kept a nervous eye on the rearview mirror.

Los Angeles County Sheriff cars, SUVs, and other police vehicles zoomed past her with sirens blaring and lights flashing as she made her way to the 105 Freeway and back to her side of town.

Later that night, news of the raid left Yvette still. She immediately started thanking God for sparing her. Every news station offered continuing coverage of the raid that resulted in more than fifty arrests. LA's chief of police came on the TV screen. He said the Watts-area arrests were only a small part of an ongoing investigation and crime-fighting strategy by the LAPD. The plan included targeting a percentage of the region's hundred thousand violent gang members.

Yvette nearly choked on her drink when the chief uttered his next words: "We are going after the real shot callers," the chief said. "The most violent of the violent gang members."

"Did he say shot callers?" Yvette whispered as her eyes fixated on the screen.

The news started showing video of the actual raid from earlier that evening. Yvette studied the screen and still marveled at the fact that she was able to just drive away. Then the one image, probably the most important one, caught her eye.

She looked on as Roshawn was walked, handcuffed, and shoved into the back of a patrol car. The news lady said the scale of Wednesday's raid caught residents and longtime gang members by complete surprise.

Next they showed a resident. Yvette sat there thinking the fool even used his real name. She watched and listened in awe as the man spoke, looking right into the camera. "I'm an OG Hunter, and I can say for sho everybody around here was shocked when it all went down. But on the real, though, most of the arrests won't stick, and it ain't gonna make that much of a difference anyway. See, what the po-po don't realize is you can move one soldier out, but it won't take long for another and another to step up to the plate and move in without missin' a beat."

Yvette couldn't believe she had been right there in the midst of all that madness. The more she thought about it, the more she was pissed about how Roshawn had played her so close. Everyone knew the Gardens were home to the Bounty Hunters, one of the largest groups of Bloods and the most lethal street gang in the Watts area.

"It was wild," he said. "I saw doors ripped off the hinges and boo-coo families huddled on their porches when the raid was going down." He shook his head and mad-mugged the camera.

Then another man's face popped up. "Somebody's gonna answer for this. You shoulda seen Five-O and how they was just roughing up innocent people. Everybody who lives in Nickerson Gardens ain't criminals, you know!"

Just when Yvette thought he was done talking, he added, "It was a nightmare; something that I thought I'd see only on TV. I saw mothers and kids just sitting on the ground shivering."

They panned to a woman who was showing the cameraman that her iron-screen door had been pierced by a bullet. The news lady started talking again. "Many residents, like Linda Sanders, who's been living here for ten years, said they were accustomed to the gangs and the raids." Then the resident started talking when the camera went from her door to her face. "It happens a lot, the shootin's, raids, and fights here in Nickerson. Ain't nobody in their right mind would live here if they could live someplace else."

Then the news lady started talking again. "The police chief said that several hours before the raid, the department received a threat from the gang. He referred to an incident in which three Bounty Hunters opened fire on an LAPD patrol car after a traffic stop. Police said it was the fourth time in the last fifty days that police had been fired upon in the Nickerson Gardens area. They turned up the heat in the area after some gang members hit a jewelry store Tuesday morning and got away with more than a quarter million dollars' worth of diamonds.

"A subsequent search for the three suspects forced delays in the openings of two nearby elementary schools. One man was captured late Tuesday. In response, the Los Angeles City Council offered a seventy-five-thousand-dollar reward Wednesday for information leading to the arrest and conviction of the men who shot at a uniformed officer in the city.

"Twenty-two-year-old Roshawn Earl Carson was one of the three suspects wanted in connection with yesterday's shooting. He was picked up during the raid." Yvette thought she was going to die when she saw Roshawn's face fill the screen. As if that wasn't enough, when Bug's picture popped up on the screen, Yvette's head started spinning as she thought of the disgusting way he continuously sucked his teeth.

"Authorities are still looking for the third suspect, nineteen-year-old Cederic 'Junebug' Banks. Police think he may be headed to Jamaica where it's believed he has family."

Yvette sat in stunned disbelief. She had no idea Roshawn was involved in such chaos. But she did know exactly where Junebug was hiding out.

# CARMEN

Even after death, confusion still surrounded Carmen's ex-man Don-Juan. She and Gina rushed out of the West Los Angeles Funeral Home on Crenshaw Boulevard. They were silent as they walked to Carmen's car. Gina didn't know if Carmen was vexed with her or if she was just hot over having to go at it all alone without Don.

She and Carmen were tight and had been close ever since Gina moved out of Compton. Her sudden move was something she never talked about, and Carmen never pressed the issue. The truth was, in her pursuit of the perfect dick, Carmen was glad to have company. She and Gina were road dogs. But their taste in men was nothing alike. While Carmen went for the roguish thug type, Gina went for the suave debonair type. Unlike Carmen, Gina only fucked with gangstas who were paid. Carmen never talked about it, but her pops broke her off proper, so money, while it was important, wasn't a must have if she really dug someone. She basically had her own bank, and she didn't have to fuck for it. But she'd be the first to tell you that it didn't hurt if her dick came with paper too. And that's what Carmen had lost when she lost Don-Juan. He'd be very hard to replace. And Gina knew this without Carmen having to say it.

"I still can't believe Don-Juan is gone," Gina said, trying to break the ice that had formed between them.

"I still can't believe he had all those kids. Did you see that in there?" Carmen was astonished at the number of women who took to the podium to talk about Don-Juan and the children they said he fathered. Carmen had stopped counting at thirteen. When the memorial service became too much for her to swallow, she had tapped Gina on the shoulder. When Gina leaned in, Carmen had quickly grabbed her purse and said, "C'mon, let's bounce."

Gina looked toward the front of the church, then back at Carmen as if to ask, *now*? But Carmen was already up and making her way through the pews and was near the aisle. Gina was glad they had decided to sit in the back. They weren't even halfway through the service, but Carmen had had enough. At a time when she should've been mourning the loss of the man she shared nearly a year of her life with, she was instead faced with the reality that she had been one of many.

On their way out, they had passed Wanda as she wobbled her way into the church and down the aisle; Carmen knew she was gonna be sick then. Wanda thought her unborn child was gonna be Don-Juan's eighth; boy, was she in for a serious wake-up call!

Once they got into the car, Gina checked her makeup, and Carmen drove down Crenshaw to Imperial and hit an In-N-Out Burger. Gina had offered something a little more formal, but Carmen wasn't in the mood. She hadn't uttered a word since they left the service, and Gina didn't know quite what to say.

"Hey, you ever hear what happened to Trina? She

get out of the hospital yet?" It was the first time Carmen had spoken about the shooting at the baby shower. After Don-Juan was killed, it was like she was in a constant state of shock. There had been so much she didn't know about him.

In her quest to find Mr. Right, somebody who could rock her world in bed and help her keep up the ghetto-fabulous image she and her friends lived by, Carmen had overlooked so much. She had no idea Don was a banger. She was completely oblivious to the fact that he had kids all over the damn place too.

"I heard she got out of the hospital, but I think she's gonna have to do a lot of rehab."

Carmen shook her head. "Shot at a fuckin' baby shower. Now that's a damn story to tell, ain't it?"

"For real."

Carmen knew Gina was trying to keep it light. She was glad Gina didn't want to throw the facts up in Carmen's face, but she hoped Gina also knew she'd be back on the prowl soon. "Hmm, the next man I get is gonna go through some serious background-check type of shit. Did you know Don was a banger? I mean, those are your girls out there in Compton."

"Girl, you know I don't kick it in the CPT like I used to. As far as those chicken heads out there, shit, I'm cool on them. I can't kick it with females I gotta keep my eyes on, you feel me?"

"Do I? They are some shiesty bitches." Carmen stuck a French fry into her mouth. "But how come you never met her baby's daddy before?"

Gina leaned in. "Look, you know how it is, Carmen. Wanda and her girls always fucked on the down low. You talk about shiesty? Them bitches fuck right after each other sometimes, like it ain't nothing. When I got up outta Compton, I was like, ain't shit for me to come back to. But you know Wanda and my cousin have always been real tight, so I wasn't frontin', 'cause them bitches really know how to get down. I don't care what kind of party it is; when they throwin' it, you better believe it's gonna be real crunk, and I'm always trying to roll. I had no idea they was all caught up in a bunch of drama and shit. I usually go around for the good time, then bring my ass back to the Eastside. I ain't got beef with none of those females, but I also ain't trying to be a part of their crew."

Carmen didn't want to say anything cross, but she was vexed. She felt like Gina should've known more about the Compton girls before taking her over into unknown territory. She wouldn't go so far as to say she couldn't trust Gina, but she kind of felt like Gina wasn't too torn up over the fact that Carmen had been embarrassed.

"Wanna go to Club Menlo later?" Gina asked, breaking Carmen's train of thought.

"Nah, I think I'ma chill tonight." Carmen figured she'd wait awhile before she shared her idea about how they could both score some real thugs. Although she didn't think Gina was in on that shit with Wanda and Don-Juan, something told her to hold off on sharing her new gold mine.

Once she checked out Frankie and heard what she had to say, she'd decide whether to let Gina in on the action. Besides, Carmen had to admit she did feel a little down; not necessarily because she'd miss Don, though she would. She had always been smart and started saving for a rainy day the moment Don started freely throwing cash her way. And her daddy had bank anyway.

Carmen knew that no matter what happened, it was hard to keep a good woman down. She'd bounce back and if this Frankie was legit, she'd do it with a shot caller of her own. And since the flyer said you could describe the perfect man, Carmen had a feeling she'd get just what she was looking for.

# VICKI

Vicki and Pam arrived at Roscoe's Chicken and Waffles on Manchester nearly thirty minutes before she was supposed to meet with Frankie. Vicki didn't know if they should get a table or wait for Frankie. She had no idea what Frankie looked like but had told Frankie's assistant that she'd be wearing a light blue strapless top.

"Vicki, are you sure about this?" Pam asked, looking around the restaurant.

"Right behind you!" a waitress hollered in Vicki's ear.

"Oh, excuse me." Vicki moved out of the way and said to Pam, "Yes, I'm sure. Hey, why don't we go check out some of the artwork that guy has for sale?"

"Cool, 'cause the aroma in here is driving me nuts."

Pam followed Vicki out of the small restaurant after putting their name on the waiting list. In the first five minutes of looking through the man's paintings, Vicki had selected three she planned to buy. A waitress opened the door and stuck her head out. "Vicki, table for three."

"We're about to go in and eat. You think you can hold on to these for me? I'll get them on my way out."

"Sure, what's your name?" the vendor asked.

She acknowledged the waitress, then said, "My name is Vicki. I'll pay when I pick them up."

"Excuse me, did you say your name is Vicki?" Frankie asked. She was stunned to see the bottle blonde near the vendor's stand. Vicki was not fat by a black girl's standards. But for a white girl she would've been considered fat. She was thick, with implants that didn't scream fake right away. Frankie knew they weren't real because there was no way anybody that busty could wear a tank top without a bra and not be sagging to her knees. Vicki was wearing big gold bamboo earrings and had both her tongue and belly button pierced. Her acrylic nails were painted in bright, two-toned colors. Her face may have been average, but the make-up put her in the pretty category, and her gray eyes reminded Frankie of a cat's.

Vicki looked like she had just walked off the set of a rap music video. In addition to the blue tube top, she was dressed in an old-school sweat suit with a pair of Louis Vuitton tennis shoes.

"You must be Frankie," Vicki said. "This is my roommate, Pam. They just called for our table if you're ready." Vicki ignored the look on Frankie's face. She knew exactly what the woman must've been thinking. She was thinking what everyone who met Vicki after speaking to her over the phone thought but didn't have the balls to say.

Seated at the table and waiting on their food, Frankie couldn't stop looking at Vicki. "You do know what kind of service we're running here, right?" Frankie asked.

"Oh, of course, girl. Hey, I'm all for keeping it real. Pam, let her know what's really going on."

Pam looked at Frankie and said, "Let me guess—

when you talked to Vicki on the phone, you thought you were talking to a sistah."

"Well, yeah." Frankie slowly nodded as she kept her eyes on Vicki.

"Now don't tell me my race is gonna be a problem for you. I hope you ain't one of those sistahs that got problems when she sees a black man with a white girl." The question took Vicki back to her childhood. She was used to those types of sistahs. Growing up, she was used to such hatred in her very own house. She had even lost her family over her preference for black men. Vicki's parents were older and set in their ways when they had her. They had spent years in Long Beach, where they owned and operated a small drugstore. And even though the success of their business was built on the backs of the blacks and Hispanics in nearby neighborhoods and cities, Vicki's parents were racist.

She grew up in a house where her father continuously talked trash about the very people who kept his business thriving each day. He had told her the worst thing she could ever do was bring home a brown or black man. It was something he had drilled into her ever since her body started showing signs of womanhood.

During her last year of high school, Vicki had started dating the star of the football team. To Vicki, he was big, black, and beautiful. She couldn't get enough of him or his thick long dick. When her father came home unexpectedly one afternoon and found that dick in his daughter's mouth, he nearly keeled over and died.

That had been two months shy of her eighteenth birthday. Her parents decided it was best if they got an apartment for her because they didn't want "those kinds" of people trampling through their house. The Michaels had never looked at their daughter the same, and she didn't have a problem with it.

"Not at all. Shit, your money spends just like mine. It's green, right?" Frankie said.

Frankie's answer jarred Vicki out of those awful memories. "Cool, well, let's get down to business." Vicki pulled a Louis Vuitton messenger bag from under the table and removed a thick packet of papers. "I filled out my paperwork and made three choices like you requested. I have a few questions too."

"Okay, shoot."

"The HIV test thing. Are these guys cool with an independent test once they're released?" Vicki asked.

"That's something you can talk to them about, but we can make that part of your request up front. I don't see why it would be a problem. We don't select anyone from the HIV wards, but ain't nothing wrong with you double-checking. What else?"

Vicki looked up when the waitress came with their food.

"Can I get anything else for you ladies?" the waitress asked.

"Umm, I'd like some hot sauce," Vicki said.

"Tabasco okay?" the waitress queried.

"Is there anything else?"

The waitress laughed and walked away. Vicki turned back to their conversation. "Okay, let's see. How long will it take? And can I choose how much time I want him to have left on his sentence?"

"The answer to both questions is it depends. We go over exactly what you're looking for and try to get a match as close as we can. You can get up to two matches, but we think you should choose only one. When you make your choice, we send him your picture and tell him a little about you. Usually after that first contact he'll call or write within forty-eight hours."

The waitress reappeared. "Tabasco." She passed the bottle to Vicki.

Frankie continued, "About the time left on his sentence. Let's say you have two options; you can choose the one with the shortest time left, but we ain't got no control over that."

"Fair enough," Vicki said.

"I know it says so in the paperwork, but we do not refund your money if it don't work out. We just do the hookup; the rest is up to you."

Pam sat and listened intently. Vicki nodded as Frankie spoke. Frankie was still hyped about nearly wrapping up her second sale of the day, and she still had two more meetings to go.

After they ate for a few minutes, Vicki looked up at Frankie and said, "I have fifteen hundred in cash. Is that okay with you?"

"Cash always works, girlfriend. Always."

# FRANKIE & ERICA

This Labor Day weekend, the Central Avenue Low-Rider Club was throwing a beach party. Erica had been trying to come up with ways to convince Frankie that they had to go. She had already bought two new swimsuits and was looking forward to showing them both off. But lately, The Hook-Up had been the only thing on Frankie's mind.

Sure they had been able to pay off the back taxes on her grandmother's house and had even bought a new ride, all thanks to Frankie's business mind and her moneymaker of a plan. But still, Erica felt Frankie didn't want to enjoy the money; she just wanted to make more.

Erica purposely told Frankie she'd be at the shop later than normal because she wanted to get with her old friend Jerome. Even though Frankie made sure she kept a nice stash of money, Erica had no desire to spend it if she didn't have to. When Frankie was busy doing other things, Erica had been secretly hooking up with Jerome. And Erica knew if Frankie ever found out what she got from Jerome, she'd flip out.

She had talked to Jerome before Frankie dropped her at the nail shop. When Erica saw Frankie pull off, she quickly called Jerome, told him it was cool, and he came by to swoop her up.

"Hey, Ma. Why your sister be trippin'?"

"I don't know. But you know how she is. Where we going? You know I only have 'bout an hour to kill before I gotta be back here, right? You got something for me?" Erica asked.

Jerome nodded. "Yeah, but, baby girl, you know you still owe me from last time, right?" He licked his lips and looked at Erica's cleavage. "I mean, a brotha ain't running no charity here, but we can always work something out."

Erica looked around. She had only the money Frankie had given her, and she needed what Jerome had. "So what's on your mind exactly?"

"You know the Snooty Fox ain't far from here, right?" he asked.

The Snooty Fox was as close to high class as any motel with hourly rates could come. Erica was familiar with room 342, the corner suite on the third level. And while she hadn't been there during the day, she figured she could get what she wanted a whole lot faster if she agreed to go with Jerome that afternoon.

Inside the room at the Snooty Fox, Erica closed the thick drapes to darken the room. Before she could turn around good, Jerome had stripped down to his boxers and wife-beater undershirt. He hopped onto the bed, stretched out, and laced his fingers behind his head.

"Yo, hit the radio over there," he told Erica. "Then hop up on the bed and shake that ass the way I like it."

Erica did exactly what he asked. It was hard for her to keep her balance on the bed as she swayed her hips to the music, but she was determined to work it out.

"That thong looks real nice on you, Ma. Here, turn around; lemme get a better look."

Erica turned her back to Jerome and shook her hips. Suddenly she bent over to touch her toes, then dropped her butt down.

"See, that's what I'm talking 'bout."

Before she could finish her dance, Jerome pulled her down to the bed. When she tried to lie next to him, he held out his arm. "Naw, girl, you gots to work for this," he said.

Erica unhooked her bra, then reached for her thong.

"No, leave those on." Jerome slid his index and middle fingers into her thong and started moving them in and out of her. "You like that?"

"Mmm-hmm!" Erica cooed.

"Cool," Jerome said. He slapped her ass and watched it jiggle. "C'mon, turn your back to me and hop on up," he said, motioning toward his stiff dick.

The sight of his huge erection made Erica happy. Suddenly she didn't mind doing what she had to do to get what she wanted. In a matter of seconds, she swung one leg over and grabbed his thighs as she lowered herself onto his stiffness. Once she was straddled in place, she adjusted herself by moving her hips.

"Aahhh. You like this, Daddy?"

All Jerome could do was release a massive belly-wrenching moan.

"I feel it way up in there, Daddy. It's so biig and haard. Mmm, just the way I like it." Erica slowly increased her momentum. First she rode him with her back upright. She used her hands to massage her titties; then a few minutes later, she switched and grabbed his ankles.

"Damn, Erica! You got some sweet pussy."

She held on to his ankles even tighter and quickly moved her hips up and down. The swooshing sound

from their bodies increased her excitement and made
her even wetter.

"You like it, Daddy? Whatchu gonna do for me,
huh?"

"Girl, Erica, Mmm," Jerome cried. "Girl, you sho
know how to . . ." He grabbed her ass, slapped it a few
times, then tried to grab her waist. "Wait, girl. You
gotta slow down. I'm 'bout to . . ."

His words made her wild. Erica humped him harder
and faster.

"Ww-wait!" he cried to no avail.

The more he cried, the faster she moved. She felt his
dick throbbing inside her walls. When she felt it tighten,
she gripped it with her muscles and humped even
faster.

"That's it, Daddy, let it go."

Erica turned around, careful not to allow him to slip
out. Facing him now, she leaned forward and allowed
her breasts to dangle in his face. Jerome closed his
eyes and stuck his tongue out.

She started gyrating and grinding her hips, slowly
and deliberately. She shook, then wiggled, then rode
him some more.

Just when Erica felt him about to explode, she jumped
off his dick and opened her mouth. She deep-throated
him, then sucked the head one good time before releas-
ing it. She knew the move would have Jerome climbing
the walls and get her everything she wanted.

Jerome's fingers clutched the sides of the bed and
his eyes rolled back up into his head. That's when Erica
moved in for the kill. She slopped his shaft, then
sucked the head. When she felt his warm fluids fill her
mouth, she lay back, spent and breathing hard.

"Damn, girl. That was the shit!" he breathed.

Later, as Erica walked away from the Quick and

Split burger stand on Vermont, she pulled out her new cell phone and hit the speed-dial number to reach Frankie. The phone rang twice before she saw the gold Benz slow to a crawl next to her.

"Say, Erica, whassup?"

"LadyRae!" Erica hit the END button on her phone. She'd wait to call Frankie. Besides, Frankie was probably working anyway.

"You need a ride?" LadyRae asked. She lowered the passenger window and pulled over to the side of the street.

"Naw, Frankie told me to call when I was ready. You know how she gets."

"Yeah, whassup with her lately? She be on one. It's like when I wanna holla at you, she be actin' all foul and shit."

"Frankie is Frankie. You know how my peeps can be." Erica looked down the street in both directions. The last thing she needed was Frankie rolling up on her in the middle of the street talking to LadyRae.

"You rolling out to the beach tomorrow?" LadyRae asked.

"Frankie still ain't said if we going or not." Erica leaned into the open window.

"Say, Erica, you a big girl. Why can't you just go without Frankie? It's like she be hoverin' over you. You can barely make a move without her breathin' down your damn neck. Don't you get tired of her ridin' you?"

"LadyRae, before our mother died, she made Frankie promise to look out for me; that's all she doing. I know she act funny sometimes, but you know how Frankie is. She just Frankie."

"Say, why don't you hop in? I don't like being out on front street like this." LadyRae looked in her rearview mirror, then at both side mirrors. "You know the jackers be out."

"Now, LadyRae, you know doggone well ain't nobody gonna try and step to you, not like that. Be for real." Erica grinned.

"Here, why don't you hop in?"

"Yeah, Frankie would have a field day with that."

"Damn, y'all act like I bite or something. Whassup? It ain't like I hound you or nothing like that."

"I know, LadyRae, but I don't want to get Frankie all worked up, so I better just call her and tell her I'm ready. She'd have a fit if I took a ride from anybody."

"Not *anybody,* Erica. Go ahead, admit it. Frankie would have a fit if you took a ride from me."

# YVETTE

Yvette looked at her bank account ledger again. She had never had so much money in her life. Even after she paid Frankie, she still had close to one hundred thousand dollars. And she had big plans for the money too. She already had Roshawn's Beamer painted and had changed the tags.

If someone had told her the night she had to sneak out of the projects in Roshawn's car that she'd be able to turn that situation around to her benefit, she would've called them a liar. But that's exactly what she had done. And she had the money to prove it.

Just as she stretched out and got comfortable on the couch thinking of ways to get the title transferred to her own name, the phone rang.

"Yvette, it's me. I'm parking and coming up," Frankie said before Yvette could even say hello.

Yvette hung up the phone and put her plate in the sink on her way to open the door.

Frankie breezed by her with a huge grin on her face.

She sat on the sofa and opened the bag she brought with her. She pulled out a large manila envelope.

"Your order came in." She extended the envelope toward Yvette, who sat there and stared at it. "According to your list, you wanted a single, caramel-colored, six-foot-two, two-hundred-fifteen-pound, HIV-free brotha." Frankie smiled. "Well, I think we've done it again."

Yvette was shocked; she didn't know quite what to say.

"Hmm, take it. Take a look at him," Frankie said as she extended the envelope toward Yvette.

Yvette couldn't believe it. When she created the list, she never really imagined Frankie would be able to make a match.

Frankie pulled the envelope back and opened it herself. "Okay, here we go." She pulled out a picture first and held it so only she could see.

"His name is Nyeree." Frankie took a deep breath, then asked, "Are you ready to see your new man?"

Still somewhat leery but more than a little curious, Yvette wanted to see exactly what she would wind up with. She moved next to Frankie on the couch. When her eyes focused on his, her heart nearly stopped.

"Close your mouth, chile; you starting to drool." Frankie laughed. This was always her favorite part.

"Dang, Frankie, he's . . . shit, he's downright man-pretty." Yvette licked her lips.

"Ain't he, though?" Frankie nodded. "And he's all yours if you still want to go through with it."

As Frankie pulled the rest of the stuff out of the envelope, Yvette couldn't tear her eyes off the picture. Nyeree's chiseled features demanded attention. He was the color of a dark Hershey's chocolate bar with dreamy brown eyes and a smile to die for. His body was ripped with a tight six-pack that he proudly displayed in a sexy pose.

"So what's his story? Why is he in prison? What did he do?"

"Bobbi said he was sentenced to twelve years, but he's up for parole in three months. He served six years. He says he's innocent, has since the day he was arrested."

"No! Really?" Yvette asked. She looked back at his picture, and her mind started thinking about all of the things she could do with a body like his.

"So she says he's innocent, huh?"

"Yep, but he was charged and convicted of armed robbery. Some eyewitness swore it was him."

"How old is he?"

"He's twenty-nine. It's all in here, everything you need to know about him."

"I can't believe this! He looks exactly like what I ordered. Um . . . I ah . . . I mean *asked* for." Yvette grinned.

"Here." Frankie smirked and passed Yvette a medical form that confirmed Nyeree was HIV negative. She also gave her two more pictures of Nyeree and a smaller envelope with Yvette's name on it.

"Y'all told him about me?" Yvette gasped and looked at Frankie, horrified.

"Told him about you? Girl, we sent him pictures. Just like you, he wants to see what he's getting into. Besides, Bobbi picks only the best. We ain't got time for no junk, chile."

Hours after Frankie left, Yvette sat and stared at Nyeree's picture. She had read at least one thousand times the letter he wrote specifically to her. She had gone over his personal information so much that she had it memorized. She couldn't wait to talk to him.

Yvette thought that if men like Nyeree were any sign of what was available behind bars, it wouldn't take long for Frankie to become a very rich woman. She had paid nearly fifteen hundred dollars. And once she looked at his picture, she determined it was money well spent.

As she looked through the information again, she started thinking about what Nyeree might think if he learned her secret. She desperately wanted for him to be *her* Mr. Right. She also wanted him to accept her wholeheartedly despite what she had done.

Frankie had told her that all she needed was Yvette's approval and Nyeree would be calling collect the very next evening. After lusting over the picture, Yvette could hardly wait to hear his voice; even more, she couldn't wait to get her hands all over that banging-ass body of his. His full-body picture left her salivating.

She hugged the picture tightly and told herself only time would tell if she would win the guy in spite of her own slipup.

# CARMEN

Carmen looked down at her diamond-encrusted Cartier watch and hoped she would not be late. This was the day she had been waiting for since she fell in love with the idea of finding love behind bars.

She and Frankie had hit it off immediately and since they'd been working together, had even become fast friends. After Don-Juan's funeral, Carmen moved out to Beverly Hills and moved into one of the buildings her father owned. Even Gina wasn't aware of where she was laying her head. She wasn't sure who to trust, so for the time being she felt it was better if she went underground.

When she moved out to Beverly Hills, she decided it was the best time to get in touch with Frankie. She still hadn't told Gina about her plans to find the perfect man. Shortly after she made that decision, she waited for Frankie.

It wasn't long after they met and Carmen filled out the paperwork that she and Frankie were heading north on I-5 toward Sacramento. When they took the Palmdale/

Lancaster exit, the butterflies in the pit of Carmen's belly sprang to life.

"Are you having second thoughts?" Frankie questioned.

"No. Not really."

"No, or not really?"

"I guess not really." Carmen flipped the visor mirror down and checked her make-up. Again.

"Carmen! You *are* nervous!" Frankie teased before she suddenly switched lanes without putting on her blinker.

Carmen didn't respond or react.

"For the entire time we've been on the road, I've watched you put on lipstick four times, put powder on your face three times, and you can't stop fidgeting with your hair."

"Hmm, and here I thought you were watching the *road*."

Frankie gave Carmen a flip look, hit cruise control, and turned up the radio.

"It's not every day a girl drives up to a prison to meet her new man for the very first time," Carmen said before frowning. "I still can't believe we are so desperate that we have to resort to finding a man behind bars."

"A good man?" Frankie's brow shot up. "Girl, yes!" Frankie smiled. "I knew it—not only are you nervous, but you're having second thoughts, too."

Carmen didn't know if she was having second thoughts. It was more anxiety. She wondered if Chip was anything like the letters and pictures he had sent over the last few weeks. What if he decided talking to her in person wasn't quite as interesting as over the phone or through letters? She knew their correspondence had turned into a fast-budding relationship, and she didn't mind one bit.

Frankie suddenly swerved her Mercedes SUV to avoid hitting the car she had been tailgating, and Carmen snapped back to the situation at hand.

"You awfully quiet," Frankie said like nothing happened.

"Just praying we make it to CSP in one piece."

"Well, you lucky in more ways than one. We only about fifteen minutes away."

From the far left lane, Frankie darted across two lanes amid honking horns to make a turn she nearly missed.

That day was nearly a month ago. Carmen may have been nervous, anxious, and everything in between. But a few weeks after that, when she stood alone outside the gates of the California State Prison, she couldn't feel her legs. She knew they were there, because she had used them to drive there and get out of the car.

It was like a scene from a movie. The gate slowly slid open, and he walked out. Only, Chip Davis looked like he was gliding. By the time Carmen was able to take in his broad shoulders and model-like features, he had scooped her up into his muscled arms, and they enjoyed the most passionate kiss Carmen had ever experienced.

"Hey, baby," he said when they separated.

"Hey, yourself." She wiped the lipstick from his clean-shaven face.

"I'm so glad to have you."

Next to Carmen's slim five-foot-six frame, he fit perfectly. In the sunlight, Chip's eyes looked lighter than she remembered from the pictures.

He glanced around, then said, "Let's get outta here before they change their minds."

Frankie had been right. Chip was everything Carmen could've wanted in a man and a little more she hadn't quite expected.

# VICKI

"Damn!" Vicki rolled over and tried to shield her eyes from the sun's rays. They crept through the sheer curtains that hung in her bedroom's large bay windows. Finally giving up, she brought her body into an upright position and swung her feet onto the floor.

She looked around her bedroom and reminded herself that this was the day she'd finally get a call from her Mr. Right. Frankie's secrecy had, at times, pissed her off. But Frankie had also promised Vicki that this catch was worth the wait and the secrecy. She kept saying everything would be explained to her really soon.

Frankie had also assured Vicki that this fish was everything she could want in a man. And she better be right, Vicki thought as she padded to the large bathroom, which was decorated in all white with mirrors up to the ceiling. She turned on the shower and started her morning ritual.

In the shower she started going over in her mind all that she knew about this man. According to Frankie, he fit her request to a tee, and there was a bonus. But the only part was, Vicki had to agree to take this hookup on blind faith. She was guaranteed that he would be everything she wanted, but she had to wait for the picture.

Since she agreed with that, Vicki and Steven West had been exchanging letters for weeks. But she had yet to hear his voice. It was kind of hard corresponding with him since he was trying to hide certain things about his identity.

Vicki had told Frankie she wouldn't press him, but honestly, every chance she got she was trying to piece things together to figure out who he was. For instance, in one of his letters, he alluded to the fact that he was in for a probation violation. Vicki then tried to call the probation department and get information on Steven West. She had almost made progress until his probation officer wanted to know who she was and why she needed the information. Vicki hadn't thought that through completely, so when the woman asked, she got nervous and hung up the phone.

Fucking with Frankie, she knew he hadn't killed anyone or anything like that, because murderers and rapists were not allowed to join Frankie's stable. And that was cool with Vicki, especially since she had had her fill of the dangerous types. She told herself they were only looking for donations and sponsors.

Two hours after she had gotten up, her phone rang. She sat and watched it for a minute, trying to gather her composure. Vicki grabbed the receiver and in the sexiest voice she could muster, said, "Ah, hello?"

"Vicki, it's me, Frankie."

"Oh, what the hell? Girl, the number on caller ID was unknown. I thought it was Steven." Vicki sighed.

"There's been a change in plans. I'm about fifteen minutes away from you. I'm about to scoop you, and we headed out to CSP."

"Today? Right now?" Vicki yelled into the phone.

"Yeah, what's up? It's a Saturday. You got plans or something?"

"Naw, nothing like that, but damn, a bitch need her roots done, and I wanted to get my hair streaked before I see Steven in person. I just wasn't expecting this, Frankie, that's all."

Now it was Frankie's turn to sigh. "Look, you need to get it together. Plans have already been made. He's expecting us, so throw on some make-up and be ready in fifteen. Can you do that for me?" When Frankie didn't get a response right away, she turned up the heat. "It's your money, Vicki, but I handpicked Steven especially for you. Now you know it would be bad for business if I had to show up alone for the visit and tell him you couldn't make it. So what's it gonna be?"

Vicki sucked her teeth and rolled her eyes at the phone. Dang, she just wasn't ready, but she didn't want to let Frankie down either.

"C'mon through. I'll be ready to roll." Vicki hurried and put her hair in a ponytail, toyed with her bangs, and then slapped on some make-up. She figured she'd finish in the car on the drive up to the prison.

She threw on a pair of jeans that made her booty look big and a Rocawear T-shirt that she tied into a knot in the back, showing off her pierced belly button. Since she couldn't wear open-toed shoes to the prison, she threw on her Louis Vuitton tennis shoes and a matching belt.

Vicki gave herself a once-over in the mirror and decided it was the best she could do with what little time she had to work with. When she heard Frankie's horn, she grabbed her make-up bag and rushed out the door. One thing she knew for sure: this visit would either leave her alone or it would be a sign that she and Steven could make a go at it.

Because she didn't need anybody to tell her what she already knew. If Vicki Michaels didn't have at least an hour to get ready, there was no way she could guarantee she'd be at her best. And she wanted to be at her very best when meeting her new man for the first time.

The trip to CSP didn't take long since they took the commuter lane on the 110 Freeway. However, things slowed a bit on the I-5, which didn't have a commuter lane. Vicki used the time to perfect her face so that when they stepped out of Frankie's SUV, she'd look like she was ready to grace the cover of *Vibe* magazine. She felt a little better knowing Steven would at least see her with her game face on.

After they went through all the crap visitors are subjected to while visiting an inmate, she waited eagerly for Steven to make an appearance. CSP's waiting room wasn't the kind with thick glass window and phones; they were actually in a large room with metal picnic tables.

Once all of the family members and friends were seated, a door opened on the far left side of the room, and inmates walked out in a single line. Frankie and Vicki were sitting on a bench in the room's far right, way in the back.

"OMIGOD! Frankie, is that MC Murderous? Damn, I love his music. What's that new song he got out now? "Die Trick Bitch Ho" I think is what it's called. It's got a dope-ass beat," Vicki whispered. She watched as the men went to their respective tables, and the room erupted in laughter, kisses, and hugs.

When Vicki saw MC Murderous walk toward their table, she looked around nervously. She didn't even know he had been sent back to jail. When she saw Frankie stand and walk toward him, she nearly fell onto the floor.

"Vicki, this is MC Murderous, but you know him as Steven. Steven, this is my client Vicki."

Vicki may have been speechless, but she did send up a silent prayer, giving thanks for finally getting herself a bona fide thug.

# FRANKIE & ERICA

Erica knew she was in trouble the minute LadyRae's Benz pulled away from the curb. She thought she had planned it perfectly, but when they pulled up and saw the white Mercedes SUV in the driveway of her grandmother's house, she almost wanted to tell LadyRae to keep driving.

She thought better of it when she saw Frankie sitting on the porch with the phone glued to her ear. When Erica stepped out of LadyRae's car, her eyes met Frankie's and that's when she knew for sure she was about to catch hell.

At least Frankie waited until LadyRae turned the corner before she started acting all foul, Erica thought. Erica opened the little gate and took her time walking up the walkway.

The minute her foot hit the porch, Frankie lit into her. "So you a ho now, right?" Frankie huffed.

"Why you trippin', Frankie?" Erica tried to pass her and reach the door, but Frankie blocked her path. She was furious.

"Answer me, Erica. You turning tricks for LadyRae or something now? Naw, naw, maybe you just a mule for her, right? Whassup? Which is it, Erica?"

"Frankie, I can't talk to you right now. You too upset." Erica turned her back, trying to hold in the tears.

"You damn right I'm upset. Why you been lyin' to me?"

Erica spun around at Frankie's accusation. For a moment her heart sank. How could Frankie have found out? How did Frankie know what she did, and if she knew, why did she wait all this time to confront her? She didn't know how to respond.

"What did I lie about, Frankie?" Erica swallowed hard.

Frankie walked up closer, so close that Erica could smell her breath. They stood there glaring at each other for what seemed like forever. When Frankie finally spoke, it was through gritted teeth. "You lied to me about going to the low-rider beach party with LadyRae."

Erica didn't know if Frankie could read the relief on her face. At that very moment she didn't even really care. If that was all Frankie thought she had lied about, things might not be as bad as she thought. Erica turned away from Frankie.

"Can we just squash it? I don't want to talk about this right now," Erica said.

Frankie spun her around. "Oh, you gonna talk about it, and you gonna talk about it now. If you rolling with LadyRae now, I need to know, because I told you from day one that we wasn't going out like that. First you go off to the beach party with her; now I come home early to take you out and your ass come creepin' up outta her ride. I saw the look on your face when you saw me."

"Frankie, what difference does it make? It's not like you really care about what I do anyway—we never together no more. All you care about is The Hook-Up.

Every weekend you go running up to that damn prison like they giving away money up there. You don't give a damn about me. Now that you rolling, you couldn't care less about me."

Frankie snatched Erica's hand up. "Look at your nails." She snatched a lock of Erica's hair. "Your hair stays done; you have Manolos on your feet; shit, you wear fine silk on your ass. That prison pays for all of that and then some, Erica. When we was broke, your ass was stressin' me. Now we finally on our way up and you still complaining!" Frankie shook her head. "I'm out here hustlin' my ass off, running these females back and forth to this prison, and you got the fuckin' nerve to be cryin' over me not spending time with you? Shit, I'm working to make sure you living the way you should be living."

Erica stood with a stone-faced stare, looking at Frankie getting herself all worked up.

"You don't want for a damn thing, Erica. I even told you that if you wanted to, I'd pay to send you to take those Driver's Ed classes so you could learn to drive and we'd get you your own ride, but you said you were fine. Now I turn my back and you sitting up getting all close and friendly with LadyRae. I don't have to tell you how dangerous she is—you already know."

Minutes of silence passed between them on the porch. Frankie didn't know what else to do. She had tried to get Erica more involved in the business, but Erica was uninspired. She'd answer the phones, take messages, then get bored. And honestly, Frankie couldn't really trust her to do that. A few times, Erica had gotten the messages all wrong and almost cost them ten grand. That was when Frankie decided to move the business to a little storefront in the Lemert Park area.

She had tried to convince Erica to go up there during the day and help out, but Erica didn't want to do that either. She had told Frankie she didn't need a babysitter. Frankie shared the office with a woman named Joy who did taxes and other odd jobs for people.

But Erica insisted that whenever she came around, the woman looked at her funny and it made her uncomfortable. To avoid useless arguments, Frankie just dropped it and Erica never brought it up again.

"Frankie . . . um . . . I'm sorry. I didn't mean to lie about the beach party, but the truth is you would've never agreed to let me go alone, and I knew you'd be working because I heard you on the phone talking about going up to CSP." Erica looked down at nothing on the ground. "I know you don't like LadyRae, but she really has been nice to me. She not even trying to get me to join her team, and the only reason I was with her today is because you left me stranded at the nail shop. She was there and offered me a ride home, that's all."

Now it was Frankie's turn to feel bad. She had forgotten she told Erica to go get her nails, feet, and eyebrows done. She figured on a Saturday she'd be in there for hours, because Man-trap was usually packed on Saturdays. But then there was the change in plans, and she had to take Vicki up to CSP. How could she have forgotten? Maybe she had been doing a little too much lately.

"Oh, snap!" She shook her head. "E, I'm sorry. I got caught up. It slipped my mind."

"See, that's what I'm talking 'bout, Frankie. Back in the day, you would've cut off your right arm before you left me stranded anywhere! Now your ass can't even remember to pick up your little sister after you dropped me off!" Erica looked at her. "I'm starting to feel like I'm slowin' you down. Like I'm in the way or something."

"Erica, I swear I'll make it up to you. You right. I've been all caught up in the business, but I promise I'll make it up to you real soon. I can't believe I left you hanging. Anything could've happened to you, and it would've been my fault."

"You damn right, Frankie. So you know what this tells me? This tells me since you ain't doin' nothing but looking out for the almighty dollar, I gots to be looking out for me! 'Cause obviously ain't nobody else going to!" Erica stormed off and slammed the iron-screen door shut.

# YVETTE

After nearly three months of corresponding by letters, postcards, and collect calls, their time had come. On the day of his release from CSP, Nyeree told Yvette not to worry, that he'd come to her. So she sat waiting, in heat.

But before the day had arrived, she went out and did some very special shopping. Since Nyeree's family was picking him up from prison, that gave her time to turn her place into a love nest. She went shopping and bought all kinds of aphrodisiac foods, from strawberries and melted chocolate to an array of seafoods. She also bought an assortment of wines and champagne.

A week before his release date, Yvette went to Frederick's of Hollywood and cleaned up. She also went to a novelty store and bought lots of body oils, edible panties, and an enormous amount of lubricant. Lately, all she could think about were the ways in which she planned to fuck her man.

The ringing phone jarred her out of her thoughts.

"Hello?"

"Baby? Is that you?" Nyeree's deep baritone voice rang in her ear.

"Yup, it's me, baby. Where are you?" she purred, struggling to contain her sheer excitement.

"I'm over at my mom's right now, but I should be by your way around six. Is that cool?"

"Is it? Shit, I can't wait!"

"Are you ready for me?" he asked, breathing heavily into the phone.

"Oh, am I ever," she said.

"Good, 'cause a brotha got a lot of pent-up frustration if you know what I mean." He giggled at their inside joke.

"Baby, I'm here for you. You just hurry and come on over. I know your family is happy to see you and all, but tell them you got business to tend to. I'm sure they'll understand, right?"

"Girl, don't make me reach through this phone," he threatened jokingly.

"Is that my future daughter-in-law you talking to? It better be," Yvette heard a woman's voice say. "When am I gonna meet her?"

Yvette was glad to know Nyeree had told his people about her. She couldn't wait to get him over to her place. In the last few weeks, she had been brain dead when it came to thinking about anything other than Nyeree coming home. She could hardly eat or sleep. And when she did sleep, she had the most erotic dreams about where they'd fuck, for how long, and how often. Sometimes she'd wake up wet from her dreams.

"Moms, chill, you'll meet her soon. Okay, babe, I'ma holler at you when I'm on my way, cool?"

"I'll be here. Hurry, Nyeree."

Four hours after that conversation, there was a knock at Yvette's door. She didn't answer right away. When the knock came harder and louder, she grabbed her wineglass and sashayed over to the door.

"Who is it?" she called out seductively.

"Depends on what you want," Nyeree said.

She slowly opened the door, starting with just a crack. When she looked at him, she could see he was clean shaven; his body looked like it was begging to be freed from the Sean John velour sweat suit he was wearing. On top of that, he smelled good enough to eat.

Not to be outdone herself, Yvette opened the door wider and stepped back so Nyeree could see she was wearing an outfit from Frederick's Seduction Collection. Underneath her black mesh slip, she wore a three-piece bralatte set that included a see-through push-up bralette, which gave her breasts the appearance of being up on a platter. She also had on the garter belt and matching thong. Yvette topped her look off with matching glamour-girl lace high-heeled slippers that helped elevate her ass a few notches as well.

"Dayum!" Nyeree shouted. "You wasn't playin' when you said you'd be ready, huh?" He stepped inside and quickly closed and locked the door. "Turn around for me, baby. Slow, nice and slow," he said, slowly rubbing his crotch.

Yvette didn't disappoint. She spread her feet apart and took her time turning as slowly as she could. "You like?" she asked teasingly.

"You damn straight I like. Baby, I want to give you a serious tongue bath." He took her into his arms, and they began a passionate kiss. Moments later, Nyeree slipped out of his clothes. His body was that of a Greek god—built in all the right places. His months of taking out his frustrations on the prison weight and exercise equipment had paid off. When he stood in front of her with nothing but his boxers on, he couldn't hide his excitement.

"Are you ready for this?" He glanced down at his growing erection. "You know a brotha ain't had sex in six long years, right?"

Yvette swallowed hard and looked up at him through lowered lashes. "Are you gonna hurt me?"

"Baby, I'ma hurt you real good."

She had started to step out of her slippers when Nyeree stopped her. "Naw, keep those on. All we need to do is take this little thing off." He lifted the straps from her slip and watched the dainty material fall to the floor. He scooped Yvette up in his muscular arms and kissed her passionately as he took her to the couch.

Nyeree reached for the bottle of champagne she had sitting in the ice bucket. He drank from the bottle and looked at her sprawled out across the couch.

"This is gonna be good," he assured her.

Nearly out of breath from the kiss, Yvette watched the bulge between his legs get even bigger. Nyeree followed her eyes to his crotch and smiled wickedly. "It's all yours, boo. You sure you can handle it? I mean, a brotha 'bout to tear it up."

He began by toying with her nipples. First he pinched her nipples between his thumb and index fingers. With each squeeze, Yvette released a deep and husky moan. As she struggled to gain her composure, he started using two fingers to enter her wetness. As he fingered her, he studied the changing expressions on her face.

"You like?" he asked.

"Mmm-hmm," she cried. "Please, don't stop."

"Oh, I'm just getting started," he promised.

True to his word, Nyeree sucked her neck, then used his tongue to lather her breasts and bury his face between them. He tasted every square inch of her body.

He didn't leave a single spot dry, and with each stroke or lick of his tongue, he had Yvette crying out in excruciating pleasure. Just when she dared not expect anything better, he spread her legs and told her to brace herself.

"Wait," she said, reaching for a condom.

"Baby, I want to, but I need to go raw. A brotha ain't had no pussy in years. Please don't make me wear a jimmy just yet. You know I'm clean; that's what you paid for, remember?"

"Yeah, but it's for your protection too," she breathed.

Nyeree shook his head. "Yo, I ain't had pussy in two thousand one hundred and ninety-one days. If something in here's gonna kill me, then please, let me go out a happy man. I've dreamed about this very moment for six hard long years; just let me feel you, baby! After today, I'll walk around with a jimmy on twenty-four-seven if you want me to—just not today, not today," he begged.

Before she could agree fully, he put the head of his dick in, and she swore she could feel it at the pit of her belly. Her heart started beating faster, and her breath got shorter, but she liked the way he felt. He was massive and stiff. Yvette swore he had spread her opening even wider.

Nyeree looked deep into her eyes. "You ready for me, 'Vette?" As he spoke, he stroked his shaft and rubbed her stomach. It was like he was trying to prepare her for what he had to offer.

She took a deep breath and nodded before he slammed into her with his entire might. Soon their bodies moved in a comfortable but frenzied rhythm.

It would be two days before Yvette and Nyeree got out of bed. They fucked for what seemed like twenty-four hours straight, till she was so raw she simply couldn't take any more. But each time she cried out in pain, he told her to use more of the K-Y jelly and they were back at it again.

It took three days before she could walk without any hint of a limp, but she concluded that those had been the happiest three days she had spent in years.

# CARMEN

The two weeks Carmen had spent with Chip had restored her faith in men. He stayed up under her, and she didn't have a problem with that one bit. For a man who had been robbed of his freedom, he didn't mind being all cooped up in Carmen's apartment, despite the fact that it meant another form of confinement.

While the sex they shared was earthshaking, Chip couldn't stop eating her pussy. There had been times when she simply had to tell him she needed a break. He would then tell her it had been so long for him, he just wanted to reacquaint himself with all that a woman, his woman, had to offer.

The more she thought about it, the more she agreed and continued to spread her legs. They had been in paradise since his release.

At first she thought it was too ghetto to ask that her man come with an exceptionally large dick, but she had to be honest with herself and admit that that was what she wanted. She still found it somewhat strange

that despite his extra-large dick, Chip always found a
way to keep his head buried between her thighs.

It was how he put her to sleep at night and how he
woke her up the next day. There were a few times she
had to break down and ask him to fuck her with his
dick and not his tongue.

The thing Carmen liked about doing business with
Frankie was that even after Chip's release, Frankie still
called to check on how things were going.

Had it not been for one such call, Carmen and Chip
would've still been in bed.

Carmen and Chip were relaxing in front of the TV
when there was a knock at the door. She sprang up because no one knew her whereabouts, and Chip's family
wasn't about to venture out to Beverly Hills.

"Who's that, baby?" he asked, taking his eyes off
*Jerry Springer* for a quick moment.

Carmen shrugged. She left the comfort of his arms
and walked to the door. When she looked out of the
peephole, she jumped back with a startled look on her
face. "Oh, shit! It's my father."

Chip sat up. "Whassup? Is that gonna be a problem?" he asked.

"No . . . um . . . I mean, I just haven't told him about
you yet."

"Oh, baby, is that all? Shit, that's cool. You need me
to go in the other room or something? Whatever you
want, you know I ain't trippin'."

With her fingernail between her teeth, she started
looking around the room nervously. "You wouldn't
mind, would you? It's just that he can—"

Before she could finish, Chip got up and walked upstairs to the loft. He went out onto the terrace to give
Carmen and her old man some privacy.

As Carmen opened the door, her father was headed

down the hall, back toward the elevator. "Um, hey, Dad," Carmen said.

"Oh, you are here." He glanced down at his watch. "I know you aren't sleeping at this hour?"

Carmen's relationship with her father was rocky at best. He didn't understand how, with all he had given her, she could live so beneath her potential. When she called and told him she needed to get out of *the* environment, he was all too glad to help. He saw it as his chance to talk her into registering for school. Carmen had dropped out of Long Beach State after only her third semester.

That was two years ago. Her father felt like she had been on a downward spiral ever since. He blamed that mostly on his ex-wife, who had been a hood rat since the day he met her and tried to rescue her from the hood.

Back in the day, Trina, Carmen's mother, had told him she didn't need to be rescued. She said she never had a problem with where she was from and couldn't understand why he did. Still, Mark wanted better for his only daughter. It was a constant battle for Mark because Carmen loved the hood. The more he tried to convince her that she didn't have to dwell there, the more it seemed she was lured back. Soon, he finally decided it was best to leave the subject alone. He figured his daughter would soon grow tired of the madness in the streets and would turn her life around.

"Carmen, I only have a few minutes. I have a meeting in the area and wanted to stop by to check on you." He followed her back into the apartment.

"I'm good. Just layin' low, trying to get my head on straight."

"Carmen, speak like the lady you are. I'm your father; don't go talking that Ebonics to me. Have you

given any more thought to going back to school?" He
sat down on the sofa.

She sighed and tied her robe's belt tighter around
her waist. "I'm thinking about it, but you stressing me
ain't . . . ah . . . I mean, isn't going to make me want to
go any faster. You said you'd give me some time, remember?"

"You're right." Her father got up and looked toward
the loft when he heard a noise. He looked at his watch.
"Well, I need to run." He removed his billfold and
pulled out several crisp bills.

At the door, her father looked again toward the loft
and pressed the folded bills into her hand. "I'll call and
check on you next week. Take care of yourself, and
stay as long as you need." He kissed her cheek.

Moments after her father left, Chip came down the
stairs. "Hey, is everything cool with you and your old
man?"

"Oh, we straight. He just, you know, caught up in
that Daddy's-little-girl shit. I ain't trying to hear none
of that right now."

"Hmm." Chip nodded. He glanced at the bills crumpled up on the coffee table.

"He thinks he can buy me off, but I ain't trying to
hear what he's talking about."

"So what do you do? I mean, you know, when your
man ain't occupying your time?"

"Nothing, really. My girl Gina and me, we roll around,
partyin' here and there, you know, trying to stay up."
Carmen shrugged.

Chip nodded. "So y'all just chill, basically."

"That's it. My pops keeps me laced, so I'm like cool."
Carmen shrugged again.

"But what would happen if your pops cut you off?"

"Cut me off? What for?" Carmen asked, frowning.

"I mean, he was talking about school. You say you

don't want to go back—what if he stopped kicking in the duckets?"

"Hmm, well, I guess I'd just go to the bank." Carmen reached for the crumpled bills. "He gave me five hundred dollars, but that's chump change, really. If he stops breaking a sistah off, I'd just go to the bank or Moms would help me out."

Chip stopped trying to get through to Carmen, but he saw her in a whole new light.

When she licked her lips and dropped her robe and asked, "How about we talk without using words?" he was more than happy to oblige.

# VICKI

Vicki was absolutely beside herself. Was it really true that *she* was about to become MC Murderous's number one? Hell, truth be told, she didn't care if she was his number thirteen. The fact was, she'd been corresponding with the one and only notorious MC Murderous, and they were making plans for the day he'd walk out a free man. And *he* was planning to walk into her arms to boot.

In the time they'd been corresponding, she'd come to learn a lot about him. He said he wanted to be with a down-to-earth female, somebody who wasn't afraid to be herself. Before she learned the truth about who he was, he said he was ready to settle down and have a woman to come home to every day. Once she learned his true identity, he'd been talking about having a female who could travel with him when he didn't want to be alone. He told her how lonely it was on the road, especially when he went on tour.

She still marveled at the fact that she had been conversating with him all that time and had no clue about who she had been hooked up with. When she told Pam, Pam didn't believe her. Or at least she *said* she didn't believe, but the very next day that bitch was on the line trying her damnedest to page Frankie herself. *Now* she was trying to be down with The Hook-Up.

Vicki had been counting down the days until Murderous's release. She had a mere thirty days to go, so in the meantime, her mission was to build up her stamina and keep doing the exercises to tighten the muscles in her coochie. She also had the time she needed to prepare herself for the rigorous challenges she knew she'd face as a rap star's girl. Most importantly, Vicki wanted to make sure that when she did give him some, she would be the very best fuck he'd had in years. She had quit her job and told herself this was serious. After all, she was fucking for a ring and a title.

The roller-coaster ride she always got and enjoyed from her relationships with men behind bars was at its height. She was amazed each time she thought about her luck. Vicki knew she could spend her entire life walking the streets of LA in search of a real shot caller, chasin' it and never hitting gold. She had Frankie to thank for this; there was no doubt in her mind. She knew Frankie could've hooked Murderous up with any of the hundreds of women who paid for her services, but she had chosen Vicki.

That's why she was giving Frankie a serious bonus. There was no way she could truly pay Frankie back for what she had given her. Vicki sat looking at MC Murderous's latest CD while she waited for his phone call. Its sales had gone through the roof since his arrest, and *Vibe* magazine still called him one of the ten most influential artists in the rap game, something that kept Vicki's panties wet.

When the phone rang, the door opened and Pam

walked in. Vicki quickly pressed the button to accept the collect call from MC Murderous.

"Vicki, baby girl, what's cracka-lackin'?" Murderous sang.

"Hey, baby, I'm just sitting here thinking about all the things I plan to do to you when you spring up outta that tank."

"Oooh wee, I can't wait."

Pam came and sat on the couch near Vicki. She took the remote and turned on the TV, but put the volume on low.

"Baby, remember when you said you want to put me in your next music video?" Vicki smirked at Pam. "Well, I was looking at your CD today, and I want to know which one of the songs you talking about."

"Well, I know three of the cuts still need videos, so we'll figure something out. You know I don't make those decisions alone."

"You sure you not just bumpin' your gums?" She chuckled.

"Vicki, I think you know me well enough now to know that I ain't one to be shootin' off at the mouth for nothing, right? I'm really feeling you, and I think we can really do some shit together, you know, if you stay down with a nigga."

"Baby, you know I'm down for you." She smirked at Pam again. "How did I get so lucky to get you?"

"'Cause you got a good heart, Vicki. You know hos just be throwin' the pussy at me; even in here, these guards be on one for real. When I heard about Frankie's hookup business, at first I thought it was the funniest shit ever. I was like this probably ain't nothing but a bunch of gold-diggin' ass hos looking for a saver—you know, some big-time niggas are up in here. Shit, I signed up at first just to help kill some of this time.

Then we started conversatin', and I was like bam! I came up, boo."

"Dang, you say the sweetest things!"

"You make it easy, baby girl. And that's on the real."

"Oooh, ask him if I can be in his video too," Pam cried.

Vicki acted like she didn't hear Pam. What kind of foul shit was that? Pam knew how valuable her time on the phone with Murderous was, considering they didn't get to talk for long, and she wanted to go dippin' into the conversation?

Vicki started to get up and walk out of the living room, but she knew if she did, Pam would probably go into her own room. Then when she wanted to brag about her conversation with Murderous, she wouldn't be able to.

# FRANKIE & ERICA

It was Frankie and Erica's very first time on an airplane. She could hardly believe they had finally made it. Frankie remembered the look on Erica's face when she told her they were going to the Belizian Keys for a vacation. She was so hyped. But when Frankie told her the flight would be six hours, the excitement quickly turned to horror.

"Flight? Why we gotta get on a plane, Frankie? Those things be dropping out of the sky left and right."

"Erica, how the hell are we supposed to get to Belize without getting on a plane?" Frankie demanded to know.

"Why couldn't you just get us tickets to the Catalina Islands or somewhere close? Why we gotta go up in the air for hours like that? I don't think I can do it, Frankie. 'Sides, what made you choose to go there?"

Frankie shook her head in frustration and decided there was just no pleasing her.

The few times she thought Erica could handle things on her own usually landed them in some kind of chaos that Frankie had to struggle to get them out of. Working with the new business was really the first time Frankie had to spend a lot of time away from her sister. But the business had turned into money Frankie never imagined they'd have.

She had the money to move them out of the hood but then reconsidered. Work would only demand more of her time, and with LadyRae lurking around Erica, it would only be a matter of time before her sister found herself in some real jacked-up kind of trouble. The last thing Frankie wanted was for Erica to start using again. She had experimented a bit, which is why Frankie wanted to keep her away from LadyRae at all costs.

"Okay, fine, if you don't want to get on a plane, we don't have to go anywhere. We can just hang around here. Remember that girl Neece? She used to always tell us stories about her family living in Belize and how pretty it was there. I just wanted to do something real nice for you, because I realized I have been spending a lot of time working lately."

"You won't be mad?"

Frankie shrugged. "If you don't want to experience anything new, why should I force you? We'll just stay here."

"But what about the tickets? Can you get your money back?"

"Naw, if we don't go, we just lose out. But I guess that's cool. I probably need to hang around here anyhow; ain't no telling how much money I would've lost takin' a vacation. Besides, maybe I'll just give the tickets to Bobbi. She would love to go and have a blast in Belize."

Silence hung between them. Then suddenly, like she had thought better of it, Erica jumped up and said, "Okay, let's go. I'm not scared, as long as you'll be there. Besides, we'll probably have so much fun, I'll forget all about those airplane crashes."

That was two days ago, and now, on the plane, everything was going smoothly. They were waiting for the flight attendants to pass out the headphones so they could enjoy the in-flight movie.

When their plane touched down hours later, Frankie and Erica were hyped. Frankie waited until everyone else got off the plane; then she grabbed the carry-on bags she and Erica had brought.

The minute they stepped off the plane, the heat stifled them. "Dang, Frankie, it's hotter than a pot of fish grease!"

"I know." Frankie looked around at the small airport and all of its buildings; most looked as if they were made of wood. The inside of the terminal still had an outdoorsy feel to it. There was no air-conditioning, which made her wonder what was worse, the hot air or the humidity. She and Erica were shuffled into the line for the country's visitors. There were about four other people in front of them. Frankie felt sorry for the workers. Although it was scorching hot, their uniforms had long sleeves, and some were topped off with a necktie.

"Welcome to Belize. Are you here for business or vacation?" the woman at customs asked in her broken English accent as she reached for the customs form and Frankie's passport. At the same time, two men picked up Frankie's bags, opened them, and started rummaging through her belongings. It didn't take long for Frankie and Erica to clear customs and go out to the waiting bus. They were headed to the luxurious Princess Hotel and Casino. Along the way, the bus driver used a small microphone to point out facts about the city.

"Belize City is home to the world's last manually operated swing bridge. The bridge is swung open daily, at five-thirty A.M. and five-thirty P.M." The driver's voice crackled through the speakers.

"Dang, that's huge," Erica said.

Frankie looked at what seemed like hundreds of sailboats in the water as they passed over the bridge.

When they got off the bus, Frankie checked them into the hotel. Erica could hardly contain her excitement. She wanted to go into the casino but saw the movie theater and gift shop right next door.

"Oooh, let's go see a movie," she cried.

"Erica, we could've seen a movie at home. We're here to have a good time, to do some things you only read about in magazines."

"Like what?" Erica asked.

"Well, we could go snorkeling and relax by the pool, or we could hang out in the casino. This brochure says they have Broadway-style shows in there."

Inside the elevator, Erica leaned over and said, "I'm so glad you convinced me to come, Frankie. I'm already having a good time, and we ain't even been nowhere yet."

"I wanted you to have a good time, Erica. We deserve this and then some."

Their room was on the fifth floor of the Princess Hotel. It had two queen-sized beds, air-conditioning, and cable TV. From their balcony, they had a spectacular view of the aqua-blue Caribbean Sea. The cool breeze blowing off the water and into their room was a welcome relief.

On day two of their vacation, they went into town and watched as the cruise ships docked. The locals went out to try and sell things they had made to the passengers. Frankie and Erica also went to JB's Watering Hole, a bar and restaurant, and had chicken with red beans and rice. It was the best Frankie had ever eaten.

It was day three that Frankie and Erica would remember most. They were walking back from one of the city's cybercafes and stopped inside JB's for lunch again. That's where they met Christopher and BD, two good-looking dreadlocked natives. BD's longer dreads made him look sexy. Christopher was fine and all, but BD was the bomb, and Frankie found him sexy as hell.

It had been months since she had paid attention to, much less given in to, her sexual urges. She could tell from the look on BD's face that she and her sister were in for a treat.

Frankie had come prepared—she was strapped with condoms galore. She could also tell Erica was digging Christopher.

BD and Christopher took them to some hot spots where they partied into the wee hours of the morning. When they were completely worn out, the party moved back to Frankie and Erica's room at the Princess.

Since Frankie didn't want Erica to leave and go anywhere with Christopher alone, they all got busy right there in the same room. They didn't exactly plan for it to go down like that, but they had been drinking some Belizean rum and learning how to dance to the music when one thing led to another. BD got up behind Frankie and held her hips to show her how to do some of the native dances. When she rubbed her butt against that huge bulge, she was instantly turned on.

Frankie turned to face him, and his mouth quickly cupped hers. Their passionate kissing and swaying to the music sparked something with Christopher and Erica. Soon, all of the kissing and dancing turned to clothes being stripped off. Before it was over, BD pulled up a chair and invited Frankie to sit and ride him. She did, as Christopher had Erica pinned up against a wall.

If someone walked in, they would've thought it was nothing but a big ole freak fest. It was just Frankie's way of trying to do her small part to keep a close eye on her sister, especially since they were in a foreign country.

Before they left Belize, they had fucked enough to tide Frankie over until she needed another tropical vacation.

# YVETTE

The more time Yvette spent with Nyeree, the more fearful she became of losing him. Her secret was sure to change the way he felt about her, and that was unfortunate because they'd really hit it off. As he lay next to her in bed, she couldn't help but think about the spine-tingling sex they just had.

Fucking Nyeree was like a serious rush each and every time. She figured that must be what happened when crackheads took a hit. She was definitely sprung, and she didn't mind one bit. He always took her to levels higher than he had before, and each time, he hit a spot she never knew existed.

There was no question about it, she was hooked, and she'd tell anyone who wanted to listen. She had been with other men before, but none like Nyeree. First she thought his stamina was due to the fact that he had been in prison for so long, but even weeks after his release, he was still laying in on her like it was their very first time. When she got tired of waiting for nighttime to come so they could get it on, they started doing it during the day, and that was real cool with her.

Yvette felt that the way to *her* heart was definitely through her thighs, and Nyeree had laid claim to the path each and every time he stroked her. Nyeree's dick was so good, she couldn't get enough of him; while they were going at it for the second time that afternoon, they were interrupted by banging on the door. It seemed one of her neighbors had actually called the law because she thought someone was hurting Yvette.

Yvette was beyond embarrassed when she had to explain to the officers that she and her boyfriend were very passionate and expressive lovers. At first the cops looked skeptical, but Yvette had assured them it was only the sex and that standing at the door meant she was missing out. She promised they'd keep it down, and the officers reluctantly turned to leave.

After dealing with the cops and once again back inside her bedroom, she flopped onto the bed next to Nyeree. She was spent, but she felt good.

"Whassup, baby? What'd Five-O say?"

"When I told 'em what was going down one smirked, and the other one just rolled his eyes."

Nyeree stroked her neck. "Well, a brotha is ready to finish what he started," he said.

Yvette chuckled. The truth was she couldn't take another stroke, pound, or anything else. "Baby, I'm straight."

His head snapped up. "You sure? 'Cause we didn't get a chance to finish up, and I'm ready." He reached under the cover and stroked himself. Yvette jumped up from the bed and looked back at Nyeree.

"How about we take a shower and get out? It's supposed to be a nice day today."

When he didn't respond right away, Yvette wondered if she should crawl back in bed. If he even thought she hadn't come, he'd roll up his sleeves and go right back to work, surely she wanted to do the same for him, but she also had to be realistic too.

She was a bit nervous at first, but when Nyeree smiled and moved to get out of bed, she figured everything would be okay. She would lie there and let him have his way with her if that's what he really wanted, despite how satisfied she was already. Yvette didn't want her man running the streets in search of pussy because he felt he couldn't get enough at home. Goodness knows she'd been down that road before. She wasn't about to lose her new man to that kind of foolishness. She felt good when he slipped behind her into the steaming shower.

Just as they were about to get out of the shower, they heard pounding at the front door.

"Damn, somebody wants inside bad," Nyeree said. He put the soap back and looked at Yvette. "You expecting company?"

She shook her head. "Nah, baby. I don't know who that could be."

"Well, you want me to get it?"

"Why don't you wait here for me, and I'll go get rid of whoever it is." Yvette got out of the shower and grabbed her silk robe from the back of the door; she jumped when the intense pounding resumed at the front door.

Yvette had an idea of who was at the door, and she knew her problems would get even worse if she tried to act like she wasn't home. It had to be somebody coming to get Roshawn's car; it just had to be. No one ever visited her without calling, because most people knew she was hardly ever home.

"Who is it?" she cried after she looked through the peephole and didn't recognize the burly man standing there.

"Ah, I'm looking for Todd," he said.

"Todd? You have the wrong apartment," Yvette said. She looked back toward the bathroom.

"Nah, I think I got the right apartment," the man said.

Yvette swallowed hard, and her heart nearly dropped to her feet. How could someone refuse to leave after she said he had the wrong fucking apartment? She didn't know what the hell to do. When she heard the shower turn off, she really didn't know if she should open the door and take her chances or let Nyeree see her standing there scared to death.

"Look, you got the wrong apartment!" She tried to sound hard, but she knew the words came out kind of squeamish.

"Bitch, either you open the door, or I'll open up for you."

Before Yvette could respond, an arm reached over her and the door flew open.

"Whassup, nigga? You can't hear or something? She said you got the wrong apartment!" Nyeree stepped up. "So whassup? You can't understand English or something?"

The man looked at Yvette, then back at Nyeree. "Naw, dawg, it ain't nothing like that. Um, I guess I got the wrong apartment." He glanced back at Yvette and nodded. "Yeah, that's it. I guess I do have the wrong apartment. My bad." he chuckled, then looked Nyeree up and down.

Yvette couldn't believe that Nyeree didn't back down. What the hell would she have done if she was there alone? She was so glad he was there, especially since the stranger was threatening to open the door himself.

"Some of these cats are sick," Nyeree said, turning to Yvette once he closed the door and locked it. He took her into his arms. "Damn, baby girl, whassup? Why you tremblin' and shit?"

Yvette looked at Nyeree. She wanted desperately to tell him, but she couldn't. Instead warm tears started rolling down her cheeks.

"Ah, baby girl, you don't have to worry. I ain't gonna let anybody come up in here and threaten what's mine. Your man is here, baby; now come on and let's get started on that wonderful day you was talking 'bout." Nyeree wiped the tears from Yvette's cheeks. "C'mon, girl, it's okay. That fool knew he was at the wrong door. Probably thought you were in here alone. Trust me, he ain't coming back," Nyeree said with great confidence.

Yvette wanted nothing more than to believe him, but deep down inside, she had a feeling the stranger wouldn't stay away for long. One way or another, her secret would get out—whether she'd still have Nyeree once it did was what worried her most.

# CARMEN

When her cell phone rang again, Carmen looked at
the caller ID and decided against answering. She wasn't
in the mood to talk to Gina. It had been weeks since
she'd seen her girl, but that wasn't what had her in a
foul mood.

She looked at the clock on the VCR again and realized she had been sitting around for seven hours, wondering and worrying. Chip had left Friday, and she
hadn't heard a word from him since. It wasn't like they
lived together, but still, not a day had gone by since his
release that they hadn't been together. Even when he
left to spend time with family, he usually returned or at
least called to say when he was coming back. It was
nothing less than maddening. Carmen had worn a path
through the vanilla-colored carpet from her constant
pacing. She was worried, and she couldn't hide her
fears. What if Chip had been picked up again? If he vi-
olated his parole, he would be sent back to the pen—
and she didn't want that.

What if he found himself another female to kick it with? "Damn!" she shrieked.

Carmen tried to think hard about where his mother lived. She could roll through and see if she spotted him hanging out. She quickly decided against that when her cell phone rang again. She figured she needed to stop avoiding her girl. When she reached for the phone, it stopped ringing. Carmen walked out to the terrace and dialed Gina's number.

"Damn, bitch, where you been hidin'?" Gina hollered into the phone, obviously very excited to hear Carmen's voice.

"Girl, I've just been chillin'; you know, needed some time alone," Carmen confessed.

"Okay, now that you've had some time, whassup? Wanna go out tonight?"

Carmen wasn't feeling it at all, but what else would she do? She had grown tired of sitting up in the apartment waiting and hoping Chip would come by or call. She knew she couldn't get a refund, but still she felt like she should be entitled to something if her man suddenly had a change of heart once he sprang up out of the pen.

Hours later, Carmen met Gina at Club Menlo. The small club on the corner of Menlo and King Boulevards was a little hole-in-the-wall. You didn't have to dress up or anything to go there, but you never knew who you might bump into once inside.

Gina was already at the bar when Carmen arrived. Before she could walk all the way inside, Gina was waving Carmen over to a waiting drink. "Damn, girl, I ain't seen you in a minute! Where you been?"

"Just here and there, you know, trying to keep it low," Carmen said. She looked at the drink. "What's this?"

"Hypnotic. I thought you could use a taste. So, how you feelin'?" Gina asked.

"I'm straight. The time away did me some good. You know, it always helps when you take a break from the streets and all its hoopla. Besides, it never hurts to get some extra beauty rest." Carmen noticed Gina was mad-mugging her on the sly. She wasn't sure what was going on, but she intended to ask Gina quite a few questions before they left the club.

"Well, you look good, girlfriend. But don't be running away like that. I missed you, dawg." Gina extended her drink toward Carmen. "Here, let's make a toast to reunions. And friends who should always keep it real."

Carmen reluctantly raised her glass. When the glasses clinked against each other, the girls took a sip.

"Speaking of keepin' it real, how about you and me keep it real with each other?" Carmen put her glass on the bar.

"Okay," Gina said, signaling to the bartender that she wanted another drink. When he walked over to them, she said, "Crown and Coke for me." She looked at Carmen. "And my girl is drinkin' Hypnotic."

The bartender smiled and walked away to fill the order.

"So, what's on your mind, Carmen?"

"Well, it's funny you should mention keepin' it real, because I feel like there wasn't nothing real about what went down with me, you, and Don."

Carmen noticed how Gina looked away when she mentioned her dead boyfriend's name. She knew then that she was on to something. She watched closely as Gina's shoulders immediately slumped. Gina lowered her eyes to her drink and began twirling the straw with her finger.

"I mean, how could you not know for sure that girl was having a baby for Don? I feel like you left me hanging, and then walked me into the pit to see my man get slaughtered."

"Dang, is that how you *really* feel?" Gina shook her head. "Look, it hurts that you would think I'd actually put you on blast on purpose like that. I mean, we supposed to be tight and shit."

"That's even more reason why the shit just don't add up. I've been thinking about this for a long time. What are the chances that you just *happen* to take me to a baby shower for some chick and she just *happens* to be carryin' my man's child?"

"See, I knew you was vexed with me. Why did you play like you wasn't? We supposed to be able to tell each other anything no matter what, right?"

"Yeah, supposed to," Carmen said. She took the last bit of her drink to the head.

"Well, here it is. Look, girl, Don had you wide open. I couldn't tell you a damn thing about him, because you didn't want to hear it. Remember that time I told you how I heard someone saw Kim, the strawberry, in his truck, and you didn't believe me?"

"I wouldn't say I didn't believe you. It's just, look at me." Carmen ran a hand along her body. "If you had all of this, you wouldn't think your man was capable of creeping with some crack ho either." Carmen shook her head. "It wasn't that I didn't believe you. I didn't *want* to believe he'd go out like that," she said.

"Well, what do you call it when you call me up on the phone but have that fool on three-way and not even tell me about it? You had me up there running my mouth while he sitting there listening to what I was saying. Then when he popped up and called me a dirty lyin' bitch, you didn't even say nothing. How you think that made me feel?" Gina looked Carmen in the eye. "Now I know you probably think a lot of these skeezers out here were jealous of you and Don, but you know I wasn't one of them. I was just trying to look out for my girl, and you wound up dissin' me over him. So this time, I figured I wasn't gonna say shit." Gina shrugged and looked back at her drink.

"What? So you knew?" Carmen asked. The bartender returned with their drinks. "You knew he was doggin' me out and you didn't say shit?" Carmen snarled.

"I didn't know shit for sure. But I did hear that someone said Wanda's baby was Don's. At first I didn't believe it, but you know my sister Shelly is still tight with her crew, so I figured if we went to the shower and he showed up, you could ask him yourself."

"What kind of shit was that? What if something would've jumped off there? You know how those Compton bitches are, and you know for damn sure how these females be hating on me 'cause I'm all that. You figured you'd just walk me into the pits like that?" Carmen shook her head in disgust. "It would've been too much like right for you to just holla at your girl *first,* right?"

"I may not have been sure about Don and Wanda, but ain't no question I've always had your back. It wasn't about to go down like that at all. You know I keeps heat, and I had already talked to my sister about it. Wasn't shit gonna happen to you there. The plan was just for you to confront Don *if* he showed up at the shower. We both know that if that baby wasn't his, he had no business rolling through. Hell, I didn't know those fools were going to try, and take him out. Well, not 'try' but you know what I mean."

Carmen and Gina sat at the bar silently sipping their drinks. Carmen didn't know whether she should be mad or grateful that Gina was trying to look out for her. Gina had been right about how things were when Don said something to Carmen. She didn't care about nothing but the dick. So if someone said they saw him with another female, Don would simply say the person was lying and Carmen would believe him, no questions asked.

Then there was the one time that Gina said she had proof that Don was kicking it with some hoochie who lived deep in the rolling-sixties hood. When she told Carmen and Carmen confronted Don, he told her to stop hanging with Gina because she was just jealous of what they had. He swore Gina was trying to hate on Carmen. And although most women were jealous of the way Carmen carried herself, she knew that much wasn't true about Gina. But there was a period where any time Gina called to go shopping, to go eat, or to go clubbing, she'd come up with an excuse about why she couldn't go. When she realized it was because of what Don had said, she hooked back up with Gina and promised herself she'd never let another man come between them.

"I swear I never kept anything else from you. It's just when I thought about telling you, I kept thinking you'd just side with him, and this time he might actually convince you to stop kicking it with me. I didn't want to lose your friendship, but I also didn't want you to be walking around looking like a fool either." Gina looked down at her empty glass. "So if you still hot with me, then I understand, but just know you still my peeps, and that's my word."

While Carmen wanted to be mad, she knew Gina had a good point. Truth was, she didn't want to see Don dead, but she knew deep down inside that their relationship had been headed nowhere fast. And even though Chip had been helping her to get over him, she really had cared for Don-Juan.

"I just wish you would have given me a chance. Things could've gone real wrong at that shower, and I would've been left out to dry."

"Never!" Gina said. "I would *never,* ever leave you hanging." Gina looked at her. "You know that, right?"

"I do," Carmen confessed. "And you're right, I probably wouldn't have believed you about Don. He just had a way of making me feel like I was the only one. I guess I'm just stupid when it comes to men."

"Shit, girl, aren't we all?"

"Well, that ain't nothing compared to what's been going on with me lately," Carmen said, finally breaking a smile, the first since she'd arrived.

"I thought you said you been chillin'." Gina looked perplexed.

"Yeah, but a bitch didn't say she been chillin' alone!"

They giggled like old times.

# VICKI

Vicki stood at the mailbox holding the envelope at an angle. She thought her eyes were playing tricks on her. What the hell was Raymond's sorry ass writing to her for? She had kicked him to the curb a long time ago. *Fuckin' scrub.* First she started to write "return to sender" on the outside of the envelope but decided against it. She had two weeks before Murderous was coming home, and she told herself if she remained a nice person, things might finally work her way for a change.

Upstairs she started going over her options for dinner. She went to the drawer where she and Pam kept menus to their favorite restaurants. She decided to order take-out from this little Italian joint a few blocks away. She ordered their low-fat lasagna, and a side salad with spinach. She had been watching her figure and didn't want to take any chances. She wanted to make sure her body was as tight as possible when Murderous came home.

The minute she finished placing her order, Pam walked through the door. "Hey, girly," she said.

"I didn't know you were on your way. I just ordered food," Vicki said, closing the drawer.

When Pam walked around to the kitchen, Vicki stopped and looked at her, sucking her teeth.

"Pam, why are you bringing pizza up in here when you know I'm trying to watch my figure?" Vicki asked with her neck twisting and her head bobbing.

Pam smirked. "I don't know what you talking about, girl. You used to love eating pizza. Now all of a sudden you're on this super diet. I can't hardly bring shit up in here without you wrinkling up your nose."

"It's not that, Pam. You know I want to look my very best when Murderous comes home. In the last two weeks, you been parading through here with all my favorite junk foods. It's almost like you trying to set me up to fail. You know all I have to do is look at that stuff too long and it goes straight to my thighs and my belly. I wouldn't do you like that."

"Girl, you being way too dramatic. If you don't want no damn pizza, then don't eat none. Shit, it ain't that serious."

"You know what, Pam? I'm tired of your little jealousy fits. It's no big secret that you wish it was you Murderous was coming home to. Ever since I told you who he was, you've had this bitchy attitude toward me." Vicki stood with her hands on her hips.

"Oh, no, you didn't!" Pam screamed. "I know you ain't callin' me no bitch!" she yelled, catching major attitude.

"What I said was—"

"Oh, I heard exactly what you said, Vicki. You think you all that 'cause you done hooked up with some jailbird rapper? Chile, please, they come a dime a dozen."

"You're just jealous, Pam. You wish Murderous

wanted you, but instead he wants me. And I'll have you know he ain't no fuckin' jailbird rapper—he is a multi-platinum-record-selling artist. You black chicks are all the same."

It happened so fast that Vicki couldn't believe it. Pam actually slapped her! And was drawing back to hit her again. This time Vicki was able to duck.

"I can't believe you hit me! Your motherfuckin' ass is dead," Vicki threatened as the phone rang.

"Bitch, I know you ain't threatening me. I'm the one who been by your side since you came down from your high-and-mighty private school to study us *black* folk. Don't you ever try to make it seem like I got something against you just 'cause you white."

"Pam, I'm blacker than you'll ever be. You don't even date thugs because you think you too good for them. See, that's why Murderous came to a white girl—he knows you black bitches are always out for money. One minute you looking down on thugs, but the minute you hear I'm with Murderous, you trying to see if you can get the hookup. You just like all the rest of 'em—a brotha ain't good enough for you until you see him with somebody who looks like me." Vicki touched the side of her face, which was still stinging. "Then all of a sudden he's a sellout. Well, what the fuck are you, Pam, Ms. Ask-Murderous-If-I-Can-Be-in-His-Video-Too?" Vicki clowned.

"You better get the fuck out of my face before you really get hurt up in here!" Pam hollered.

Vicki grabbed the phone. She pushed the button to accept the call from Murderous. Suddenly, she started crying, and Pam stormed into her room.

"Vicki, baby, what's going on, what's wrong?"

"Oh, boo. Me and Pam just had a fight. She slapped me, and then she started cussin' me out, all because of you."

"What?" he yelled into her ear. "I don't believe this shit. I want you out of there, Vicki."

"But this is *my* apartment, Murderous. Besides, I don't have no place else to go," she sobbed. Vicki was so mad at Pam, she didn't quite know what to do.

"Listen to me, baby. I'ma make some calls, and I'll holla back at you in a few. In the meantime, I want you to go into your room and lock your door," he said. "You hear me?"

"Yeah, baby, I hear you," Vicki sobbed.

She went into her room and waited by the phone. She couldn't believe Pam was acting like a jealous bitch because *she* had snagged a real thug. Nobody could say Murderous wasn't the real deal. All you had to do was turn on any radio station in LA and listen to the lyrics of his songs. Yeah, she had finally snagged the real thing.

The phone rang again. This time Vicki grabbed it before it could ring again. Pam had picked it up too. Instead of the normal recording asking if she wanted to accept a collect call from an inmate in the California State Prison, Murderous's voice rang through.

"Yo, Vicki, baby, grab some shit. One of my boys, DJ Spin, is on his way to pick you up."

"Murderous, I told you, I don't want to leave. This is *my* apartment."

"I understand that, boo, but I don't want you there with somebody who jealous of you. 'Sides, I got this spot in Beverly Hills; that way you can go there and chill until I get out."

"But I don't have time to pack all my stuff," Vicki said.

Still listening on the other phone, Pam rolled her eyes.

"My publicist, Lydia, is coming too; she'll take you shopping so you can buy some new shit. I just want you out of there, boo. What kind of man would I be if I didn't do all I could to keep my girl safe?"

Pam thought she was gonna be sick as she listened to the way he was being all goo-goo over Vicki.

"Okay, baby," Vicki cooed.

"When I get out, we'll go back to your place together. I'd like to see that bitch put her hands on you then."

"Who the fuck are you calling a bitch, punk? You don't even know me," Pam said.

"Obviously you don't know who the fuck you talking to!" Murderous hollered.

"Pam, why are you on the phone? Can I even talk to my man without you dippin'?"

"Last I knew, I lived here too," Pam said. "Since when am I not allowed to answer the phone in my own fuckin' house?"

"Well, it won't be your house for long. You wait till I get out. And you had the nerve to slap my fuckin' girl?"

"You don't know what the fuck you talking about. Your so-called girl ain't nothing but a prison ho! You think you special? Ask her how many other inmates she done hooked up with. Baby, you ain't the only one, and you damn sure ain't gonna be the last! You think you got yourself a prize, huh?"

"Why you hatin', Pam? Why you hatin'?" Vicki asked.

# FRANKIE & ERICA

Frankie could hardly believe how quickly she was blowing up. As she maneuvered her way down Wilshire Boulevard, she prayed she'd be on time for her very first live radio interview. She couldn't believe it when she received the phone call asking *her,* of all people, to be a guest on her favorite morning radio show.

When she pulled up to 5900 Wilshire, she even lucked out and found a parking meter out front. That had to be a good sign, she thought. According to her information, 100.3 The Beat's offices were on the nineteenth floor. Frankie thought Steve was the best DJ on the radio, and the fact that he was a comedian made his show even funnier.

All week long she listened as he and his sidekick, Shirley, talked about this new business where women were paying to be hooked up with men behind bars. Yes, there were some times when the jokes had made the service sound real bad, but still Frankie was glad to have the chance to appear on the show.

When she arrived, the receptionist greeted her and

offered her coffee or something cold to drink. Frankie was so nervous she didn't want a thing; she just hoped Steve was as down-to-earth in person as he came across on the air. *Wonder if he likes "Mr. Harvey" better than just "Steve."*

Before Frankie knew it, she was inside the greenroom and listening to the show. Although she wasn't going on until the nine o'clock hour, she had arrived at eight sharp. She listened as Steve and Shirley joked with callers and gave away tickets to upcoming events.

Then at 8:30, Steve announced the topic of the day, the issue he and listeners would be discussing in honor of their special guest. Frankie thought she'd die sitting right there inside the radio station's waiting room.

"Okay, y'all, as everyone knows, today we're talking to none other than Frankie Brown. For those of you who don't know her, this young lady started this business called The Hook-Up. Now you might ask what's so special about some dating service."

That's when Shirley chimed in. "Yeah, but this isn't your regular run-of-the-mill dating service. You see, Frankie took that old saying 'All the good men are either married, gay, or in jail' to a whole 'nother level."

"For real," Steve said. "And that's what we're talking about today. We want to know if you would wait for your man if he was behind bars doing time, 'cause Frankie is betting that you will. As a matter of fact, she's going a step further and laughing all the way to the bank, because some of you women out there are so damn desperate, you're paying *her* to hook you up with a convict."

"We'll have more after the break," Shirley said.

At that very moment, an assistant came and escorted Frankie into the booth. The introductions were brief and fast. Frankie couldn't get over how handsome Steve was in person, and Shirley looked good too.

They gave her a headset and directed her to the microphone.

They also told Frankie to pretend she was just having a conversation with them, to forget about the blinking lights that indicated who was calling in and to just get ready for a good down-home conversation. Frankie took a deep breath, exhaled, and prepared herself for the show.

"Okay, we're back, and now we're joined by Frankie Brown. And let me tell you listeners, she's a fine-looking sistah too."

"Man, you sound surprised, Steve. Whassup with that?" Frankie joked.

"Oh, nah, I'm just saying you know how it is sometimes—most women who write romance novels are old as dirt or they look like somebody's grandma, but deep down inside they ain't nothing but freaks." Steve shrugged. "Girl, I didn't know what to expect when Shirley came in here with this flyer. But, girl, you a fox!"

Frankie noticed one of her flyers that had been circulating around LA and the surrounding cities.

"Steve, let's stay on topic here. You see these phones lighting up? People want in on this topic."

Steve shot Shirley a look that said, "This is my damn show," and Frankie chuckled. She enjoyed the vibe between the two hosts.

"Okay, well, like I was saying," Steve said, "the topic is whether you women would wait for your man if he was doing time in the pen. Let's take our first caller." Steve pressed a button, then said, "One-hundred-point-three, Donna, you're on. What do you think about our topic this morning?"

"Mr. Harvey, I love you! I love you, I love you, I love you! I lo-ve you!" Donna cried.

"Donna, I love you, too, baby, but we're trying to have a conversation here, so I need you to answer the question. Make a comment or something, but it's got to be related to the topic we're discussing. And call me Steve like everybody else."

"Oh . . . um . . . okay, Mr. Harvey. Um . . . ah . . . I mean Steve. Am I live on the radio right now? Oooh, can I send a shout out?"

"You 'bout to be hearing this dial tone if you don't answer the question, Donna."

"Oh, okay, Steve. Um, yes, I would wait on my man if he went to jail."

"Okay, how long would you wait?"

"Hmm, let's see. I'd probably wait about six months," Donna said.

"Six months!" Steve screamed. "Girl, puh-lease. We talking about some serious time here, not no damn six months." Shirley and Frankie started laughing.

"Steve, well, six months is serious time if you ask me. Hey, a woman got needs, you know. I say six months, then I'ma have to do what I gotta do. I know the sistahs out there feel me. Y'all in radio land, Steve is phoine in person. I saw him in that comedy tour he did with Cedric the Entertainer and the rest of 'em. I love you, Steve."

"Yeah, okay, thanks Donna." Steve clicked the button again.

"One-hundred-point-three The Beat. Beverly? You're on the air."

"Hi, Steve, Hi Shirley. I love the show," the caller said.

"Thanks. You have something to say about our topic of the morning?"

"I do. I think what this Frankie person is doing is brave. We tend to give up on our brothas and sistahs when they go down for a crime. And I think if we start treating them like somebody before they're released, maybe they wouldn't go back."

"Okay, Beverly, so I take it you would wait for your man?"

"Naw, Steve, I ain't saying all that, but I am saying I think it's pretty good what she's doing. I like my man right where I can see and touch him, if you know what I mean."

"I feel you, baby, I feel you," Steve said.

"Oh, can I ask Frankie a question, Steve?"

"Yeah, sure."

"Ah, Ms. Frankie, I know you hook other women up with these prisoners, but would you date one yourself?"

"In a heartbeat," Frankie said. "But you know, I'm so busy these days, I don't have time for a date. Seriously, I'm either running back and forth to the prison or I'm meeting with the hundreds of sistahs who keep callin' and begging for a few minutes of my time. While my cousin Bobbi handles most of the interaction with inmates, I'm the central person customers deal with. And they keep me busy too."

"Damn, it's like that? You got that many women calling and willing to pay?" Steve asked as he stroked his mustache.

"Steve, the thing with The Hook-Up is, you actually decide what type of man you are looking for. We give you a detailed questionnaire, then in addition to that, you can say, 'I want him to have a foot fetish,' or 'I want him to be a nondrinker, a nonsmoker, and so on,'" Frankie said.

"What about his shoe size?" Shirley queried. "I mean, can you say, 'I want a man with, say, a size-sixteen shoe'?"

Frankie started laughing.

Steve looked at Shirley and said, "See, you wrong for that, Shirley."

"Whaaat? I'm just asking the questions women

really want to know about." She winked at Steve, and
the producer announced it was time for another break.

"We'll be right back with the woman who found a
way to make money off women willing to date men behind bars. And she's making a killing too. No pun intended," Steve said, half-laughing at his own joke.

After the break, a caller named Jewel was up next.
"I think what you're doing is disgusting," she said to
Frankie. "How dare you exploit these men who are al-
ready being exploited by the system?"

"Look, sistah, I'm not exploiting anyone. I simply
found a way to make an honest living while helping the
hundreds of lonely women find someone. If it works
out for them, I'm glad. If it don't, at least we tried. The
men participate voluntarily, and each month we have to
turn down hundreds of brothas who we can't accept.
I'm just filling a void."

"Yeah, but what happens when you hook one of
these women up with a killer or a rapist?" she pressed.

"You'd have to know more about my service to know
that would not happen. We do not hook people up with
offenders who are serving time for violent crimes. We
just don't do that. I've had women who thanked me for
helping 'em find someone. I've had some women who
tried it and found it wasn't for them, but the majority of
people who paid for The Hook-Up have been satisfied."

"I'll bet they have," Shirley chimed in. Again,
Frankie laughed when Steve shot her the familiar
scolding look.

"One-hundred-point-three, Letasha, you're on the
air," Steve said.

"Steve, I love your radio show."

"Thanks, LeTasha. Do you have a comment or question about our topic of the day?"

"Yes. Frankie, how old are the women who use your service?"

"They range in age, but typically it's women who are in their late twenties, early thirties. I've had a couple of women over forty. But keep in mind this is a service, and these women are paying to be hooked up."

"Can I ask one more question, Steve?"

"Yeah, shoot."

"Why would someone pay for this when they could go on the Internet and find a jailbird for free?"

"The service we offer is like I said before—exactly what the customer wants. On the Internet, you never sure what you're getting. Here, we find that person right down to the exact weight you want."

"Damn, is it like that?" Steve asked.

"You wouldn't believe, and even though we are selective, there are still more than enough men to choose from. I haven't had an unsatisfied customer yet."

Steve took the next call from Lynette. She said, "I think women who get themselves involved with criminals are not only desperate, but they're also stupid. I would not be wasting my time on a man behind bars. I know it's hard to find a man, but I'd rather share a man than go to someone in jail."

"Well, I'm happy everyone don't think like you. And I need to add, not everyone behind bars is guilty. Innocent people are convicted each and every day in this country, and sadly, I've learned it's the brown and black people who are least likely to be able to afford the good lawyers and are often the ones thrown in jail, guilty or not."

"She ain't lying about that. Wait, we got a brotha who wants to weigh in on our topic, right after this break."

"You're doing really good, Frankie," Shirley said.

The door to the booth opened, and a young woman wheeled a cart in. It was filled with drinks and pastries.

But the conversation was going so well, no one even bothered with the food.

"Yo, Frankie," the next caller said. "I'm Bo, and what if I contacted you to kind of help you out with all these desperate women? 'Cause if they willin' to pay, me and my boys ain't got no problems servicing them, and we out here on the streets."

"Look, man, you got a question or something? We ain't trying to *give* you the hookup; we're discussing something here, brotha," Steve scolded.

"Ah, yeah, Steve, all I'm trying to say is, why these women gotta pay when they can get it for free from brothas who are out here roamin' the streets already? That's all I'm saying."

"I don't ask my customers why, but I can tell you that some of them come to me because they're fed up. I've had customers who've told me that they're tired of being one of many. And besides, I think what you mentioned may be part of the problem. These women don't want their men roamin' the streets. This way they always know where he is."

Everyone laughed at that as Steve greeted the next caller. "Hi, you're on the air," he said.

"I'd rather not say my name. But I wanted to let you guys know that I did time with this dude, three long hard years. And it was all gravy when he was in the pen. I was working to help him out with his commissary, putting money on his books, sending care packages, and taking the bus to see him. He was in San Quentin. Things were straight as long as I was accepting the collect calls and so forth. To make a long story short, he got out and at first we were real tight. Yeah, the sex was the bomb! And it was all good till he got back on his feet."

"What happened?" Shirley quizzed.

"Well, like I said, it was all good at first. But then

later, he started staying out at night, and he'd come up with all these tired excuses. Then one day he just never came back, just like that. Later I found out he had another family. It seems I wasn't the only one he had been writing to when he was locked down. My question to this Frankie is, what does or can she do when these users—'cause that's all they are, users who want someone to do time with them—get out and things aren't all that wonderful?"

"Well, I don't think there's anything for her to do," Steve said. "We all adults here. And these women know the chance they're taking, I'd think."

"You're right, Steve. Caller, we don't guarantee you'll find your future husband in the pen or through our service. All we do is give you exactly what you pay us for and what you ask for. The rest, and I do mean the rest, is entirely up to you and him."

"Well, I guess what I'm asking is, do I get my money back if he just bounces when he gets out?" the caller asked.

"Nah, you don't get your money back. Do you get your money back if you don't like a movie you paid to see? No. This is the same thing. You are paying me to provide a service. Once I provide that service of hooking you up with a man, what happens after that is all on you and that man."

Frankie's appearance was supposed to last for only thirty minutes, but she ended up staying until the show was over at ten. She continued to answer questions about her business and listened as callers told her about their experiences. Some people had funny stories and others had serious questions. Throughout the entire program, Steve and Shirley kept cracking jokes, which helped make her feel right at home.

When Frankie got up to leave, the receptionist gave her an entire stack of messages. They were from women who had called during the show. They did not want to be on the radio, but they did want more information about Frankie's business. A few even said they wanted the hookup.

During the program, she didn't want to say exactly how much her services cost, but after much prodding, Steve got her to admit that the women better have at least five hundred dollars if they wanted her to help them in any way. In spite of the dollar amount she threw out there, she still had close to one hundred messages from women who wanted the hookup.

# YVETTE

"What made you want to do this?" Nyeree asked as he stood on the hotel room's balcony. He looked out at the waters of Marina del Rey. The sun was moments from setting, and the view was breathtaking.

"I just felt like we needed to get away for a little while." Yvette walked up and wrapped her arms around him from behind. She squeezed him tightly and immediately got excited when she thought about how hard and strong his body felt. It was so good to touch a man and have everything be completely solid. She felt so safe in his arms, just being in his presence. "Besides, if I want to do something nice for my man, who's gonna tell me I can't?"

Nyeree turned without escaping her embrace. He bent down and kissed her forehead.

"Don't get me wrong, baby, this is real nice. And I'm glad to be here with you. This is real nice," he said. He rubbed his hands up and down Yvette's back and ass. "Now, it's the other part of this romantic weekend I'm not too sure about."

Yvette playfully pulled away from his body. "You promised you'd try different things, Nyeree." She pouted for effect.

"I am, I am, but I don't see why we can't just kick it up in here in the room together, and alone."

"What kind of way would that be to spend Halloween? Besides, we went and picked out these bomb-ass costume; now you trying to back out? C'mon, Nyeree, don't be a chicken." She stepped closer to him. "Besides, I promise I'll make the after-party worth it for you," she teased.

"We don't know these people is all I'm saying."

"Nyeree, it's a costume party. It'll be fun, I promise. We can just go there, have a few drinks, party a little, then come back up to our room. Baby, I'm telling you, it's gonna be the shit, but you gotta at least give it a chance. That's all I'm asking. Don't knock it till you at least give it a try."

"I'm just not used to going to parties like this. I mean, this shit is kind of wild."

"It's different, Nyeree, but it's just a party."

"Yeah, but, baby, we don't know nobody who's gonna be there. A cat like me ain't used to being out all exposed and shit."

"Exposed?" Yvette shrugged. "What are you talking about? This is gonna be a nice party. This ain't none of that gangsta shit where you gotta be watching your back or you can't roll because ain't none of your boys gonna be there. See, that's what I'm talking about, Nyeree; ain't nothing wrong with stepping outside your norm every once in a while."

Nyeree exhaled. He didn't want to upset Yvette, but he just didn't feel comfortable with what she wanted to do. He honestly felt like this was all mostly a waste of money. This was something he had started wondering about since he'd been out. Yvette didn't work. They could lie in bed all day, and she didn't have any place to be or anything to do. He found it odd. The other trip part was she didn't seem to be hurting for money either.

The other day, Nyeree tried talking to her about him looking for a job, and she actually asked him why he needed one. He liked her tight-ass Beamer and liked the fact that they weren't hurting for money, but, hell, he was still a man, and he didn't feel right with his woman having to foot the bill every time they went out.

True enough, Yvette did take him shopping when he got out so he'd always look sharp, and he did like that. But he wanted to know exactly what her hustle was and why she didn't have to work at it.

The knock at the door brought him back to the conversation at hand.

"Okay, we'll go, and I promise I'll try to have a good time," he finally gave in.

Yvette was glad he finally agreed to the party downstairs in the hotel's ballroom. This was different for her, too, but she came up with the idea as a way to escape and give herself some time to think.

The way she saw it, the strangers might have tried to revisit her on Halloween or close to it. She wasn't sure what they wanted, but she knew it couldn't be good. Yvette was surprised that in all the months Roshawn had been put away, no one came or called about his car. Then she told herself that keeping the car was the very least she deserved. Shit, hanging out with Roshawn almost cost her her own damn freedom.

Then there was the issue with the money. Well, there was no doubt in her mind that she deserved it. The more she thought about it, the more she was convinced she should move. The only problem was how she'd explain it all to Nyeree.

Just the other day, he asked questions about her family. He said it was kind of strange how she kept to herself at all times. She told him she just wanted them to get to know each other better without having a bunch of people hanging around.

He seemed to have bought it, and she was relieved. She rushed to the door when she heard the knock. It looked like Nyeree couldn't believe she had called room service.

As the bellhop wheeled in the cart with food, strawberries, and champagne he stood by silent. Yvette felt him watching as she gave the young man a tip and closed the door. She turned around to find shock still across his face, but she chose to ignore it.

"I thought you might be hungry, baby." She smiled as she lifted the metal covers off two entrées. "Hmm, T-bone steaks, potatoes, and veggies." She picked at the green beans. "Gotta have the veggies," she said. Yvette looked up at Nyeree. "What? Don't tell me you not even hungry?" she asked.

He rubbed his stomach. "Nah, I can eat something, and a good steak would probably hit the spot."

"Well, c'mon, let's eat, drink, then let's get dressed and get ready to go party."

Reluctantly, Nyeree moved toward his plate and prepared to dig in.

Hours later, they stumbled off the elevator and back to their room. There they fumbled with Nyeree's wallet, searching for their room key. "See, I told you we'd have a blast," Yvette mumbled.

"You were right, baby. I did have a good time. I'm glad we decided to go. I ain't never partied like that before."

"And wasn't it live? I mean, we even won the dance contest. I never thought I'd run across people who ain't seen the crip walk before."

"For real. But they could've given us some Dom instead of this cheap-ass champagne." Nyeree held up the bottle. He finally retrieved the card key and slipped it into the door.

They stumbled inside the room and tore at each other's clothes. Throughout the night, Yvette had been eyeing Nyeree with pure lust. She couldn't wait for them to make it back to their room. She was ready to get her freak on, and she wanted him to tear it up. The costume party had been fun, but to her, this was about to be the *real* fun part.

She and Nyeree hadn't fucked nearly all day, and for them that was a long time. Nyeree could barely get his clothes off before Yvette was moaning and carrying on. It got him all worked up, and he couldn't wait to plunge into her.

Suddenly she stopped. "I have an idea," she said with a devilish smile.

"As long as it involves us both being naked," he huffed.

Yvette pulled him toward the balcony. "How about we fuck out here, under the stars, way up above the waters and out in the open?"

"Damn, girl, you wild, huh?"

"Just wild for you, boo." She rushed out of the French doors, ripping the remainder of her clothes as she moved. Nyeree could hardly keep up, but he didn't dare hesitate to try.

# CARMEN

It had been nearly two weeks since Carmen had heard from Chip. She didn't know if she should send out a search party or just call Frankie and place another order. She did feel like a weight had been lifted from her shoulders concerning Gina. Sitting next to Gina in her Range Rover, she had finally told Gina about her little hideaway in Beverly Hills. They were headed there since they were going to Reign, the restaurant owned by NFL Star Keyshawn Johnson.

When they pulled into the underground garage and Carmen had to show her ID, Gina looked impressed. "Wow, your pops owns this building?" she asked.

"Yeah, and two others just like it."

"Dang," Gina said as they cruised to find a parking spot. "I don't get it, girl."

"What?"

"Well, most people in the hood are there because they don't have a choice. If they had a way out, they wouldn't be there."

"Here, pull into this one, near the elevator," Carmen said.

"Well, here you come from all of this, but still you hang in the ghetto. Girl, if my daddy had all this, shiiit, you would never see me."

"I guess it's just the way you look at things," Carmen said as Gina swung into the parking space. "When my parents divorced, I didn't want to stay anywhere but my grandmother's house. You know my mom moved back there because she stays in the air, traveling and spending up my daddy's money, but I always felt more at home right there on the Eastside."

"I'm glad you did, 'cause we would've never met if you had stayed out here, huh?"

Carmen shrugged. They walked to the elevator and stepped inside when the doors opened. She selected their floor and rode up in silence.

Just the hallway alone was nicer than most places Gina had been. "I can only imagine what your apartment looks like on the inside," she said as they walked down the hallway.

"It is nice. It's a loft with two bedrooms. The lady in charge of decorating for my dad did a pretty good job too. The furniture is laid and I've got all of the newest electronics. Oh, I can't wait for you to see the plasma screen my dad installed in the living room."

They arrived at Carmen's apartment, and she had to fumble through her bag to find the keys. "Okay, I think I found 'em," she said, as she dug deep into her bag.

When Carmen opened the door, she dropped everything from her hands. "What the fuck?" she shouted. Her voice echoed right back at her. The entire place was empty.

"Damn, somebody straight cleaned you out!" Gina said.

From the living room to the bedrooms to the loft and

even the bathrooms, absolutely everything was gone. Carmen ran back and forth between closets—shoes, toiletries, clothes, everything was gone. When she stumbled back into the living room, Gina was standing right where Carmen left her.

"Are you okay?" Gina asked.

Carmen shook her head and looked down at her keys and the key card. She shuffled through her purse and swung the door open. The number on the key matched the number on the door. She was definitely in the right apartment.

"You don't understand," she said to Gina as she strolled into the kitchen, opening empty drawers. "Two days ago, everything I owned for years was here. How could it all be gone now?" Carmen looked around. "Just like that?"

"This was done by a pro," Gina said. "No doubt. A real pro pulled this off."

"I can't believe this shit." Carmen ran and found her cell phone. She paged Frankie first. Then she punched in the numbers 911, and two seconds later she paged Frankie again.

"Who are you callin'?" Gina asked.

"I never told you this, but Frankie. That's who I'm paging. Let me make a long story short. Okay, this is how it went. I don't know if you've heard of The Hook-Up, that new dating service?"

"The one where you basically order a man and they fill the order from the pen? I heard about that, but honestly I thought it was just some kind of joke."

"Oh, girl, no joke whatsoever. I paid her about fifteen hundred dollars, and she delivered. Okay, remember when I told you I've been hiding out here? Well, we were here together. It was like heaven at first. We were just kicking it, you know, eating, fuckin', sleeping, fuckin', drinking, and whatnot."

"Damn, sounds like paradise." Gina giggled.

Carmen paged Frankie again. "Well, one day he left and didn't come back, just like that—no phone call, no nothing. It's like he just fell off the face of the fuckin' earth."

Gina looked around. "So you think he ripped you off?"

Carmen shrugged. "He *is* an ex-con. I mean, how else do you explain everything being cleaned out like this? All my shit is gone. How the hell am I gonna face my dad? Shit, I'll never hear the end of this."

When her cell phone rang, Carmen expressed a sigh of relief. But she nearly dropped it when she realized it was her father calling and not Frankie. She tried to calm her nerves and placed it on the table.

"Oh, God! I can't talk to him right now. I'll let voice mail pick it up." She picked the phone up. "Oh, God, what to do? What to do? What the fuck to do?" She paced the floor quickly, unable to keep still.

"I'll tell you what we gonna do. Let's go find this motherfucka and get your shit back!" Gina screamed.

# VICKI

Vicki yawned and stretched her now-lean body between the satin sheets. She opened her eyes and looked around the room. "Ain't no fuckin' way!" she screamed as loud as possible.

She looked around the room again; she could hardly begin to believe she was lying in MC Murderous's luxurious bed. *Oh, a bitch could get used to living lovely like this*. It was the day before his release, and the minute she got up, she had tons of errands to run. The week and a half she had spent in his house was simply heavenly.

There was a cook, a maid, and another person at her beck and call. "Now this is the way a bad bitch like me should be living," she said. Vicki walked into the master bath and started a hot shower.

Later, the butler came into the office, where Vicki had started going over her list of things to do. "There's a delivery of the beverages for Friday night's event. Where would you like them?"

Vicki put the pen to her pursed lips. "Hmm, I think

we can put them in the sitting room for now. When are the planners coming to decorate?"

"I believe noon," he said before turning to leave.

Before she could get comfortable, Lydia showed up at the doorway. "Hey, Vicki, whassup, girl?"

"Nothing, just chillin' waiting on my man to come home." Vicki started squirming in her chair. "Then I'll really be working it." She laughed.

"I know that's right. Well, we've got the menu set, and the drinks are here. Now all that's left is for you to take care of what you need to do. Do you want to go to Rodeo Drive or to the Beverly Center?"

Vicki looked up from what she was writing. "Rodeo Drive, shit, that would be the move right there. But if I go, how will all the stuff get done for Murderous?"

Lydia walked around to where Vicki sat. "Okay, how do I put this without hurting your feelings? This party would've gone on without you. What I mean is, all you need to do is show up and look good. The food, drinks, music, and all of that will happen without you lifting a finger to do anything."

"Really?" Vicki asked.

"Girl, puh-lease. His record company is footing the bill, so everything is already arranged and paid for. Besides, he told me to take you shopping, but I guess if you don't want to go, I'll just use the money on my out-fit and a day at the spa."

"Okay, okay, you twisted my arm," Vicki joked. "A spa day too?" she asked, getting up from the desk.

Vicki's mind immediately went to Pam. She wished she could call and invite her to the party, but then she remembered they were no longer speaking. She felt a pang of regret, but the thought of going shopping along Rodeo Drive with MC Murderous's money made her forget all about not having Pam around.

Lydia had a good point, Vicki thought. When she

stepped out next to MC Murderous, she had to look amazing.

They strolled out and got into a waiting car. "I want to go to the La Perla boutique," Vicki said from the backseat of the town car she and Lydia were riding in.

"Wow, you have good taste." Lydia and Vicki had just finished spending a few hours at the spa, where they had the full treatment. Their next stop was the boutique.

Vicki walked right in and went to the back. She found a salesperson and said, "I'd like to see the Black Label collection."

"Right away, ma'am," the woman said, and walked behind a pair of velvet curtains.

When the saleswoman emerged from the back, Vicki looked at her and said, "I'd like the black wrap silk robe, the garter set, and matching top and bottom."

"I like a customer who knows exactly what she wants," the saleswoman said. She looked at Vicki and said, "You've made wonderful selections. That will be one thousand one hundred eighty-five dollars and twenty cents."

Lydia produced a credit card and they were off to Dolce & Gabbana. Vicki played it cool.

After seeing several evening dresses, she leaned over to the saleswoman and said, "Here's an idea of what I'm looking for. I want something my man will take pleasure in removing from my body. Something sleek and sexy. Capice?"

When the woman returned, she was carrying a black satin stretch dress. The minute Vicki laid eyes on the dress, she knew it was the right one.

The saleslady began describing the dress. "This has an antique lace trim deep V-neck, with an empire waist. The body-loving fit—"

"Hold up, lady. I'm already buying the dress. How

about you find some shoes to go with it?" When the woman went off to find shoes, Vicki went to the fitting room and tried the dress. It looked great and felt wonderful against her skin. She was stunned as she looked at her reflection in the mirror.

"That will be two thousand six hundred twenty-five dollars."

Again, Lydia produced the card and signed for Vicki's clothes.

"I could get used to this," Vicki said as they walked out of the store and back toward their car. "Lunch now?" Vicki said to Lydia before she could speak.

Lydia shrugged. "Okay, but I thought we'd go to the Beverly Center now."

Vicki frowned. "I have everything I need for the party. And, what, it took us only four hours. I think I did okay. Considering I'm usually in the stores for hours." They stopped at a light. "Besides, I'm starved. Ain't you hungry after all that shopping?"

"Well, I still need to get something to wear," Lydia said.

"Oh, snap! Girl, I wasn't even trippin'. Why didn't you say something? Here I am shopping for myself and not even thinking about you. I didn't realize you needed something to wear too. I thought this was all about me. Is Murderous paying for your clothes too?"

"Girl, puh-lease! I wish. No. I was only to buy your things. That's why I wanted to go to the Beverly Center, where I could find something in Nordstrom or some place a little more my speed."

Vicki didn't know what to say. A part of her didn't like the idea of having to do more shopping. She was exhausted and wanted to eat, then go back to the house and relax in the hot tub. Here this heifer waited until the last minute to say she still needed something to wear. Vicki couldn't understand it, but she reminded herself she needed to be nice. The last thing she wanted was for Lydia to go report back to Murderous that Vicki was difficult. After all, she had a ring to think about.

"Not that they take pictures of me or anything, but I still like to look nice just in case I wind up in any of the pictures."

"What do you mean?" Vicki asked as they neared their car.

"Well, when the label does events, they allow a certain number of photographers, you know, *Vibe*, *Sister 2 Sister*, and a few other rags. They're good for MC's image. It's a great way to cross-promote, and with the new video dropping next week, it's good to get as much pub as we can."

"I had no idea," Vicki said as the driver stepped out to greet them.

"You 'bout to enter a whole new world," Lydia said.

# FRANKIE & ERICA

"Well, I heard you on the radio last week, and I was calling to get more information about what you do." Frankie had heard it over and over again. Since appearing on the morning radio show, she couldn't keep up with the phone calls. She had no idea how most of these women had even gotten her cell phone number.

And most of the women who were calling were from surrounding areas. She had one meeting in Santa Monica, one in Moreno Valley, one in Sherman Oaks, and two on the UCLA campus. It had long since gotten to the point where she needed help. She had already commissioned Erica, but her sister's attention span lasted all of fifteen seconds, tops.

When Frankie stepped into the storefront office she shared with Joy, she saw that the woman was about to lose her mind.

"God, I'm glad you're here. This phone won't stop ringing, Bobbi says she couldn't reach you on the cell, and"—she lowered her voice and pointed toward the back—"you have some visitors back there. They've been waiting for hours even though I told them I had no idea when or if you would be coming in today."

"Joy, I think we should look at hiring someone else to help out around here."

"I'm glad you said that. I've been interviewing a few people for a receptionist position. I figured we could bring someone in to help answer the phones and help with some of this paperwork."

"Good thinking." Frankie picked up a stack of messages. "Let me guess, women wanting more information about what we do."

"You have no idea," Joy said.

"Oh, Joy, Bobbi and I wanted to talk to you about how much time you can give me to help with the business. I mean, I know you still have to do your thing."

Joy put her hand up to stop Frankie. "Girl, I've already told Bobbi that I got all the time you guys need. This is the most work I've had in ages. You know my busy time is right around tax season, so I'm cool, and you know how to break a sistah off, so just let me know what you need me to do."

"Whew! Great." Frankie passed the stack of messages to Joy and started walking toward the back. "You can start by telling these ladies what we charge; separate the ones who just want information from the ones who want the hookup." She stepped into the back area of their office and was greeted by twelve eyes watching her every move.

"Okay, ladies, who's first?"

A woman dressed in a fierce business suit stepped up. "My name is Stephanie Swanson. We spoke earlier in the week. Do you remember me?"

Frankie nodded, but honestly, Stephanie, Cynthia, Pam, Kenya, Yolanda, Sandra, Rachelle, and Trisha names were all starting to sound the same.

They walked back to Frankie's office, and Stephanie

sat across from Frankie. "So, not only did I hear you on the radio, but a friend of mine said you helped her out, and I was just wondering if you'd be able to do the same for me."

"I'm sure we can, Stephanie. I take it you've already filled out the paperwork."

Stephanie produced a stack of papers and placed them on the desk in front of Frankie. "Yes, I did, but I wanted to go over some of the information with you. You should know, I've never done anything like this before," she said as Frankie took in her information. She and Joy had updated the form to learn a bit more about the clients, instead of just finding out what they wanted in a man.

According to Stephanie's paperwork, she had a master's degree in sociology. She was divorced with no children and was very detailed about what she was looking for in a man. That was nothing new to Frankie, she had learned that when you tell a woman she can basically pick the perfect man, she tends to get real specific.

Stephanie was no exception. She wanted a light-skinned man with eyes any color other than dark brown. She wanted him to weigh 175 to 190 pounds but not to look too muscular. She wanted someone who didn't mind getting manicures and who was open-minded.

When Frankie frowned at the throbbing in her head, Stephanie spoke up. "I know you're probably wondering why I want him to not look too muscular."

Frankie shrugged. She never turned down additional information. It helped her get the best matches for her clients.

"I believe if you see a man who looks really muscular, people immediately know that he's been in prison. I attend a lot of social events, so what I'm looking for is more of an escort than anything else."

Frankie put the paperwork down and looked at Stephanie. "If you're looking for an escort, Ms. Swanson, there are several other agencies that might be better for you, and they're probably cheaper too, I might add," Frankie said as she reached for the Rolodex on her desk.

"Well . . . um . . . I, ah . . . ah-hem." Stephanie patted her chest. "How do I say this?"

"Just spit it out," Frankie said, then caught herself. She wasn't sure what Stephanie's problem was, but she had a room full of women waiting to see her, and Stephanie seemed to be beating around the bush.

"Well, my girlfriend tells me she is experiencing the very best sex she's ever had. And . . . um . . . well, I was told you provide detailed documentation of the men's sexual background, so while I do want an escort, well, I want someone who wouldn't be against, well, sex," she said.

"Oh, okay." Frankie leaned back.

"So, do you think you can help me?"

"Of course. Was there anything else you wanted to tell me before I begin the search?"

"Well, can I say I want his penis to be at least thirteen inches long?"

Frankie was so glad when the phone on her desk rang. Stephanie jumped up from her chair and nervously thanked Frankie for her time and promised she'd be in touch; then she rushed out the door.

While Frankie was up to her elbows in new clients, Erica strolled into the Man-trap nail salon across town. Although she spent some time helping Frankie with the business, most of her days were filled with appointments. If she wasn't getting her hair done, it was the nail shop for the works.

LadyRae noticed Erica before Erica saw her. One of the nail techs came up front and stood next to her. "LadyRae wants you in the back," the woman said.

Erica looked toward the back of the shop and saw LadyRae and her entourage being serviced. She held up her finger to signal wait to LadyRae as she spoke to one of the women waiting for her turn.

"Erica, what's up? I've been callin' Frankie for two weeks now, and she ain't even called me back yet," a woman named Jerri complained.

"Girl, we have been swamped. Ever since Frankie did that morning show, the phones been ringing off the hook."

"Oh, I heard her on that morning. Steve is so hilarious, and Frankie hung with him toe-to-toe," Ronda said.

"Yeah, Frankie did really good. So I don't have to tell y'all how many people heard her, and now they want the hookup too." Erica started to walk toward the back. "I'll make sure she calls you soon, though," she said to Jerri.

When she moved to the back where the nail shop employees surrounded LadyRae, everyone looked over at her and said hi.

"Say, Erica, what's crackin'?" LadyRae cried. "C'mon, sit here next to me. I need to holla at you for a minute."

"Whassup, LadyRae?"

"Look, I've been hearin' a lot on the streets about The Hook-Up. Seems like y'all struck gold with this one. I'll bet y'all flippin' mad ends over there."

Erica nodded. "Yeah, Frankie really did good with this one. I can't believe how much things have taken off. We are sooo busy."

"I was wondering if you could pass along a message to Frankie for me. I tried to call her myself, but I understand what it's like when business takes off—sometimes you can't even call your old friends you knew on your way up."

The technicians were wrapping up their work on LadyRae, and one of the women brought the bill. LadyRae took a look at it and said, "Oh, this ain't got everything on there." The woman took the bill back and shook her head.

"I'm paying for Erica too," LadyRae said.

Erica began shaking her head. "No, that's okay. I can pay. I got money," she quickly offered.

LadyRae tilted her head to the side. "Oh, so you big-time now, huh? Since when have you been too good to let me pay for your services?"

Fear quickly enveloped Erica. She didn't know what to say, and she wished Frankie was there.

"Like I said"—LadyRae raised her voice—"I'm takin' care of Erica's services too. So go ahead and put her bill with mine. You getting the works, right, E?"

Erica nodded.

"Like I was saying—I need you to tell Frankie to call me. I'd like to talk to her about partnerin' up. I think we could make a killin' if we went in together."

"I don't think that's a good idea," Erica said. "You know how Frankie can be sometimes. She likes doing things on her own. Besides, our cousin Bobbi is already a partner."

LadyRae leaned into Erica. "You know, back in the day, you used to come to me for things that I'll bet Frankie would be very interested in hearin' about. Now, I know Frankie likes to do her own thing, and I can't say I blame her. But it's getting hot out here in these streets, and I was thinking about turning legit myself, and I think Frankie's little idea might be just the thing to get me going. But I'm gonna need you to convince your sister that it would be to her benefit and yours to hook up with me."

"But, LadyRae, you know I can't make Frankie do anything she don't want to do," Erica pressed.

"That's your sister, and I'm sure you know ways to get to her that I could never imagine. Besides, if it was up to me, well, let's just say it would be best for you to talk to your sister before I do."

# YVETTE

The second day at the hotel, Yvette was able to slip away from Nyeree for a few hours. They were only staying about twenty minutes from her mother's house, so she told Nyeree she had a hair appointment with her mother. While she did go to the hair shop, she first dropped the Beamer off at her mother's and put it in the garage; she then had Enterprise drop off a Cadillac Escalade.

On the last day of their stay at the hotel, Yvette woke up to find Nyeree's side of the bed empty. She panicked momentarily, then remembered they were at a hotel in Marina del Rey. If someone was looking for her, they'd never find her there of all places.

She wondered how she had gotten herself into this mess in the first place. It was no fun having to look over her shoulder every second of the day. What if that stranger had followed her and Nyeree out to the Marina?

When she got up to go to the bathroom, she noticed the French doors were open. She was a bit thrown off until she peeked outside and saw Nyeree's bare back. He was sitting on a stool with his arms leaning on the railing in a way that displayed the various muscles in his massive back. Just looking at him turned her on immensely.

She went to the restroom, then crawled back into bed. She was toying with the idea of extending their stay. After three days of trying to think of how she could move without alarming him, she still had not come up with a solution.

If only she could find out who was looking for her and why; that might help ease her nervousness. She thought about going back over to the Gardens just to poke around but decided against it. She didn't even know anyone over there. What would she look like going there to ask questions? And what would she ask anyway? And what if someone spotted Roshawn's car and recognized it? She'd really have some explaining to do then. That was why she figured it would be best to park it for a little while at her mother's.

So far, the fact that she didn't know any of Roshawn's friends had worked to her advantage. But she knew all too well that many thugs were able to reach out to the world from behind bars. Not a day went by when she didn't think about what would happen if Roshawn had been able to talk to her.

Then the other idea she had been contemplating popped back into her head. What if she just laid all her cards on the table with Nyeree and seen what happened? But something deep down inside told her not to risk it. He was so good to her; she didn't want to risk losing him, and she had a feeling she would if she fessed up about what she had done.

"Hey, baby?"

Yvette jumped at the sound of his deep voice. She never heard him enter the room.

"You sleep good last night?" he asked.

"Last night?" She lifted her upper body from the

bed. "You mean this morning? We spent most of the night going at it like rabbits," she said.

"You complaining?"

"Oh, hell no, baby! I'm not complaining at all. I was just mentioning that we didn't fall off to sleep till something like three or four."

"It was three-thirty," Nyeree said.

"Dang, and how long you been up?" she asked.

"Oh, I got up at five-fifteen."

"Five-fifteen? What the hell for?"

"Prison mentality, baby. It takes a while to break it. I get up at five-fifteen every morning. I don't wake you, but I get up and chill for a little while. Today, I watched the sunrise. It was real tight."

"Oh, I'll bet seeing the sunrise out here is something," she said.

"No, I mean being out and free to see it from here. Things like sunrises and sunsets are foreign when you locked up in a cage. It makes you realize what you really took for granted out on the streets." Nyeree lay down next to her.

"So, what do you want to do today?" she asked.

"I don't know. What time we gotta be outta here?"

"I was thinking about extending our stay. We could hit some of the restaurants on the boardwalk, go to happy hour, and just hang. What do you think of that idea?"

"Nah, baby, this has been real nice and all, but I'm ready to bounce. Let's go back to your crib. I'd like a nice home-cooked meal. That is, if my woman don't mind moving around in the kitchen."

Yvette really wasn't ready to go back to her apartment; she wanted to stay at the hotel for as long as she could. But she knew it was time to go. She wasn't ready to start explaining anything to Nyeree, so she decided the only other option was packing up and going back home.

"Okay, we can go back home, but first let's do a little shopping. Then I promise I'll fix you whatever you want for dinner."

"Whatever I want?" he quizzed.

"Yep, you can think about it while you carry my bags." She jumped up out of the bed.

"See, I knew there was a catch to this shopping shit. You just need a brotha to follow you around and carry the bags," he teased.

"Yeah, but I'm willing to pay real good for that job. So whassup? You interested?" Yvette dropped her robe, exposing her naked body. When Nyeree reached for her, she stepped back.

"Oh, so you into teasing a brotha now, huh?"

"No, ain't no teasing jumpin' off in here. But you have to come and get a down payment in the shower first. After that, I expect all my bags to be carried without so much as a whisper of complaint. Then after we shop, we head back to my place and I'll make sure you're paid in full."

"I'm down," Nyeree said as he followed her into the bathroom.

They later checked out of the hotel and spent the entire afternoon shopping. When it was all said and done, Yvette had spent close to five thousand dollars without batting an eye. She wondered if Nyeree knew something was up. If he didn't then, she knew sooner or later he was bound to get curious and would probably be determined to find out exactly what was going on. When she hit the alarm to the new Escalade, Nyeree stopped. "What happened to your ride?"

"Oh, I had to put it in the shop. It needs major work, so they got me a rental. I hope you like it," she said.

Nothing could've prepared them for what they saw the moment Yvette unlocked her front door and they stepped inside her apartment.

# CARMEN

It was like the good ole days. Carmen and Gina were rolling once again. They had been hitting corners for hours all throughout the Eastside, the bottom, and other parts of south central LA.

While she drove, Gina kept trying to help Carmen remember where Chip said he was from. Carmen had called and paged Frankie with no luck, so it was up to her and her girl to find him and confront him about the things missing from her apartment.

So far, she had avoided five phone calls from her father. While finding Chip might not get all of her stuff back, at least she'd know what to tell the old man when he asked about it. She knew that by now he had to have gone to her place and seen that everything was gone.

Gina pulled up in front of the beauty college on Vermont. She was tired of driving around and still not being any closer to finding Chip. Carmen had long ago stopped giving advice, because she didn't know how to go about finding anyone, much less the newly released-from-prison Chip Davis.

"Dang, why didn't I think of this before? We need to find my sister. You know she either knows how to find this fool or she knows someone who knows him."

"But I thought you said your sister hangs out in Compton," Carmen said.

"Girl, Shelly hangs everywhere. I'll bet she can help us." Gina flipped open her phone and hit the number to speed-dial her sister.

"Shelly?" she hollered into the phone. "Where you at?"

"Getting my hair done," Shelly said. "Why, what's up?"

"I'm with Carmen, and we're looking for someone. What shop are you at?"

"I'm at Cuttin' Up in Lemert Park," Shelly said.

"How long you gonna be there?" Gina could barely hear what Shelly was saying.

"Huh?"

"How long you gonna be there?" Gina asked louder.

"Girl, I've been here for two hours already, and I've only been based. I'll be here for the rest of the day," she yelled.

"Cool, we on our way," Gina said.

Cuttin' Up hair salon was packed when they walked in. Loud music was pumping through the speakers. Some women were grouped off with others, laughing, while others were watching music videos on BET. Every chair in the shop was occupied, and a few kids were running around keeping up even more noise.

By the time Gina and Carmen arrived, Antoinette, Shelly's stylist, had finally started parting her hair to apply the perm.

"Tony, you remember my sister Gina, don't you?"

The stylist smiled at Gina as she grabbed a bunch of Shelly's hair.

"This my girl Carmen," Gina said to the stylist. Antoinette nodded and started pasting the perm onto Shelly's hair.

"Okay, here's the deal. We're looking for this dude named Chip Davis. He just got out a few weeks ago. You heard anything about him?" Gina asked.

"Was he in CSP?" Shelly asked.

"Yeah," Carmen said.

"Nah, I ain't heard nothing about him, but if he was part of Frankie's crew, you know her office is just a few doors down."

"Frankie's crew?" Gina asked.

"Yeah, Frankie, that's who I met him through," Carmen admitted.

"What? Girl, NO! You got the hookup?" Antoinette asked. Before they knew it, a small crowd had surrounded Gina and Carmen.

"Girl, what's it like?" a customer asked.

"What did you have to do?" another woman wanted to know.

"Somebody told me she charges something like ten Gs," a different woman said.

"What? Ten Gs? Ain't no dick worth that much," Antoinette said.

"Oh, there's some dick worth that much," a different woman said, and the crowd broke out in laughter.

"Ten thousand dollars? Nah, I didn't pay that much at all. I paid what, close to fifteen hundred. And I described exactly what I wanted. About three weeks later, she brought two people who matched what I wanted, and I picked the one I wanted. We started writing and talking on the phone, then hooked up when he got out."

"Whaaaat?" Antoinette said.

"You don't have to put all your business out there," the older woman said, "but, baby, what was the sex like?"

Carmen took a deep breath, then exhaled. The crowd again burst into laughter.

"That's it, I'm signing up right now. I ain't never been too proud to beg for some dick, so you know I ain't got no shame in paying for some if I could get exactly what I want."

"So her office is around here?" Carmen asked.

"Yep, about three doors down." Antoinette pointed over her shoulder. Carmen and Gina gave each other knowing looks.

"Y'all about to go over there?" Shelly asked.

"Yeah," Carmen said.

When Carmen and Gina walked into Frankie's little office, they weren't sure they were in the right location. It was filled with women, but the sign on the outside of the building had some kind of tax preparation name.

There was no one at the front desk or anything, but women lined the walls, and a few were looking through photo albums.

"Now, that one there, he looks way too sweet to be trying to hook a woman," a woman said as she held the photo album.

"Well, you know some of them probably go both ways," another woman commented.

"What?" cried the woman standing next to her.

"Well, yeah, what if a woman wants a bisexual man? I'm sure you can ask for that too."

"Chile, please," the woman retorted.

"Think about it; if I can request his shoe size, his eye color, and anything else, why wouldn't I be able to request something about his sexuality?"

"Well, I guess you got a point there."

Carmen and Gina looked at each other, then around the crowded room. "Who's in charge around here?" Gina asked no one in particular.

"Oh, um, a lady will come up front in a few minutes. She calls your name from the sign-in sheet on that table over there."

"Thanks," Carmen said.

As they waited, Gina leaned closer to Carmen. "So you just walk in here, look through these photo albums, and pick the one you want? Huh, this is some wild-ass shit."

"She wasn't this big-time when I met her. Actually, I've never even seen the photo albums before. She just had a bunch of paperwork back in the day. I guess business has picked up, though, because when I met her, you literally filled out the papers, being as specific as possible, and she matched you according to what you asked for."

"Uh-huh." Gina was tickled by the entire idea. They looked around the room at women from all walks of life. There were the ghetto girls, the business types, and everything in between.

When Joy walked up front and picked up the clipboard, Carmen quickly approached her. "I need to see Frankie. Is she here?"

"Ah, yes, she is. But she's with a client. Did you sign in?"

"I don't think you understand. This is an emergency," Carmen said.

"Yes, it always is," Joy said. She was about to turn her attention back to the clipboard.

"No, I think Frankie would definitely want to see me. I'm already one of her clients."

"Okay, I think she'd want to see you, too, but look around—all these other women want to see Frankie too. But they were all here before you, so you have to wait your turn."

"You don't understand. I need to see her about the

man she hooked me up with." By now, Carmen's frustration had begun to surface. "He's gone, and so is everything in my house!"

Joy dropped the clipboard. Complete silence fell over the entire room, and every woman stopped talking or stopped what she was doing and looked at Carmen and Gina.

# VICKI

Vicki felt like Cinderella as she stood at the top of the spiral staircase and watched the sea of lights flashing beneath her. It didn't matter that she wasn't the focus of the photographers and their trigger-happy fingers; she enjoyed being near the spotlight. *This is the shit. Damn, Murderous is large.* She had never felt so important or alive in her life.

It had been hours since MC Murderous's release from CSP. He walked out to TV cameras, newspaper reporters, and even a small group of fans. Just the way he rolled had her nose wide open. The only thing that upset Vicki a bit was the fact that she and Murderous weren't able to ride in the limo by themselves. Two assistants remained at his side, as did a rep from the record label and some chick who claimed she was writing a book.

It didn't take long for Vicki to feel like she had been played, and faded into the background. She told herself it would be okay, because later she'd have him all to herself. The party was winding down, and it had been one helluva party. There were several times she had to fight off the star-struck urge; well-known R & B singers and entertainers flooded the place.

Vicki had seen some of the video hos, and some other well-known rap stars. She also saw how the women clung to Murderous like he was single, and it made her mad. She didn't want to act out at a party in his honor, but the shit was starting to make her sick.

The one incident that really got her heated was when a photographer asked Murderous to pose with his girl. Of course, Murderous reached for Vicki. But as they were standing there preparing to pose, this skeezer with a big fat booty came and bumped Vicki out of the shot, just as the photographer snapped the picture. "Hey, boo." She kissed Murderous on the cheek. All of her ghetto-fabulous black girlfriends thought it was funny and started cracking up. Before Murderous could turn to her, the skeezer's girlfriends all gathered around and the stupid photographer kept snapping away.

Vicki was seething. She felt bewildered when she thought about how these gold-digging tramps were treating her. Even Lydia was acting like Vicki was some kind of groupie instead of Murderous's new lady. The more she thought about it, the more she wished she would've never even attended the party. Vicki knew the females would be jocking; hell, she felt the same way when it came to the roughnecks, but, damn, did they have to be so deliberately disrespectful? Part of her felt like the women, who were mostly black, looked at her and thought she was unimportant. She wondered if they would've pulled that kind of shit if Murderous had a sistah on his arm.

As Vicki sulked toward the bathroom, she started thinking of just how much she hated black women. Not only did they have this nasty attitude all the damn time, but they acted like they had a right to *her* man just because he was black.

"Giiirrl, he did not say he would put you in one of his videos," a thick one with a bad hair weave said.

"He did. I also heard he only went down to promote his new single. Girl, I heard it's hot. And while he was on lockdown, his shit blew up even more," a skinny, broke-down-looking one with a jacked-up grill said.

"Girl, no!" Bad Weave squealed.

Vicki stood behind the two, simply disgusted by them and their actions. Here they stood waiting to use the bathroom, acting like she wasn't standing right behind them. And she hated the way they were running their mouths. When Bad Weave stumbled back and bumped right into Vicki, she didn't even bother to say she was sorry.

"Um, excuse you," Vicki said, serving up more attitude than they expected.

They stopped laughing and looked at Vicki, then looked at each other and burst out laughing again. Vicki just rolled her eyes at them. *Skanks*. The skinny one was wearing a pair of what looked like cheap Payless shoes. She could see where the girl had used white shoe polish to try and go over the straps. But obviously she did it while the shoe was on her foot, because traces of white cakey paint were all over her right foot. *How fuckin' tacky*, Vicki thought.

"So you believe him?" the skinny one asked.

"Girl, why wouldn't I?" Bad Weave said.

Vicki looked around the two and wondered when the bathroom would become available. She was tired of being behind the two rap-video rejects. The thick one had the nerve to be wearing what looked like cheap Victoria's Secret lingerie. Who in their right mind would step out wearing underwear as clothes? *How do they expect to attract anything looking like that?* Vicki wondered. She was ready to walk away when six little words stopped her cold in her tracks. It was the thick one who said, "You know I'm staying here tonight."

"'Scuse me?" Vicki said with her neck twisting.

The two looked at each other, then back at Vicki. "Bitch, I know you didn't," the skinny one said.

"Was somebody talking to you?" Bad Weave looked Vicki up and down like she was scum.

"You didn't have to be talking *to* me for me to set you straight." Vicki was in full effect. "You said you were staying here tonight." Vicki had her hands on her hips now. "MC Murderous is *my* man, and you ain't staying here if I got anything to say about it."

"Bitch, who the fuck are you?" Bad Weave hollered.

Vicki started taking off her earrings.

"I know you ain't takin' off your cheap-ass earrings like you 'bout to do something," Bad Weave said.

"You did not call my earrings cheap. Bitch, these are Anthony Nak originals. Wait, let me break it down for you, because it's obvious you don't know what that means." Vicki took the earrings off and held one up. "Okay, these gold earrings cost forty-five hundred dollars. More than every item both of you have on your bodies and your feet. You know you wrong for wearing those cheap-ass shoes; then you had the nerve to try and use white shoe polish while the shoes were on your feet. You black bitches are all alike—no class but think somebody owes you something because of the color of your skin."

By now the skinny one was holding back the thick one.

"Hell, let her go. What's she gonna do? Better yet, lemme go get my man so he can toss you street skeezers out on your cheap asses."

Before the thick one broke free, Vicki was off to the main living room where she had last seen Murderous.

# FRANKIE & ERICA

When Frankie heard all the commotion going on up front, she left her client, Lee, in the office.

"What the hell is going on out here?" she asked as she walked down the hall.

Before she arrived up front, Joy met her in the hall.

"There's a woman out here; she's real upset. She said one of the inmates cleaned out her house. She said he took everything. Are we liable? I've already put a call through to Bobbi."

"Okay, Joy, I'll handle it. I'll handle it." When Frankie walked to the front, she spotted Carmen right away.

"Carmen, hey, girl, whassup?"

"Frankie, I really need to talk to you about Chip."

"Oh, are you the woman she's talking about?" Frankie glanced at Joy, who was still upset and shaking.

"Yeah, is there someplace we can talk in private?"

"Yeah, I was meeting with a client, but let me reschedule with her, and you can come on to the back."

Carmen soon saw Frankie escort a woman to the front door.

"Okay, Carmen, why don't you follow me to the back?" Frankie had heard the women whispering among themselves.

Before she and Carmen disappeared down the hall with Gina on their tail, a woman spoke up. "I know these are criminals we're dealing with, but I thought you guys checked these inmates out. I don't want anybody robbing me," she said.

Frankie stopped and looked at her. "Ma'am, the only thing I guarantee is getting whatever you ask for. I am not responsible for what these men do once you take them into your home. That's something you should think about before you give us your hard-earned money, because there are no refunds."

Two women dropped the photo albums and rushed to the door. A few others started whispering among themselves. Frankie walked Carmen and Gina to the back and hoped at least some of the women would be there when she got to the bottom of the problem at hand.

"Okay, what's going on?" she asked Carmen once she sat behind her desk.

"I don't know where to start."

"Let's try the beginning." Frankie spoke slowly, hoping to calm Carmen.

"Okay, everything was gravy with me and Chip. Then one day outta the blue, he said he was gonna spend some time with his family. I didn't hear from him for the next three days straight."

"Okay?" Frankie asked, still not sensing the urgency.

"Well, I went to my other place and returned home after being gone for nearly a week, only to find everything in my apartment gone. Absolutely everything. The place was cleaned out completely."

Frankie felt bad for Carmen. "And you think Chip had something to do with this?"

"What else should I think? I mean, how could all my stuff be gone, just like that?"

As Carmen spoke, Frankie took notes and asked questions at just the right time. Gina looked around the office.

"Okay, so you still haven't heard from Chip, but you believe he ripped you off?"

"I have no other explanation, and I need to get to the bottom of this before I talk to my father. We're here because I need you to tell me where I can find him," Carmen said.

Frankie turned to a small file cabinet. She flipped through several folders until she found what she was looking for. She pulled a file from the cabinet, then picked up the telephone and started dialing.

"Hello, ah, may I speak with Mrs. Davis? Yes, this is Frankie Brown. I'm a friend of Chip's. I was wondering if I could give your number to a female friend of his." Frankie stopped talking and listened. "Okay, yes, ma'am. No, she's sitting right here. Her name is Carmen. Yes, I'll put her on if you can hold a minute."

"Chip's mother wants to speak with you, Carmen." Frankie got up from the desk. "I'll let you talk in private. You can take as long as you need. I'll work up front until you're done."

When Frankie walked to the front of the office, a crowd was still gathered. She looked around and walked over to where the clipboard was lying on the table. Before she could pick it up, one woman walked up to her.

"Did that woman say one of your inmates robbed her?" she whispered.

"Okay, first of all, I don't have any inmates. These men do not belong to me. They are inmates who volunteer to take part in a dating service. I'm not responsible for what these men do once they're released from prison. Have we ever had anyone rob or steal from someone they've hooked up with? No. But is it possible?" Frankie shrugged. "Anything is possible. That's why when we hook women up with these men, we suggest you question them and try to find out as much as you can. We do have a very good screenin' process, but we don't claim to be perfect. I'm sure some not-so-perfect men will slip through the cracks."

"Ah, you do know these men are in prison, right?" another woman asked loudly.

"I don't know about you all, but my luck with those clowns who ain't behind bars has been nothing less than sad. So if you don't want to do this, leave so she can keep calling names off the list."

"I know that's right," a different woman said.

The woman looked at the other women, then back at Frankie. "I was just asking a question. I wasn't trying to piss everyone off." She rolled her eyes. "And I wouldn't be here if I wasn't interested. It ain't like her service is free," she mumbled.

Frankie wanted the day to be over. She had had enough excitement to last for a week. Before she could turn her attention back to the clipboard, her cell phone rang. She only answered because it was Erica. "Erica, whassup?" Frankie breathed into the phone.

"Frankie . . . um . . . can you talk?"

"I have a few minutes. Is everything okay? What do you need?"

"Um, I think we should team up with LadyRae. We could make a killin', you know, with all the people she knows. I think it would be a good idea. And remember when she offered to give you start-up money, Frankie?"

"Erica!" Frankie couldn't get a word in. "Erica! Is that what you called me for? Girl, I'm in the middle of a meeting."

"Okay, but, Frankie, will you at least think about us

teaming up with LadyRae? She said she been looking for the chance to turn legit, and she said The Hook-Up is just the thing to help."

"Erica! We will talk about this later. I'm busy right now. I already told you how I feel about her. We would be asking for trouble to make a move like that. Now, I need to go."

"But, Frankie," Erica sobbed. When she realized Frankie had hung up the phone, she threw hers into the wall. What the hell was she going to do now? Frankie hated LadyRae, and nothing was going to make her change her mind. There was no way Frankie was going to agree to work with LadyRae.

Erica thought about calling a cab and going up to that office and talking some sense into Frankie. She should've waited until Frankie came home. This wasn't the kind of thing to ask over the phone. Yeah, that's where she messed up.

When Frankie finally got home, Erica didn't want to rush her right away. She wanted to give her sister a chance to get settled. She was a bit surprised to see Frankie home so early. Usually after she left the office, Frankie headed over to a customer's house or met someone at a restaurant for dinner. Each week Frankie had at least ten to fifteen potential client meetings.

"You home early," Erica said.

Frankie looked at her. "Yeah, but it's been another rough one."

"Hmm." Erica nodded. She was eager to bring LadyRae up again, but something told her to hold off. The problem was if she waited too long, she ran the risk of LadyRae approaching Frankie herself. And she did not want that.

"I thought we'd go out to dinner tonight, but I'm dog tired. So I figured we could order pizza." Frankie dropped her bag near the door of their room.

"But, Frankie, you know they don't deliver around here."

"Shit! I forgot. Well, I guess we need to go get something. But I want to come back and try to get some rest."

"Besides, I got a taste for Tam's. We can get pastrami," Erica offered.

"Okay. Let's go before I get too comfortable."

They piled into Frankie's SUV and headed to the burger stand. At first it was quiet; then Frankie looked at her sister. "Erica, I told you why I didn't want you hanging around LadyRae, right?"

"But she's not the way you make her out to be. She's real nice, and she really needs help right now."

"You don't understand. She says nice things to you, pays for your nails here and there, and you take that for being nice. But the truth is, Erica, she ain't one of those wangsters—she's the real thing. Aside from the fact that she's a very dangerous drug dealer, she also pimps those girls out. Now, granted, she ain't out there on the streets like she used to be, but she is nothing but a lowlife. If she thought somebody was getting between her and her money, she wouldn't hesitate to pull a one-eighty-seven. It's just that simple. Not to mention, Erica, she's turned so many people out, I just want you to stay away from her." Frankie pulled into the parking lot. "I think we should switch nail shops. As a matter of fact, we moving. I wanted to surprise you, but I think this is the best time for me to tell you—I got us a spot in Baldwin Hills."

"Baldwin Hills?" Erica frowned. "That's so far, and we don't know anybody up there."

"Yeah, but it's close to the office, and, Erica, you can get to know people there. That's what it's all about. Before I go in tomorrow, I'll take you by so you can see the place. Oh, and I need you to come in for a few hours in the morning."

The news should've been music to Erica's ears. Instead, all she could think about was coming up with something drastic so she could change Frankie's mind—before LadyRae dropped the bomb. Once that happened, she'd really be in hot water.

# YVETTE

"What the fuck!" Yvette shrieked. "What the fuck!" She stood at the door looking around as her eyes quickly filled with tears. The farther they stepped into the apartment, the more their senses were attacked. A strong stench invaded the room. Yvette's eyes started burning; then she realized she was inhaling bleach.

The odor was so strong it was almost overbearing. Her couch, the love seat, the entertainment center, all turned over. The couch and love seat were shredded. Magazines, pictures, and what looked like paper towels from the kitchen were strewn all over the mess.

Nyeree stepped over some debris and looked around, taking in the mess. "Damn, baby. Is there something you wanna tell a brotha?"

Yvette walked back into the bedroom and started to cry. Every room in her apartment was trashed. All of the clothes from the closets were on the floor, bleach poured all over them. Everything had been soaked in bleach.

"Who would want to do something like this to you?" Nyeree asked.

Yvette was just hot. "We cannot stay here! Let's go back to the hotel. I need to move. This is crazy." She carefully stepped over clothes, shoes, and other belongings. When she stood at the bathroom door, she saw a repeat of what was in the living room, bedroom, and kitchen. It was like a tornado had touched down inside her apartment.

"Maybe it had something to do with that guy who showed up the other night. I don't know." She shrugged and squeezed past Nyeree in the hall. "We need to get the hell out of here."

Nyeree looked around the apartment. Yvette was all over the place, but as she moved around the apartment, she felt his eyes piercing through her. She couldn't think straight or even talk straight. He could barely keep up with her.

When he followed her into the living room, he saw her looking around frantically. She wasn't trying to clean up; instead she was searching for something. All the while, Nyeree appeared just as pissed. Yvette knew for sure he now suspected she had been hiding something.

"What are you looking for?" he asked.

"We need to get out of here," she said, searching through the drawers of her broken entertainment center. "I don't want to be here when whoever did this shit comes back." Still, she moved around the junky room, flipping over debris, boxes, and other things.

The faster she moved, the slower Nyeree stirred. He wanted to grab her by the neck and squeeze the truth out of her. But Nyeree knew better. He had spent time for losing his temper. He didn't want to go back down that route.

Nyeree looked at the bags from their shopping spree. They were still near the door where they dropped them after they had come in. He walked to the door and waited there. He figured the moment she found what she was looking for, she'd meet him there.

"C'mon, baby, let's go," Yvette huffed.

"Wait, before we go anywhere, I need to know what the fuck is going on. Baby, you wanna tell me what's up? Or you gonna leave your man in the dark?"

Yvette rubbed the sides of her face with open palms. She exhaled. "Can we talk someplace else? I just feel like we really need to get out of here."

After she was able to convince Nyeree to leave the apartment and they were in their car, Yvette punched the gas pedal in the Escalade and burned out of the parking lot. She had no way of knowing whether or not they were being followed. By the time she pulled into a restaurant parking lot, she had calmed a bit. They walked inside, holding hands. Once they were seated, Yvette took a deep breath and looked deeply into Nyeree's eyes.

"Okay, here's the truth. I think my ex is trying to sweat me into getting back with him."

Nyeree looked at her. He chuckled, but he didn't question her any further. After studying the menu they ordered.

"We need to go to Target so we can buy some stuff to hold us over for the next few days."

They ate their food in silence. Yvette felt good that she was able to think fast and diverted what could've been a messy situation with Nyeree. If she knew all of this was going to happen, she would've given up Roshawn's car and the money.

As they ate, Yvette's mind was racing. She had to think of a new place to live because she couldn't stand the thought of being caught up if those fools came back. And what the hell did they want anyway? As much money as Roshawn had, she knew he wasn't tripping off a car that he couldn't even drive. Shit, he was about to be locked under the jail.

Suddenly, an idea hit her like a brick in the head. She could sell the damn car. Quite surely she could get something for the Beamer. But without the pink slip, she'd probably have to sell it dirt cheap. Still, she knew some people who could help. That would, of course, mean coming up with yet another explanation for Nyeree.

She looked up from her food and smiled at him. She felt that guilt starting to creep up on her again. It wasn't right that she was lying to him, but there was no way she could come clean.

After dinner, they stopped by Target, then it was off to a nearby hotel. She got a room for five days. She figured that would give them enough time to decide what to do or where to go.

Once they settled into the room, she started searching for the bag with her toiletries. "Ny, did you bring the red Target bag in?" she asked.

"I must've left it in the car. Here, let me go get it. I'll be back," he said.

Nyeree went out to the parking lot. But before he found the Escalade, he walked over to a purple Blazer and slid into the passenger seat.

"So, whassup?"

"I don't know, man. Y'all did a number on the place."

"We didn't do nothing to her place. What are you talking about? Man, you been kicking it with her ass all this time and you still ain't figured nothing out?"

"Well, I probably would've got real far if Big Boy hadn't showed up at the apartment. I told you fools to let me handle this."

"While you fuckin' around playin' the dating game

and shit, we are missing out on some serious cheddar, and I ain't gotta tell you what's gonna happen if we don't find what we're looking for. Where's the Beamer anyway?"

"I don't know, man. She said she put it in the shop, but ain't nothing wrong with that car. I need to find out where her people live."

"Well, we need to find it before the Bounties come looking. You ain't got all day, so either you help out or step aside so we can handle this our way. And if the place was tossed, them fools are probably already on to her. We didn't touch the place. You sure you don't want to let us take care of this?"

"Nah, I got it, I got it. Just let me handle this."

Nyeree left the Blazer and got the Target bag from the Escalade, then went back up to their room.

"Babe, is that you? I ordered room service," Yvette's voice shouted from the bathroom.

"Cool," he said. Nyeree was trying to think of a way to get the truth out of Yvette. He had to admit she was one down-ass bitch. At least he knew she'd go down for the cause no matter what. She wasn't giving up shit. But damn, he didn't want anything to happen to her, so he had to figure out a way to get to the truth before somebody else came looking.

# CARMEN

The Davises lived in a brownstone fourplex off Jefferson and Van Buren Place. When Gina pulled up in front of the address Mrs. Davis had given them, they saw a petite woman standing outside with old-school pink sponge rollers in her hair.

"Are you Carmen?" Mrs. Davis asked, looking at Gina as she stepped out of the truck.

"No, I'm Gina. That's Carmen." Gina pointed toward the passenger side of her truck.

Carmen walked over to the driver's side and went up to the woman.

"I'm Charlene, Chip's mother. It's good to meet you." She crossed her arms at her chest and glared at Carmen. "Now, what's the problem?" she asked.

Carmen couldn't get over the resemblance between Charlene and her son. He was the spitting image of her, except she was petite. But they shared the same light brown eyes and the same demeanor.

"Well, I was wondering where Chip is. I haven't heard from him since Friday. And I thought he said he was coming to spend some time with his family. It's very urgent that I talk with him."

"He made me promise not to say where he is. He told me even if *you* called that I'm not to tell you," Charlene said in a sharp tone.

Gina and Carmen exchanged knowing glances. That was definitely a sign as far as Carmen was concerned.

"I'll bet he don't want me to know where he is. But check this out." Carmen was trying to keep her attitude in check. "Here's the situation, Mrs. Davis. I think your son stripped my apartment of all my stuff."

"What?" Charlene frowned.

"I came home and found my place completely empty!" Carmen felt herself getting worked up.

"Okay, look here. My son didn't steal a damn thing from you!" Charlene snapped.

"You his mother—what else would you say?" Gina added.

Charlene rolled her eyes, then looked at Carmen. "Chip has been in the hospital since Friday afternoon. He left your place Friday morning, and came here. He was here about two hours before we took him to Kaiser."

"Uh, the hospital?" Carmen asked. She eased back a bit, unsure of just how she could take back everything she had been thinking about him.

"I guess just because he's got a record y'all think he's some kind of crook. Well, he's innocent, just like he was innocent when those people convicted him of a crime he didn't commit." She looked at Carmen. "I'm ashamed of you. My son really liked you and said nothing but good things about you, talking about how lucky he was that you chose him. But deep down inside, you don't see nothing other than his record. I don't know who in the hell ripped you off, but it damn sure wasn't my son. So maybe you need to check out some of your *other* friends." Mrs. Davis glared at Gina. Before either of them could respond, Charlene turned and stormed away.

Carmen leaned up against the truck. "If it wasn't him, then who could've moved all my stuff like that?" Her cell phone rang.

"We don't know it wasn't him. Look, girl, he may not have done it himself, but who's to say he didn't have someone do it for him?"

"Damn, it's my father again. I guess I better stop avoiding him and face the music." Carmen smacked her lips and flipped the phone open. "Hello?"

"Carmen, I've been trying to reach you for the past few days. Your voice mail is full, so I couldn't leave a message. I guess you haven't been by the apartment or I would've heard from you by now. I had to move you to another apartment. We sold the one you were in for nearly three times the asking price. I'm sure you understand, honey. You're on the sixteenth floor now. If you go by during office hours, the manager will have your new keys."

Carmen shook her head. "Why didn't you tell me?"

"I've been trying to call you, but I kept getting your voice mail, which was full. Look, I need to catch a flight. I'll be out of town on business. I'll be back in a few days."

"Have a safe trip, Dad." When she closed the phone, she looked at Gina and shook her head. "You will not believe this shit."

Gina started laughing. "Let me guess," she said. "Your father cleaned out your apartment."

"Damn, how could you let me go out like that? I made a fool out of myself. You know Chip's mama is gonna go and drag my name through the mud. Damn, would you take me back if you was him?"

"With your fine ass, hell yeah," Gina said, still laughing as she hit the alarm and opened the door. Before she started the truck, she looked at Carmen. "Maybe you should go apologize to his moms—you never know," she said.

Carmen bolted to Mrs. Davis's door and knocked on the black iron screen. When she saw the woman walking toward the front door, she started talking. "You were right about everything you said. I made a huge mistake, and I am so very sorry. Please don't say anything to Chip about all of this."

"So what happened to all of your stuff?" Charlene asked without opening the door.

"My father had to sell the apartment. He moved me to a different floor. I'm so sorry."

"My son is a good man. Bad things happen to good people. He did not commit that crime. He knows it, I know it, and so did that DA, but I didn't have the money to get him a real good lawyer. Like I told you, he's had nothing but good things to say about you. But if every time something goes wrong you're gonna blame him, I'd rather you just walk out of his life now. He's had enough of that shit. And I can tell you, being blamed for something you didn't do ain't fun."

"You are right, and I'm sorry. I hope you won't tell him about this, because I really like him, and I think he really likes me. I know he didn't want me to know why he was in the hospital, but can you at least tell me if he's gonna be okay?"

"He had to have surgery for a hernia. That was Friday evening, but there were complications. He's supposed to be getting out later this afternoon. He didn't want you to worry about him, so he asked me not to tell you."

"Can you call me when he gets home? I'd really appreciate it."

"I'll do better—I'll have him call you."

When Carmen got back in the truck, Gina wanted all the details. "What did she say?"

"Well, I think she forgave me. She said he's coming home later this afternoon. So we'll see."

"What's wrong with him?" Gina asked.

"He had to have surgery for a hernia."

"A hernia? Damn, just how much fuckin' y'all been doin'?"

"Shut up!" Carmen squealed as Gina drove off and headed toward the Santa Monica Freeway.

# VICKI

Vicki arrived in the main room where she had last seen Murderous. He was nowhere to be found. She spotted Lydia talking to a group of women. Vicki couldn't get over how trashy most of the women looked. She hadn't seen so many Lycra, see-through, lace, or sheer outfits under one roof in a long time.

She sashayed over to Lydia and her friends. "Lydia, I need to talk to you right now!" she demanded.

The women standing around Lydia looked at Vicki as if she were a space monkey.

"Ah, Vicki, can't you see I'm busy?" Lydia said.

A few of the women shook their heads as if to dismiss Vicki. That only made Vicki more upset. She stood for a few more minutes unsure of what she should do. It was one thing for her to be dissed by strangers, but by one of her man's employees? She wasn't about to have it.

"Look, Lydia. I have a problem that I need you to take care of. I can't find Murderous. And I need you to tell a couple of hoochies to leave." Her neck was still twisting when she finished her demand.

"Is that all?" one of the women said jokingly.

"Hey, why don't you tell me where they are so we can go and beat them down?" another woman yelled. The others, including Lydia, started chuckling. That's when Vicki realized these women weren't half naked like the rest. The more she thought about it, the more she realized they didn't seem to be cackling and talking about which rapper they were going to fuck and so forth.

"Let me guess," another woman said. "Is she the flava of the month?"

Lydia didn't even bother answering. She moved away from her friends and put her arm around Vicki's shoulder. "Look, Vicki, I'm actually off. I'm here as a guest just like you. So if you're having a problem with someone, maybe you should go talk to security. Or try to track Murderous down."

Vicki was furious. "So what am I supposed to do, let these tramps just say whatever they want about my man?"

"If you and Murderous are going to make it, you need to develop a tough skin—this ain't nothing, girl. Now look, my friends and I were just about to go grab something to eat before things really start getting wild around here."

"You not staying?" Vicki asked.

Lydia frowned. "Puh-leeease! Staying? For what? The only people who typically stay after, say about another hour or so, are staying for the after-party. You know, the private kind, and we don't get down like that." She turned toward her friends. "For us, this is work. We not on the clock, but still, our bosses are watching."

That explained why Lydia was dressed in a simple

black suit. Vicki first thought maybe it was all she
could afford. When she looked at Lydia's friends, she
saw they were dressed all homely looking too.

"So how am I supposed to find Murderous? I ain't
seen him in nearly an hour."

"Vicki, I know this is a party in his honor, but he's
sort of working too."

"Well, why would he have me here if he was working, if he didn't have time to spend with me? He ain't
even been introducing me as his woman. I'm confused."

"Vicki, his image ain't that of a settling-down family type of man. He's a rapper, for God's sake. He has
to have most women here thinking they're able to be
with him tonight if they want. If he has them thinking
it's possible, that somehow translates to CD sales."

"I'm just saying this ain't what I signed up for. I
thought I'd be kicking it with Murderous, not hanging
by myself and being dissed by these little gold-digging
hoochies."

Lydia shrugged. "It's all part of the game." She
started walking back toward her friends. "And it don't
get no easier."

When Lydia reached her friends, one of them said,
"Are y'all ready to leave?" Then just like that, they
walked down the hall and out the front door. Vicki
couldn't believe it. She didn't understand why they
wouldn't want to hang around and see if they could
snag themselves a baller. *If they had, maybe they
would've been able to dress better. Shit, don't everybody want to get their shine on?*

Vicki went upstairs, still in search of her man. She
was getting tired of moving around alone. She wished
Pam was with her. When they went out on the prowl,
they always had a good time. Even though they never
tag-teamed a thug, they often joked about doing it.

Vicki had been down, but it was Pam who said that would mean taking their friendship to a whole new level.

As she rounded one of the corners, she bumped right into Murderous and his entourage. "Ah, baby, I been looking for you," Vicki cooed. "Where you been? These girls were messing with me downstairs, and I wanted you to put them out."

"Vicki, boo, I'm in the middle of something right now. Here, why don't you go into the bedroom and wait for me there. I know this is a party, but I got some business to tend to. Just go into the room, lock the door, and I'll bring a bottle of Cristal for us later."

He pecked her on the cheek before she could say anything else and moved on.

# FRANKIE & ERICA

The day of their move, Erica told Frankie she was sick, and she was. But she wasn't suffering from the type of illness medicine could cure. She was sick over the thought that she had not been able to change Frankie's mind about LadyRae.

And LadyRae kept calling to remind Erica of all she had to lose. She wished could just pack up and leave California for good, that way she'd be far beyond LadyRae's reach. But deep down, Erica knew they wouldn't leave California, because this business had turned into a serious gold mine for Frankie. She was also pissed because at a time when she should've been enjoying a new lovely lifestyle, with enough money at her disposal, she was instead worried about what LadyRae might do to bring them down.

Yeah, she was sick all right, and she didn't see herself feeling better any time soon.

The movers came and packed up their small room. "Is this all?" one man asked, looking around the cramped room.

"Yeah, you need more or something?" Erica asked, irritated more by her dilemma than by the men.

"It's just you guys could've saved yourself some money if this is all you had."

"Money is not a problem; we just need the stuff moved. It's mostly clothes and shoes. And you know what, we're not even taking the beds and dressers, so it's mostly clothes and all these boxes." She pointed to boxes stuffed with paperwork and other things related to the business. The phone rang, and she was actually afraid to answer it. When the men looked at the phone, she picked up the receiver and hoped for the best.

"Hello?"

"Erica, are the movers there?" Frankie asked.

"Yeah, they here." She looked at one man as he taped up a box.

"After they move that stuff, I need them to go pick up our new furniture. I know you don't care about stuff like that, so I just picked out everything. I figured that would make it easier."

"That's cool, Frankie. Where are they going?"

"This spot right on the corner of Manchester and Vermont. They need to get with Marvin LeFlour when they get there. They're picking up a living room set, furniture for both bedrooms, and a dinette set."

"Okay, I'll let them know."

"You feeling any better?" Frankie asked.

"A little bit. I probably just need to rest."

"I wish I could've changed the moving date, but I figured it was best if we got it over with. After they move the stuff in, why don't you just make up your bed and lie down for a little while? I'll come up and check on you when I get a break around here."

"Okay."

"Oh, catch a cab up there and wait for the movers to come. There ain't no point in you hanging around;

there's nothing for you to do. I would tell you to come by here, but you know it's a zoo around here. So I'll check on you later."

Even empty, the condo Frankie bought was tight. As she walked around the empty space, Erica couldn't help but feel like they had finally made it. Their living room was large and spacious, with sliding glass doors that led to a balcony area.

The dining room was its own little area, separated from the kitchen by one of those islands Erica saw only in the movies. She was in awe when she thought about the fact that Frankie had done it, and she had done it all on her own. Of the three bedrooms, two had bathrooms. Only one bedroom had its bathroom, but the other had a bathroom right outside the door. Either way, they'd be living large.

Erica walked into what was going to be her room, smaller than the master bedroom but bigger than the one in their last home. It had a huge walk-in closet; again, something she had seen only in the movies and magazines. She loved the place, and she loved Frankie for making it happen. It was so hard to believe they were out of the hood, just like that. She couldn't wait to decorate the room just the way she wanted.

"Heelllo?"

Frankie's voice jolted Erica out of her daydreaming. Erica ran out to the living room.

"Hey, what you doin' here?"

"Well, you know the office is only like ten minutes away once you get down the hill. So you looked around—what do you think?"

"This is the shit, Frankie! Straight up! This is tight!" Erica looked around as if she was seeing the place for the first time. "I can't believe it. And it's ours?"

"Ours! I bought it outright. No fuckin' mortgage or rent. It belongs to us, baby! Me and you! Didn't I tell you we could make this happen? Didn't I tell you to just give me some time and I'd get us up outta there? Did I work it or what?" Frankie laughed. "And we don't owe nobody a damn thing. We could sit our asses here and stare at the fuckin' walls all day and night and nobody would be able to say shit to us about it. This is ours!"

Erica couldn't remember a time when she'd seen Frankie so hyped. She was in rare form, walking around the empty living room.

"Wait till you see the furniture I picked out. I even got us a big-screen TV for the living room."

There was no way Erica could piss all over Frankie's good mood. She decided once again to hold off on talking to Frankie about LadyRae.

"Okay, I just ran up here to check in on you. I gotta get back to the office. I'm meeting Bobbi in an hour. I hope you're feelin' a little better." She dug around in her bag.

"Here, I brought you these menus to places that will deliver up here. Because you have to wait for the movers, you can go ahead and order some food. Don't worry about me; I'll grab something on my way in. Call me if you need anything else."

As quickly as she came, Frankie was gone. Erica sat in the middle of the living room floor looking over the menus. "Now ain't this some shit," she mumbled. She should be happy, sharing in her sister's excitement; instead she was facing her biggest nightmare.

When she flipped her phone open, she heard someone say, "Say, what's up?"

"Ah, hi?" Erica said, confused.

"Aeey, girl, so how you like your new crib?"

"LadyRae? Is that you?"

"Yeah, Ms. Thang, it's me. Whassup?"

"How did you know we moved?" Erica asked, looking out the patio door.

"Baby girl, lemme tell you something right now. It ain't shit that go down around here that LadyRae don't hear about. I stays on top of mine, and you just as good as mine, so you know I'ma be on point." She covered the phone and said something Erica couldn't hear.

"Now, I'ma give you some time to get settled and all, but by this weekend, I want you to tell me all about the meeting you're setting up with me and Frankie. Then after we set if off straight, the three of us are gonna take a little vacation to Vegas or something like that."

"But, LadyRae, I can't make my sister do nothing she don't want to. You don't understand."

"So what you're telling me is I'm gonna have to convince her to do it? Damn, Erica, I was hoping it wouldn't come to this, but if that's what you telling me, then I guess I'ma just have to do what I gotta do."

"But—" Erica cried.

"Nah, boo, I got this. I'll be seeing ya!"

The line went dead, and Erica started bawling.

# YVETTE

Nyeree and Yvette had been in the hotel for two days and she still didn't want to go back to her apartment. Despite his urging to see what was going on with the place, she refused to even give the idea any consideration.

"I have nothing there to go back to," she said to him the last time he asked about how she could walk away from all of her stuff.

Nyeree had long since given up on trying to get her to tell him the truth; it was obvious she wasn't about to spill the beans no matter what. And the truth of the matter was, he was running out of patience. He didn't understand how he could've read her so wrong. He thought he had her and things under control; still, he was no closer to the truth than when he first met her.

On day three, Nyeree was behind the wheel of the Escalade, driving as Yvette sat numb in the passenger seat. She didn't know if she was coming or going. They had just finished looking at the second of four apartments on her list.

She was already tired, and they hadn't even been searching that long. She kept asking herself if it was worth all of this. Yvette knew her mood had changed dramatically, and she knew Nyeree noticed the difference. She just wasn't sure what to do about him. Every time she toyed with the idea of coming clean, something convinced her it wouldn't be a good idea. She was glad when they had finally decided to go back to the hotel. When she turned on the TV, she nearly passed out right in front of Nyeree.

The news lady said, "So authorities are on the lookout for two of the three gang members. You'll recall several were picked up in the raid on Nickerson Gardens earlier this year." Yvette watched as they showed video of the raid.

"What happened?" She turned to Nyeree.

He shrugged, watching her closer than he was watching the screen. Besides, he already knew what the story was all about.

Yvette gnawed at her fingernails. "What happened?" she shrieked toward the screen. It didn't take long for her to start pacing.

"And the jailbreak happened as the inmates were being transported to the Los Angeles County Jail for a court appearance."

"What!" she screamed. "Jailbreak? What jailbreak? What are they talking about?" At that point, she had blocked Nyeree completely out. He sat back, closely watching her reaction.

Yvette quickly ran to the phone, but she still kept her eyes on the screen. The news lady was still giving background information.

"Ma, anybody come by there looking for me?" she asked nervously.

"Nobody I know of," her mother said.

"Okay, cool."

"'Vette, when are you coming to get that car out of my garage? You know I don't like parking my car on the street," her mother complained.

"Soon, Ma, soon. I'm just trying to sort out some stuff right now."

"If anybody comes looking for me, make sure you call on my cell right away. You still have the number, right?" Yvette twirled the cord through her fingers but kept her eyes on the TV.

"Yeah, I have it still," her mother said.

"To recap if you're just joining us, police are looking for several men who broke out of custody while being transported to the LA County Jail. Authorities are also investigating whether the men had inside help. Some eight inmates escaped when the van they were being transported in was stopped because of what looked like a deadly accident. The officers left the vehicle to provide assistance and were ambushed.

"Authorities say they believe members of the infamous Watts street gang, the Bounty Hunters, may have had something to do with the escape, because two of the inmates who escaped were members. At least one of the two had originally been picked up during a massive raid on the Nickerson Gardens earlier this year."

When the images of the two escaped inmates appeared on the screen, Yvette couldn't control the tears that flowed down her cheeks.

"Girl, what's wrong with you?" Nyeree asked in a voice he had never used with her before.

But his tone was the very last thing on her mind. She kept looking at the bigger-than-life pictures of Roshawn's and Bug's faces on the TV screen.

When she finally glanced over at Nyeree, the cold glare he was giving her made her wonder if she should fear him more than the two fugitives who she was sure would soon be hot on her trail.

# CARMEN

Carmen walked from her bedroom to the bathroom. The floor plan to her new apartment was similar to the one she had had to leave. The new apartment was a few feet smaller, and the balcony was in the living room instead of the bedroom like the old apartment.

After investigating the bathroom, she walked to the kitchen and nearly jumped out of her skin. "Dang, girl, you scared the hell out of me," Carmen said to Gina.

Gina had spent the night after they had gone to a serious-ass party at a club on Western Avenue.

"I didn't know if I should go in there and check your breathing or not. You were out cold. Shit, it's almost noon," Gina said as she strolled into the living room.

Carmen rubbed her forehead and sighed. "Girl, how did you even find that spot?"

"I'm telling you, sometimes the hole-in-the-wall is jumping more than the clubs you pay twenty dollars to get into."

"Well, that one was serious. Did you see all those old-school playas up in there?"

"Were they doin' the most or what?" Gina cracked up with laughter.

Carmen walked into the living room. "Girl, they were serious! I ain't mad at them either. You know me, I hope to be that broad all up in the club with my walker, getting my groove on."

"And I hope to be that broad right next to you too. I don't see how people can get tired of clubbing. But I must say, you were in rare form, working it," Gina said.

"Now what you look like talking about me when you had all those geriatrics lining up to buy you a drink with their Social Security check money. Then you had the nerve to dance with each and every one of them." Carmen and Gina broke into wild laughter.

"So, what's on tap for today?" Gina asked.

"I'm just trying to sober up." Carmen ran back to the kitchen. She grabbed a bag of vegetables from the freezer and used it as an ice pack for her throbbing head. "Those old-timers sure know how to party."

"For real," Gina said. "I wanted to go to the alley to-day. We could go do some shopping, look for new outfits to wear to that birthday party I was telling you about."

Carmen frowned. "What party?"

"The one for that guy who plays with the Lakers," Gina said, getting all hyped up thinking about it.

"Well, I'm about to go jump in the shower. We can head out after we get some grub."

"Cool," Gina said, turning up the volume on the *Jerry Springer* show.

Later, Carmen walked out of the bathroom with a towel wrapped around her body and one wrapped around her hair. Even after nearly thirty minutes in the hot water, she still felt sluggish. She and Gina had been partying nonstop for days. It was finally catching up with her, but she was determined to not let it beat her down.

As she walked to the living room, her doorbell rang.
"You order something?" Carmen asked Gina.

"No, girl, I don't know nobody or no place around
here."

Carmen walked to the door and looked out of the
peephole. "Oh, snap!" She jumped back. "It's Chip."

"Oh, it's about time I get to meet the cat who had my
girl on hiatus for more than a minute," Gina said.

But Carmen wasn't sure if she wanted to open the
door. She didn't know if Chip's mother had told him
what she accused him of doing. She was still embarrassed. And since she hadn't heard back from him, she
figured she'd chalk the entire experience up as something she had been curious about and had tried but
failed. The doorbell chimed again. Damn, he was per-
sistent, she thought.

"You better get the door, before I do," Gina said.

"I can't. Look at me. You get it if you want," Carmen
said as she rushed into her bedroom and closed the
door.

"Don't mind if I do." Gina got up and sashayed over
to the door.

When she opened the door, she was speechless. She
stood looking at a handsome face attached to a fierce
body.

"Ah, I'm looking for Carmen. I was told she had
moved to this apartment," Chip said. "I must be at the
wrong apartment." He looked up at the number on the
door.

"Nah, you got the right apartment. She's changing
right now. Why don't you come on in? You must be
Chip," Gina said, eyeing him closely. She took special
interest in his bulging arms and legs. He was a fine
specimen of a man.

"I'm Gina," she said, still eyeing him like he was a
piece of candy.

When Carmen appeared at her bedroom door, she looked different than the half-clad woman who made a mad dash for her bedroom nearly twenty minutes earlier. She had dug through a mountain of clothes and shoes to find the right outfit; then she slipped into a thin sheer dress with no underwear and a pair of sexy heels. She quickly slapped on some make-up and dabbed perfume behind her ears and between her breasts.

"Aeey, Chip, what's up?" Carmen said when she sashayed out of the room.

"Nothing much. Can we talk? I mean in private." He looked at Gina and flashed her a perfect smile.

"Yeah, why don't you come in here? Gina's a big girl. She can sit alone for a few minutes."

Gina winked at Carmen when Chip walked into her bedroom. "Don't do anything I wouldn't do. And you know I'm down for just about anything, right?"

Carmen smirked and closed her door behind Chip.

The minute she turned, she found herself wrapped in his arms. "I've missed you, boo."

Carmen inhaled as much of his scent as her lungs could hold. It felt good to be back in his arms and to be close to him. She couldn't deny what she felt for Chip, and she was so relieved that she was wrong about him.

"I've missed you too," she whispered. "Why did you leave and stay away so long?" she asked, backing up to see his face.

"My moms didn't tell you?" he asked. "She said she didn't, but I didn't believe her. My moms is always running her mouth," he said.

Before Carmen knew what was happening, she was on her back on the floor next to the bed and Chip was sucking on her neck. It felt so good, she didn't want him to stop.

"Damn, I missed you, baby." His hands moved the thin dress that separated him from the prize. She quickly pulled the dress over her head, revealing her naked body. Chip was like a kid at an amusement park. He didn't know what to do first. He fondled her breasts, sucking, then kissing each nipple. He took one breast into his mouth and suckled it roughly at first. Then he nibbled the nipple and moved down to lick a trail from her stomach and to the spot just above her thighs.

She wanted him so badly; she thought she'd die if he didn't satisfy that fire. "Here," she breathed hot and heavy. Carmen reached into the nearest nightstand drawer and pulled out the gold and black wrapper. "You gotta get strapped," she said.

He looked at her, grabbed the condom, and tore it open with his teeth. When he reached down to put it on, she noticed the small scar near his groin. She traced over it with her finger as if it might hurt him.

"What happened?" she asked.

"Later." Chip slipped the condom on and spread her legs even wider. Soon they were deep in the throes of passion.

"I missed you; I missed this. Don't leave me again." Before she could catch them, the words had escaped her mouth.

Chip kept working, moving at a comfortable pace with her body and hips matching each of his movements.

"You ready for me, boo?" Chip whispered in her ear.

"Come deep, baby, come deep," she cried.

Nearly an hour after they first locked lips, they collapsed onto Carmen's bed, breathing heavy and hard.

Three orgasms later, two for her and one for him, Carmen jumped up from the bed. "Shit, I told Gina we could go to the alley today. I know she probably hot," Carmen said, searching for her robe.

When she rushed to the living room, Gina was gone. Carmen found the note Gina left taped to the TV.

C—

*I'm running out for a bite to eat and to give you some time alone with your man. Girl, he is all of that, and then some. I'll make sure I stay gone for a couple of hours, so if you ain't got your freak on by the time you read this, girl, whatchu waiting on?*

*Peace,*
*G*

Carmen found Chip fully dressed when she walked back into the room. "She went to get something to eat," she said.

"Cool, 'cause we need to talk," he said.

# VICKI

When Vicki woke up in Murderous's spectacular bedroom the next day, she was furious. She looked around the room, unsure of exactly when she had finally fallen asleep. Vicki couldn't believe she had sat there like a fool waiting on him. He had never even shown up.

Vicki told herself she didn't have time to be dealing with any playas. Shit, she had been there and done that, she thought. She got out of bed and dropped to her knees, looking for her shoes. Once she found them, she walked over to the mirror and looked at her reflection. Man, she looked bad; sleeping with make-up was never a pretty sight. Her mind was racing with thoughts that Murderous must've hooked up with one of those hot-ass skeezers.

"I don't need this shit," she spat as she opened the door and prepared to leave the room. She was considering going back to her own damn apartment. Hell, she was used to being alone, and she'd be damned if she'd have some man, thug or not, string her along. At the top of the stairs, she heard voices. One, she was positive, was Murderous's.

"Dawg, I can't believe you let that crack head suck your dick," Murderous said.

"I can't believe you didn't," the other man said.

"I'm all about this paper, man. I ain't got time to be sidetracked by a piece of ass. Besides, my girl was waiting on me. Why go take chances with a strawberry when I got a tight-ass bitch waiting for me in my bed?"

"Fool, you never even made it up to bed last night. Trust me, if I was suppose ta be between some thighs last night, you fools would've been on your own," the other voice said.

"I feel you, but I've been gone away from business far too long; ass will always be waiting on me. You know what's up," Vicki heard Murderous say.

"Hmm." She tiptoed back to the room. She had no idea he was in the house. When she woke and he wasn't there, she assumed he had spent the night with one of those skanks. Vicki sat on the edge of the bed thinking about what she should do.

Being together was all she and Murderous talked about when he was behind bars; now that he was on the streets, free to do whatever they wanted, she found herself more alone

She sat picking at her fingernails. Just when she thought she had landed herself a real thug, she wasn't sure where she stood with him. They hadn't even touched each other, if she didn't count the little kisses they exchanged. After months of being alone, she was ready to get busy. Vicki couldn't understand why he wasn't ready to do the same.

She ripped the stockings off her legs and finally stepped out of the dress. "I'd better get in the shower," she said to herself.

Vicki stood and reached back to unzip her dress. When it fell to her feet, she glanced at the expensive lingerie she had hand-selected just for Murderous's eyes. He hadn't laid eyes on it or the tight-ass body she'd been working to develop.

"Damn, I'm a lucky man."

Vicki jumped at the sound of his voice. She was mad, but his comment still made her blush. He walked all the way into the room and closed the door. "Turn around; lemme see whatchu working with."

*It's about time,* she thought. Vicki didn't waste time second-guessing how she was feeling. She had spent hundreds of his dollars on the lingerie, and she'd be damned if she didn't strut her stuff like she was on the catwalk.

"I was about to get in the shower," she said.

"Cool, 'cause I need one myself."

When Vicki reached back to unhook the bra, he stopped her. "Not here; let's get in the shower," he said. Inside the bathroom, she watched as he stripped out of his clothes. She was more than satisfied when she looked down between his legs.

Vicki smiled inwardly. She couldn't wait. She wanted to say, "Skip the shower; let's take care of some other business." But she figured if she could wait for months, she could wait for a few more minutes.

He opened the shower door and turned on the water. "C'mon." He looked at her with lustful eyes.

"Not in my lingerie. You know how much this cost?"

"I paid for it, didn't I?"

She smiled and stepped into the steaming shower.

Murderous didn't waste any time attacking her. He pinned her up against the shower wall. With the hot water prickling their skin, he sucked and kissed every inch of her body. With foreplay over, he moved her

thong to the side and shoved his massive dick into her
before she could protest.

Vicki didn't care about him going raw; she knew she
had found her soul mate.

But only minutes after it started, she felt Murderous
explode, then go limp. She shook her head thinking
she must've been tripping. She was just getting started.
She didn't even get a chance to clamp her tight pussy
around him. She had dreamed of the day when she'd
swallow him up, then squeeze him tightly. Vicki thought
surely he hadn't had another woman love him like that,
and obviously she wasn't about to either.

When he started soaping up like nothing had gone
wrong, Vicki dropped to her knees, prepared to bring
him back to life. She hadn't spent months doing her exercises for a minuteman performance.

She also wanted to make sure he knew he had stumbled onto some spectacular pussy, and he shouldn't sleep
on it. But when she tried to take him into her mouth, he
actually brushed her off. Vicki was confused, but, more
importantly, she was horny as hell, and she wanted her
needs met too.

"Oh, I know you ain't," she said, giving him a glimpse
of the attitude she had been working to keep in check
around him.

"Look, Vicki, I got a meeting in thirty minutes," he
said.

"A meeting? Then why did you get in the shower
with me? And you wasn't thinking about no meeting
when you was humpin' me like you were in some kind
of race against the clock."

He leaned over to kiss her. "I'll make it up to you
later, baby. I just need to be on my Ps and Qs," he said.

A few minutes later, he left Vicki in the shower. She
was distraught, telling herself this just had to be some

kind of anxiety thing. Then she reminded herself that he had just come out of jail. From her past experiences, old boyfriends had told her how they suspected the government of putting drugs in the food to help suppress the inmates' sex drive. Vicki told herself the drugs must still be in his system, and just like any man, he wasn't willing to discuss it. When she was confident he wouldn't be back in the bathroom, she masturbated until she came.

# FRANKIE & ERICA

Stuck in traffic on the 110, Frankie was hot. She could still hear Joy over the phone even though the call had ended nearly three hours ago.

"Ah, Frankie, I think you need to get over here right away. There's some woman in here, LadyFae, saying she's our new partner. I told her I didn't know what she was talking about, but she insisted that you knew all about it. I told her you would not make any decision like that without telling me, but she said to just wait till you come back."

"Where is she now?" Frankie had asked.

"She's sitting in your office with her feet crossed on your desk," Joy had said nervously. "You want me to call the police?"

"No, just tell her I'm on my way, but I won't be there for at least two hours." Frankie had hung up, because there was nothing more she could do. Talking to Joy again wouldn't do any good since Frankie was out at CSP meeting with Bobbi and a new recruit when she got the call.

While sitting in traffic, Frankie seethed with anger. She had no idea why the hell LadyRae was bringing madness to her place of business. But she was sure she'd soon find out. What drove her nuts the most was being so far away from the office and not being able to see firsthand what the hell LadyRae was talking about. Frankie hoped LadyRae would still be there when she arrived at the office.

Frankie was glad she hadn't scheduled any office visits. She had already had a very long day. She had been on the phone with the people who would help expand the business to San Quentin and Soledad prisons. And Bobbi had a new stable of recruits she insisted Frankie meet. Things were blowing up faster than Frankie could handle. But she was happy, because this meant she and Erica would be able to live the way she envisioned.

Now all she had to do was make it through traffic, to the office, and to LadyRae to find out exactly what the hell she was talking about. How did LadyRae even know where her office was? But Frankie was able to answer that for herself—there wasn't too much that went on in South Central that LadyRae didn't know about.

She thought about calling to check in on Erica but decided against it. She knew how her sister was under pressure, and it wasn't good. She'd start asking a lot of questions that Frankie couldn't answer, and that wouldn't do either of them any good.

When Frankie finally pulled into her parking spot behind her office, she quickly locked the car and went rushing inside. Joy heard her coming and met her at the door.

"She's still here; been here since I talked to you earlier, refusing to leave and acting like she owns the place. She's on the phone right now."

Frankie walked into her office and sat and waited for LadyRae to wrap up her conversation. LadyRae winked like Frankie should've been happy to see her. Frankie knew she had to handle LadyRae delicately. She was fully aware that she was dealing with a callous female.

"You know how I roll." LadyRae chuckled. "Say, peep this. You know I'm goin' legit, right? Now that don't mean a bitch is getting soft; far from it. It's just I'm ready to broaden my horizons. I've just been lying low, chillin' and waiting for the right opportunity to come along."

LadyRae's pager went off. She picked it up, looked at it, then told the caller she had to go. She hung up the phone, disconnecting the first call and was preparing to make another when Frankie pulled the cord from the wall.

"Damn, Frankie, what you do that for?"

"LadyRae, whassup?" Frankie asked in a pleasant voice.

LadyRae leaned back in the chair. "Shit, not too much. You know how it is."

"I mean, what are you doin' here?" Frankie asked.

"I came to check out our little operation down here. I thought it was time I took a more active role in *our* business." LadyRae inched up in her chair. "A bitch like me ain't trying to sleep on operations around here."

Frankie's eyebrows inched upward; otherwise, she maintained her poker face.

"And I really ain't been fair to you. Damn, Frankie, you are like a fuckin' workhorse. A bitch can learn a lot from you. But I'm here to help, so we need to talk about how we gonna split profits."

"Okay, LadyRae, I'm not sure what you're talking about, but I do have some things I need to do, so it would be good if you could let me get back to work."

"You gonna have to help me out with the computer, though, 'cause I ain't got no computer skills. You teach me that, and I'll teach you how to coldcock a bitch in less than thirty seconds."

Frankie chuckled. "You know, LadyRae, I don't think I need to learn that skill, but thanks for the offer. What I do need is for you to leave so I can try and get some work done." The last thing Frankie wanted was LadyRae as an enemy. But she wasn't stupid either. She wasn't about to let her walk in and take over what she and Bobbi had worked so hard to establish.

"I won't make a lot of changes, but there is one thing I refuse to bend on—that bitch up front, what's her name, Joy? Yeah, that bitch, she's got to go. How the fuck can she look at me like I'm trash? Then she told me I ain't got no business here. Ain't that some shit?" LadyRae nodded. "Yeah, we need to let that bitch go fast like. But don't worry. I got a girl that would fit right in around here. Of course, I'd have to find her replacement before I could move her in, but trust me, as soon as I do, we getting rid of that stupid bitch Joy."

Frankie sighed. She was starting to lose what little patience she had left. "LadyRae, I'm not sure what's going on, but Joy is a real important part of my business. Let's not even get into that right now. How about you get up, leave, and let us go back to work?"

When LadyRae got up, Frankie thought she had finally gotten through to her. She picked up her Louis Vuitton purse and slung it over her shoulder. "So are you trying to tell me you really don't know nothing about us teamin' up?"

"Not a thing," Frankie said.

"Hmm, that's strange, because I thought this was something your sister started working on months ago. Well, since she didn't, let me put it to you this way—I am not asking you to join forces; I'm saying that you owe me. You got a nice little setup here; you probably makin' a killin', and I want in. Now, I do understand Erica can act a little special at times, but the fact remains this is her fault. She was suppose ta let you know about this weeks ago. She kept saying she was working on it. I shoulda known something was up when I didn't hear back from you personally. But here I thought you were just busy working to protect our interests."

"LadyRae, we don't need a partner, and I don't know why Erica didn't tell you that when you talked to her. But that's neither here nor there. The fact remains, we don't need a partner and I'm not about to be strong-armed into anything."

"I suggest you take some of that base out of your voice when you talk to me, 'cause ain't nothing changed. I'm still that mothafucka who don't take no shit."

Frankie nodded. "Yeah, I feel you. I really do. But I still don't see what that has to do with me."

"I suggest you give that sister of yours a call." LadyRae turned and left.

There was no way Frankie could simply call Erica and tell her about LadyRae's visit. This was something she had to talk about face-to-face. She needed to read Erica's body language; she needed to see her expression when she told her how LadyRae said it was up to Erica to hash out this so-called partnership.

"Oh, God, is she gone?" Joy asked, peeking around the corner and into Frankie's office.

"Yeah, for now, but knowin' her like I do, she'll be back."

Joy stepped into Frankie's office. "Who is she? She looks like some ghetto queen. And what's with those long-ass nails? Oooh-wee, that has to be unsanitary; she couldn't cook a single thing for me to eat."

"Trust me, I don't think she lifts a finger to cook a

thing. She's got enough money to have people do that kind of stuff for her."

"Well, she looks like she belongs in one of those rap videos to me, with all that jewelry, the long nails. Even her big toe had the longest nail I've ever seen on a human. But why does she think that she's gonna be working here with us?"

Frankie was already getting tired of the questions, but she knew she'd be just as curious if the tables were turned. The truth was she had no idea why LadyRae felt like they owed her anything. But she was definitely going to get to the bottom of it.

"Joy, I am about to find out everything I can about that situation. Right now, I'm in the dark just like you."

"Hmm, well, I don't like her; she scares me," Joy said.

"I need to run out. I'll be back in a few hours." Frankie grabbed her keys and ran out the door before Joy could ask any other questions.

# YVETTE

"Lemme get this straight," Nyeree said. "I'm supposed to believe that there ain't nothing wrong. But you see these cats on TV and you start shakin' like you going through withdrawals?" That menacing glare returned to his face. "What kind of sucka you take me for?" He hovered over her.

Yvette knew she was in way over her head, but she wasn't really sure why. If it was the car, she was willing to give it back; quite surely Roshawn knew she had it. And the money, the seventy-five thousand dollars, there was no way they could've tied that to her.

It was simple. When she called Crimestoppers, she was issued a number. When everything went down the way it was supposed to, she used the number to collect the money. There was no way to trace it back to her— or was there? She had started wondering lately. As her man hovered over her, she reviewed her options. She could either tell him what she had done and risk losing him, or she could continue to carry on the way she was, but she could tell he was getting tired of that.

She couldn't sleep, she hadn't eaten, and problems were starting to pop up between her and Nyeree. This shit was ruining her life. Yvette closed her eyes and swallowed hard.

"Okay," she said, "let me tell you what happened, but you've got to promise me you won't leave me when you find out the truth." Yvette looked at him, struggling to read his expression. "I couldn't handle you leaving me," she admitted.

Finally, Nyeree thought. It had taken long enough. But he was glad he was finally getting the truth out of her, and who knows, maybe he'd still stick around to hit it every once in a while. Yvette was fine, no question there. He didn't mean to scare her. It wasn't his style to bully women, but shit, he had to do something to let her know he meant business. If he didn't, somebody else would, and he was afraid they wouldn't be as nice.

The moment she was about to come clean, the phone rang. She looked at the phone, then looked at him. "It could be important. I think I need to get that," she said.

Nyeree sat silently and simply nodded. He didn't want to have to start all over again.

"Hello?" Yvette said.

"May I speak to Yvette Madison?"

"Speaking," she said.

"This is Mel Copper. I'm calling about the apartment you looked at the other day. The one off Wilton and Van Ness."

"Yes?" Yvette said.

"Well, I was calling to say you could have the place if you're still interested. It'll be ready by the end of the week."

"Great, and yes, I do want it. Can I bring you a money order tomorrow?"

"Sure, how about six-thirty?"

"I'll see you there. Fourteen hundred, right?" Yvette asked.

"Yes, first month and security."

When Yvette hung up the phone and turned to Nyeree, she forced a smile. He didn't smile back, but at least he wasn't looking at her with the stone face that sent fear running through her body.

"We got the apartment," she offered.

"Oh, really?" He liked the fact that she said *we*. Nyeree actually felt like she was someone he could really make it with. But still they had business to discuss. And the fact remained she wasn't being up front with him.

"I thought you'd be glad," she said.

"I am, but, Yvette, we got a situation on hand here, and I really want to take care of it so we can move on." He looked away from her. He was trying not to show his frustration. But she was making it hard. Why couldn't she just spit it out?

"Okay, well, I don't even know where to begin, because this shit is gonna be wild. And I have no idea how you're gonna react after I tell you."

"Damn, you act like you killed somebody," Nyeree said.

Yvette's head dropped. She began sobbing almost uncontrollably. Nyeree reached out and took her into his arms. "C'mon, babe, it can't be that bad. Let's talk about it. That's all I'm saying; let's just talk about it."

"Okay," she sniffled. Soon she sat upright and looked him in the eye. "I did something I know you will never be able to forgive, and um, I just don't wanna lose you." She started crying again.

"I'm not going anywhere," Nyeree said.

"You're just saying that, 'cause you don't know what I'm about to tell you. Once you hear what I did, I'm sure you'll leave me," she sobbed.

"You don't know that," Nyeree interjected. "Try me. Remember, this is me, the man you took a chance on. Baby, I was in the pen when we hooked up. What could you have done that was so bad?"

Yvette bit her lip, and the tears started rolling down her cheeks again. "I dropped the dime on somebody," she sobbed. This time she used her hands to cover her face and started crying even louder.

Nyeree was lost. He had no idea what she was talking about.

"I know that's probably the worst thing I could've done. But I did, and now he broke out of jail, and I think he's after me."

"What? You talking about those two cats they was talking about on the news today?"

"Uh-huh." Yvette was still crying.

"Wait, they are Hunters, right?"

"Yeah, but I didn't know—I had no idea. I went out with one of them, and we stopped off at this hotel before we went out. That's when I saw his friend. After the raid, I saw they were offering seventy-five Gs for this guy at the hotel, I remembered who he was and where he was, and I called and told the police." She started crying again.

That was the last thing Nyeree expected to hear. But it was as if she needed to get it off her chest. He sat there and listened, hoping she'd give up the information he needed.

"Remember when that guy showed up at my door?"

Nyeree nodded.

"I think that's why he showed up at my door. Roshawn must've told him where to find me."

Nyeree knew better, but he didn't say anything. He knew more was coming, and he also knew she'd eventually give it all up. "So you think yo boy sent someone after you because you ratted out this cat?" He was trying to help her along.

"If it wasn't for me, Five-O would not have found him. He was headed out of the country." She paused to wipe her face with the back of her hand. "There's more," she said.

"Okay?"

"I kept Roshawn's car. The Beamer we rolled around in isn't really mine. I had it painted, but that was Roshawn's car, and I think they may have been looking for that too. I know it was a stupid-ass thing to do, but I figured I didn't know any of his peeps, so I thought I could at least floss a bit while he was in jail. Then when I heard the kind of time he was looking at, I didn't really think about it anymore."

The more she talked, the more Nyeree realized something. She had no clue. She thought these fools were looking for her because she snitched on somebody and kept the dude's car. Man, he thought. This was gonna be a lot harder than he expected.

# CARMEN

Carmen and Chip were reunited, and she felt good. It had been nearly a week since they had started back up again, and it was like the days when he was first released.

They were all over each other, and Carmen didn't have a problem with the daily sex they were having or how they were having it. At first she was a bit leery because he showed her the scar from his hernia, and she thought that might slow him down, but once they got started, it had all been gravy again. The only thing she didn't like was the fact that Chip had gotten a job. Carmen had never been with a man who had a real nine to five. Chip's hours weren't exactly nine to five, and he had to work weekends. But that wasn't totally a bad thing.

While Chip worked from eleven to seven Friday and Saturday nights, Carmen and Gina were in the streets. Carmen wasn't really sure why she was still in the clubs as hard as Gina. But she still had fun. Gina hadn't found a baller yet, but they figured she was bound to since they basically stayed on the prowl.

Carmen told herself she was only out there like that to help her friend. But one night she was so drunk that, after she and Gina had been kicking it in the VIP section with some pro basketball players, she slipped up and fucked one of them in the alley behind the club. When Gina found out what happened, she was vexed, because after that, he and his teammate changed their minds about taking her and Carmen back to his place.

For a few days after that, Gina didn't call Carmen to go out. Carmen didn't understand the problem, because she said there were times when Gina caught the vapors and fucked on the first night, and she didn't judge her. She just hoped that Chip wouldn't find out.

When Carmen got home, she sat in a tub of ice and used lemon juice to tighten up her pussy. She and Gina had done that in the past when they messed up and fucked more than one man in less than a twenty-four-hour period. Gina had sworn by it, and after Carmen tried it, she thought it worked just fine. She was able to fuck Chip later that morning when he came home, and he couldn't even tell she'd been with someone else.

Before he left for work the following Friday, Chip told Carmen he had a couple of days off coming up and he wanted to do something special. He asked her to have a bag packed by the time he got off, so they could leave right away.

Several hours after Chip left, Carmen finally broke down and called Gina. "What's up, dawg? Why you trippin'?"

"Oh, girl, I'm over that, no doubt. I just hate missing out on mad paper like that when you know how hard it is out there."

"Yeah, I feel you. But I really couldn't help it. That

fool was talking mad shit, about how he could get down and how big his dick was and how he was just this helluva freak, and how he did all kinds of shit. Girl, I got his ass out in that alley, and he did lay it for a minute. He was hitting it real good, you know, telling me all the shit I like to hear about how fine I am and how sweet and wet my pussy is, but he was selfish. So after about an hour—"

"Whoa! Hold up. An hour straight?" Gina asked.

"Yeah, his shit was tight; I'll give it to him on that. But, anyway, after about an hour, he burst a vicious nut. That nigga was almost reduced to tears, 'cause you know I know how to work my shit. Anyway, after that tremendous release I gave him, he straight left me hanging."

"What? Like that?"

"Girl, yes! So he started getting up like he did big thangs. I was like, oh no, this can't be over. So I was like, 'Nah, paht-na, you got some unfinished business over here.' I'm pointing between my legs, and he looked at me like he didn't know what I was talking about. I was like, 'If that's the best you can do, you need to get back down there, you know, and use your tongue.'"

"You didn't!" Gina squealed.

"Girl, I did."

"And what did he say?"

"That fool had the nerve to say, 'I don't know you like that,' and walked back into the club like nothing happened."

"Whaat?"

"I'm serious," Carmen said.

"So what you do?" Gina asked.

"Shit, I came home, soaked, juiced up, then had my man eat me and fuck the shit out of me. Basically finish what the baller started." They laughed hard.

"You rolling out tonight?"

"Nah, I can't. Got plans with Chip."

"Em. Then I won't tell you where I'm going with Shelly," Gina teased.

"Where are y'all going?" Carmen pressed.

"Girl, we going to see Chocolate Crème." Gina giggled.

"Nooooooooo, I can't believe it. How could you?" Carmen pretended like she was crying.

"Girl, yes, we are. And I can't wait. You know we should think about kidnapping his fine-ass self."

"We could tie him up and keep him in your apartment. Then we could take turns having our way with him."

"Yeah, that sounds like such a plan," Gina joked.

"Okay, I need to run. I have to get ready. I don't want Chip to come home and find I'm not ready."

Carmen hung up the phone and slipped off her bed. She yawned and stretched her body. As she was about to walk out of the bedroom, she bumped right into Chip. The somber look on his face told her something was very wrong. And he was silent, he hadn't even said hi.

"Aeeey, you, how long you been here?"

"Long enough," he said.

An arched eyebrow inched up. "What's that supposed to mean?" Carmen asked with her heart beating faster.

"Long enough to hear about you and the baller in the alley," he said sadly.

Carmen's mouth dropped.

# VICKI

Vicki didn't know what to do. She was absolutely miserable and completely sexually frustrated. She picked up Murderous's latest CD and again went over the track titles. She shook her head at tracks like "I'm Hung," "An All-Nighter," and "Cum to MC-M." The lyrics were just as amazing, considering.

> *I can go all night if that's what the job calls for.*
> *I can give . . . it, just say you want more, more, more . . .*
> *When I said I'm a soldier I meant a real fighter . . .*
> *A real all-nighter . . . A real all-nighter . . . ho, watch me go*
> *A real all-nighter . . . A real all-nighter . . . ho, it's what you been begging fo.*
> *When I lay pipe, you ain't gotta worry 'cause you know I'ma do it right . . .*

*And you know, I'm MC Murderous . . .*
*and I do it all night . . .*
*I'ma hit your spot and I'ma hit it right . . .*
*like an all-nighter . . .*
*A real all-nighter . . . A real all-nighter . . .*
*ho, watch me go*
*A real all-nighter . . . A real all-nighter . . .*
*ho, it's what you been begging fo'.*

Vicki certainly had something to say about that. She looked at the lyrics from the other tracks; they also talked about how good MC Murderous could kill the twat, but she couldn't believe it. Didn't some of this shit have to be true? She thought rappers talked about shit they experienced. And she knew for sure he ain't never killed shit with that useless dick of his.

She and Murderous had tried to fuck three times since the big letdown in the shower. And each time was worse than the time before. Vicki thought this was kind of funny the more she thought about it. Sad, but funny. She wanted to cry, just crawl up somewhere and cry until somebody came and fucked her out of her misery.

For years, Vicki wanted nothing more than a thug just like MC Murderous. Then she finally landed a true thug, and he couldn't even get down in the bedroom. He had it all, a phat-ass bank account, a fly crib, numerous cars, a fierce wardrobe, and enough bling to fill a jewelry store. Still, none of that mattered when the lights went out and it was time to get busy. He couldn't do it, couldn't finish what he started. What the fuck was she supposed to do?

A man with a big dick and an even bigger reputation and he couldn't fuck worth a damn. She thought about keeping him and getting a little something on the side.

She was convinced it was the only way she'd be able to survive.

Vicki thought about calling Frankie back again, but she decided against that. Or at least she'd save that for her trump card, when times really got hard. That's what she'd do. But until then, she had to figure out how to fix the problem.

She sat in his bedroom while he and his crew worked in the studio he had connected to his house. They spent hours upon hours in the studio, and it was really starting to drive her nuts.

The sick thing about this misery she called a relationship was she had no one to talk to about it. She still wasn't speaking to Pam, and Lydia, well, she and Lydia could never be like that.

And who would believe her, anyway? To see Murderous's posters, everything looked like he could hit it. How did he expect her to survive? She had thought about trying to talk to him about it, but how would she do that?

Vicki didn't know a black man alive who would admit to having a problem in the bedroom. She certainly never thought she'd be going through anything like that with a thug. Lately, Vicki had started having wet dreams at night. All she could think about was sex—hot, steamy, good spine-tingling sex—and the sad fact that she wasn't getting any.

If only she could exchange some of her riches for sexual relief. Vicki could get up and go shopping in any of the finest stores on Rodeo Drive. She was able to order any piece of jewelry, especially since Murderous loved to see her all iced out. But the truth was she'd exchange all that shit for a good decent fuck.

From the outside, Vicki knew she was envied by so many. Boy, she thought, if only they knew the truth.

Vicki kept her eye on the clock because they were

supposed to be going out. But if she didn't go down to that studio and bang on the door, Murderous and his crew would be in there for hours. She didn't want to look like she was preventing him from getting his work done, but still, she'd be damned if she was gonna be sexless and not get something out of this arrangement.

She picked up the phone and dialed the number to his studio.

"Murderous, how much longer, baby?"

"Ah, we up for a break in about an hour, babe. Why don't you start getting ready? Oh, yeah, and wear that red dress I like, the little tight one that shows off your legs."

*What the hell for?* she thought. Instead she said, "Whatever you want, baby. An hour, right?"

"Yeah, we'll be ready to roll."

That was the other thing—any time they went out, he couldn't go without his entourage tagging along. So even if Vicki wanted to try and talk to him about their little problem, she couldn't without a crowd around.

Vicki eased back onto the bed and turned on the TV. The commercial she saw gave her an idea. She suddenly became hopeful again. "Damn!" she squealed. "Why the hell didn't I think of this before?"

# FRANKIE & ERICA

When Frankie walked into the living room, she didn't hear the TV or the radio. She wondered where the hell Erica was. She was still pissed beyond words, but she wanted to give Erica the benefit of the doubt.

She had planned to ask Erica why LadyRae thought they were going into business together, and what Erica had been discussing with LadyRae to give her that impression. Then she'd give her a chance to explain. The last thing Frankie wanted to do was make it seem like she was trying to come down on Erica, because her sister would just clam up, and they'd get absolutely nowhere.

"Erica?" Frankie called, still listening for any sound throughout the house. There was none. She checked Erica's room, and it was empty. There was no sign of her anywhere in the house, and Erica knew how Frankie felt about her leaving without a note.

She decided to order food and wait for her sister to come home. Frankie went to the bar and poured herself a drink. One drink turned into several, and after a few hours she had eaten and drunk but was still alone.

Whenever her cell phone rang, it was mostly clients or Bobbi, not her sister. Soon she stopped answering. Frankie hadn't given much thought to what LadyRae had said because she was sure it was some kind of mix-up.

Erica might have been gullible, but she wasn't stupid. She especially knew how Frankie felt about LadyRae. While Frankie didn't want to cross LadyRae, she wasn't about to go into business with some low-life thug. Even if the thug was a woman. Frankie just hoped things wouldn't get violent.

It was close to midnight and still no word from Erica. Frankie knew for sure something was wrong, and she didn't know where to start. At first she tried to tell herself Erica might have hooked up with Jerome, and he had her all caught up doing something she knew she had no business doing. Frankie suspected Erica still talked to Jerome, but she had no real proof, so she wasn't about to go stressin' it.

But the more Frankie thought about it, the more she realized that even if Erica did still talk to Jerome, it probably didn't go any further since they were paid beyond their wildest dreams, and Erica wasn't strapped for cash. The next time Frankie thought about Erica, the sun was coming up.

"Shit," she grumbled. She got up from the couch, where she had fallen off to sleep, albeit a night filled with tossing and turning. She looked around but already knew the answer to her question. There was no way in the world Erica would've come in and not waken her to talk about wherever she had been, or whatever she was doing.

It was 6:30 in the morning, and her sister had not

been home. Erica didn't spend the night out without letting Frankie know. And it had been years since she had dated anyone seriously.

Frankie jumped into the shower and changed into fresh clothes. She transferred the house phone to her cell and went down to M & M's for breakfast. By 10:00 she was strolling through her office door.

At the front desk, Joy was talking to a sistah Frankie had never seen before. She didn't want to get Joy alarmed, and she didn't want to interrupt the instructions Joy was giving the new office girl.

"Tracie, this is Frankie. She's the president of The Hook-Up." As Frankie passed by the desk, the girl stood.

Frankie looked at her and said, "Aeey, whassup?" She slipped by them both to get into her office. By noon Frankie was really wondering where the hell Erica had gone.

As Frankie was about to leave for lunch, a tall and slender woman, wearing the haircut Halle Berry made famous, strolled through the door.

"I'm here to see Frankie," she said.

Frankie noticed her from the hall as she left her office. She started walking to the back to jump into her car, but she shrugged and walked up front. "I'm Frankie," she said before Tracie could ring her office phone.

"I'm Brandy. I had an appointment with you about an hour ago. You said we'd meet at M and M's. When I mentioned it to my waitress, she told me where to find your office."

Frankie slapped her forehead. "Damn, Brandy, my bad. I'm slippin' today. Yeah, I remember. I got so much on my mind."

"Well, can we meet now?" Brandy asked.

"You know, I was just about to leave for lunch, so I guess we can head back over to M and M's if you still hungry." Frankie grabbed the strap of her bag. "My treat of course."

At the table at M and M's, Brandy started to tell Frankie her life story and why she felt it was time for a change. Frankie, of course, had heard it all before. It didn't matter to her why the women felt they needed her help finding a man. She was just in the business to match them with exactly what they wanted. And things had been going well for so long, she began to wonder if her success had alienated her sister. Frankie was so busy, she had little free time to spend with Erica.

As Brandy talked, Frankie thought about how she should've pressed Erica to take the driver's ed course. Maybe her sister felt isolated. Since they had moved, Frankie was working more and more. She had expanded to add two prisons to the roster. And she had been featured in both the *Wave* newspaper and *People* magazine. The more popular the business became, the busier Frankie was.

She and Bobbi had hired a guard in both prisons, and they were in the process of establishing the business and doing publicity in nearby cities. Joy had even talked her into hiring someone to handle advertising. They had a Web site, thehookup.com, and they were kicking off a huge advertising campaign two weeks before Valentine's Day.

There were things that still amazed Frankie. Here they were, a week before Thanksgiving, and Joy was already working on an advertising blitz for Valentine's Day. She didn't mind, because Joy was wonderful at that sort of thing. Frankie still handled most of the face-to-face meetings. Obviously she wasn't able to meet with inmates in San Quentin or Soledad, but she was still able to meet with the new inmates they added in CSP. Overall, things were good.

"So you see, I'm really ready to try something new." Brandy smiled, like she had just finished a great performance. "You have any questions?" she asked Frankie.

That's when Frankie realized she had pretty much tuned out most of what Brandy was talking about. "No, I guess all I really need is your paperwork. You were specific about exactly what you wanted, right?"

"Right down to his shoe size."

"Good, we'll take care of the rest." The waitress brought their food, and Frankie was more than ready to eat.

As they were preparing to dig into their meal, Frankie's cell phone rang. She answered it before it could ring a second time.

"Hello?"

"Frankie, it's Joy," she said frantically.

"Joy, what's wrong?" Frankie asked.

"I think you need to come back to the office. Your friend is back."

Frankie was not in the mood to deal with LadyRae. She had other things on her mind, and finding her sister was priority number one. "Tell her I'm in a meeting. I don't have time for her foolishness."

Just as Frankie was about to hang up, she heard LadyRae's voice through the phone.

"Say! Frankie, now ain't this some shit? Here I am waiting on you, and you acting like I'm some little busta. I'm trying to be nice, Frankie, but you making it real hard. Now, I suggest you drop whatever the fuck you doin' and get over here. I ain't got all damn day; I am a businesswoman, you know."

Before Frankie could respond, LadyRae had hung up. Frankie hadn't even finished her food, but she figured she needed to at least go and get LadyRae out of the office.

As soon as she got to her car, her cell phone rang

again. This time, when she heard Joy's voice, it was muffled. "Frankie, are you coming? You know this woman gives me the creeps."

"I know, Joy. I'm headed over there. I should be there in less than ten minutes. What is she doin' sitting in my office?"

"No, she's up front. Thank God we didn't have any clients since it was lunchtime. But you really need to hurry. The way she's eyeing up Tracie is nothing short of disgusting." Suddenly Joy paused. "Oh, my God! Oh, my God! Here she comes. I gotta go!"

Frankie shook her head as she held the phone. "Damn, I don't need this shit today." She tried again to call Erica, but the voice mail kicked in immediately.

Minutes later, Frankie pulled up in front of the office. She could see LadyRae sitting in front of the reception desk. Frankie hit the alarm button on her key ring and walked into the office.

"It's about damn time!" LadyRae hollered. "You must got me all mixed up. You betta ask some damn body. I ain't one to be waiting around for nobody!"

# YVETTE

Yvette sat baffled and alone. She didn't know what to think. In the middle of her tearful confession, Nyeree abruptly got up and left. Sure, he said he needed to make a quick run, but what the hell could be more important than what she was trying to tell him?

Honestly she knew deep down that she would lose him once he learned the truth, and he had proven that she was right when he just up and left. She didn't have to be locked up to know that snitching is the worst thing you can do to a person who's from the streets. She knew what would happen once she told him, but she felt she had no choice.

Since their hotel was off Imperial, not far from the airport, Nyeree figured he'd just ride it out to Alameda. He turned on to 103rd and pulled up near Jordan High School. Ever since the raid on the Gardens, he had been leery about going into Jordan Downs, the projects that were located right next to the high school. That area was home to the Grape Street Watts Crips, the second largest gang in the area and the biggest rival of the Bounty Hunters.

He didn't have to worry about venturing over there, because within minutes, two men walked over to the Escalade. One hopped into the passenger's side and the other into the backseat.

"Whassup, cuz?"

"She don't know shit about the heist. She think these fools are coming after her over some reward money she collected."

Nyeree knew Joker was skeptical. He had wanted to smoke Yvette from jump, but he had told them she was of no use to them dead, and everybody agreed. They knew she had hooked up with Roshawn, but they didn't know she turned Bug in. It wasn't until after word had gotten out that Nyeree had been selected to take part in the prison hookup ring that the Grape Street Crips devised the plan.

Word through the jailhouse grapevine was that Roshawn, a member of the Bounty Hunters, had a female he was rolling with when he went down in the raid. The Grape Street Crips had searched long and hard for a member in CSP who fit the description Yvette had filled out on her paperwork, and that's when they approached Nyeree. He was no longer active but was willing when some OG approached him about what needed to be done. He was down for whatever, because he knew the homies would break him off real proper once they caught up with the jewels.

"So you saying we ain't no closer than when this thing first went down?" Joker asked from the backseat.

"Where is the car?" Devon asked.

Nyeree shook his head. "I don't know. But we saw on the news that those fools are out, so I have a feelin' they probably posted outside her old place waiting to see if she shows up."

"So, we ain't got shit. Man, we need to get to that shit before they do. Why don't you just tell her the truth? You said she was down, right?"

"I say we put a cap in her ass. I bet she'd be willing to talk then," Joker said.

"Nah, that ain't gonna work."

"Don't tell me you got feelings for this broad. She was kicking it with some Bloods. When this is over, we need to silence that bitch for good."

"She wasn't kickin' it with him. She told me they got together and were about to go out for the second or third time when the shit went down. Let me handle it, and I'll find what we looking for."

"You been saying that for a while now, cuz. The only problem now is that them Hunters are roaming the streets, and they might know exactly where to look. So you need to put a rush on this shit before we handle it our way."

"I'm with cuz," Devon said.

Nyeree looked at Joker, then at Devon. "We ain't got no reason to go back to her old place, so I ain't worried about those Bloods. I'll get the information and holla at y'all as soon as we can roll."

"We should go blast on them niggas, Joker," Devon said. "We can catch 'em slippin' and smoke 'em."

"Let's worry about getting our hands on the jewels and think about blastin' those niggas later. I'm trying to get paid first and foremost," Joker said.

"I'm serious, cuz," Nyeree said.

Back at the hotel, Yvette decided to take a shower. She figured she could clear her head and think about her next move. At least she was safe if she didn't go back to the apartment. It was obvious they knew where she lived now. Damn, she was mad at herself, because this shit could've been avoided. But hell, she needed that money, and she thought when you called Crimestoppers, you remained anonymous. She was tired of learning shit the hard way.

Yvette nearly had a stroke when she finished her shower and walked out of the bathroom. She was happy to see Nyeree, but still, he had scared the shit out of her.

"When did you get back?" she asked.

"A few minutes ago. I picked up some chicken. You hungry?"

"Yeah, I could eat something," she said, eyeing him suspiciously. When he fled in the middle of her confession, she thought he was walking out for good. She had long felt unworthy and that only confirmed what she was feeling might have been warranted. She didn't want to pick up the story because she didn't want him to leave again. Besides, she thought, it's not like there was much more to tell anyway.

As they ate chicken from El Poyo Loco, Yvette watched him watch her.

"You know we need to talk, right?"

"Yeah. I figured as much," she said. "Why don't we eat, then go down to the bar and have a drink? I could really use one."

"Cool, that sounds like a plan." Nyeree reached over and took her into his arms. He had developed feelings for her. He wasn't soft or nothing like that, but he could see himself with her. He just hoped she'd be around after the shit went down. At that moment, he told himself he'd do whatever he could to make sure she was.

# CARMEN

*Think fast! Think fast!* Carmen's mind was racing, but still she couldn't come up with a way to explain away what Chip had overheard. It wasn't like he wasn't man enough for her; he was, and then some. The truth was it was Gina. Whenever she hooked up with her girl, Carmen felt like she had to be down for whatever.

Carmen wasn't looking for a baller. She didn't have a cash-flow problem. But the fun she had with Gina was priceless. They were tight, and whether it was chasin' paper or ballers, they always had a good time. And it wasn't like she was ready to get out of the game, but Chip made her feel like something more than any of the so-called ballers ever had.

Now she had hurt him by being unfaithful. When she was getting busy with that player in the alley, she wasn't thinking about Chip or what would happen if he ever found out. She and Gina ran around fucking so much, she never had a reason to think about anyone else.

Chip stood staring at her, and she had a feeling it was over. He had come at a bad time for her. He

wanted to play fair and fly straight. She didn't know
what she wanted. When they were together, she wanted
all he could give her. Then the minute he was at work,
she felt alone and ignored, telling herself she was too
pretty to suffer like that. That was usually when she
hooked up with Gina and the trouble started. Looking
at his face now, she didn't know what to say.

"How could you?" he finally asked.

Should she deny it? Why had he been eavesdropping
any damn way? How could she take back what she had
said when she could barely even remember the words?
She knew he heard the part about her fucking the
player in the alley. Why else would he be mad?

"What are you talking about, Chip?" She avoided
eye contact.

"So you just gonna play me like that?"

She slipped by him and walked into the kitchen.
With her back to him she opened the refrigerator and
acted like she couldn't decide what to get. After a few
minutes she closed the door and leaned against it.
Carmen closed her eyes and started sobbing softly.

When she opened her eyes, Chip was inches from
her face. He had invaded her space, and she didn't
know what to do. She was usually on the receiving end
of this kind of shit. Now here she was dishing it.
Carmen felt so bad. She knew her silence was basically
admitting guilt.

"You picked me," Chip said. "I thought you said you
was through with these tired-ass cats and the games
they play. I'm trying my best to be a better man for
you, and you out there running wild, spreading your
legs and letting these fools run up in you and shit?
Damn, I thought you was better than that." Chip shook
his head.

Carmen felt dirty. She had been caught cheating,
and there wasn't a damn thing she could say. He was

right; she *had* picked him, and paid for him too. She wanted to be honest with herself, and the truth was she had long been tired of the games she and Gina played. It was different for Carmen because she wasn't trying to fuck for money. She never had to. The truth was, she just fucked because that was all she thought the men wanted. So before she got her feelings hurt, she figured she'd get hers and move on before some two-bit hustler had her sprung and fiending.

She didn't want to hurt Chip, and now that she was faced with losing him, she was praying he'd give her a second chance.

Chip backed up, allowing her to move from the spot next to the refrigerator.

Carmen watched as he walked out to the living room. He picked up his things and looked back at her.

Before he walked out the door, he said, "I don't understand how you could let some strange nigga run up in you just like that. I can't make you believe you're worth more than being fucked by some punk ass nigga in an alley. You've gotta find a way to love yourself before you can let me or anybody else love you, baby girl."

# VICKI

Vicki had swallowed her pride for more reasons than one. She threw on a light green Baby Phat sweat suit and a white pair of tennis shoes and a baseball cap. She put on just enough make-up and picked through the jewelry Murderous had given her. She wanted to keep it simple.

She stood at her old apartment door and waited. Vicki knew Pam was home because she had called, and when Pam answered, she hung up. She figured Pam had looked out of the peephole and knew it was her at the door.

A few minutes later, the door swung open. Pam stood there with her arms crossed over her chest. Vicki had a large Papa John's pizza box and a large bottle of Hypnotic with a bow tied to it. "A peace offering," she said.

Pam looked at the pizza, the drink, then at her girl-friend. "You mean you not here to toss me out?"

"You know I would never do anything like that, Pam. I admit, I was having a bitch moment, but I'm over it, and I want my best friend back." Vicki faked like she was pouting her thin pink lips.

Pam eyed her suspiciously, then looked at the pizza box.

"The longer I stand here, the colder it's getting," Vicki sang.

Pam moved to the side and allowed Vicki into the apartment. They sat in the living room and ate pizza and washed it down with Hypnotic.

"You know I was on one. I had no right to talk to you the way I did. Can you ever forgive me?"

"Of course I forgive you, Vicki, but you know you said some pretty hateful things to me."

"I did and I'm so sorry. Sometimes I can get so caught up, and well, it's just been lonely without you."

"Whhaat? Lonely? I've seen you in the rags hanging on to your new man's arm. You don't look lonely in this month's issue of *Vibe*," Pam joked. "And is that bracelet real?"

"Girl, yeah, Murderous knows how to spend some money." Vicki reminded herself not to sound like she was bragging. That wasn't what she had come for. And she was being truthful; she had missed Pam. Usually it was during the times she was mad at Murderous or Lydia and had no one to talk to, but still she missed her friend.

"So what brings you back to the slums?" Pam asked.

"Girl, this ain't no slum. I still got all my shit here. Of course, Murderous bought me a whole new wardrobe, shoes, and jewelry to match."

"Hmph," was all Pam said.

"Like I said, I miss you, and I miss our friendship. That's it. You have to admit we had some helluva good times together. I didn't want to be one of those stupid broads who let a man come between her and her true friend."

"Good, I'm glad you finally came to your senses. Now tell me, what's it like to live the glamorous life?"

"Girl, you wouldn't believe some of the places I've been and how that fool spends money. It's like nothing I've ever seen before. The only thing that bugs the hell out of me is we have to travel with an entourage."

"What do you mean?"

"We can't go nowhere without his bodyguard, his publicist, people from marketing. I think we even have a portable lawyer."

"No shit?"

"And I mean everywhere we go. To the club, to dinner, shit, even shopping. I can't even get five minutes alone with my man. Then at his house, it's like there's always a party going on. The messed up part is, his entourage will bring their peeps, so when Murderous goes into the studio, I'm left with a bunch of fuckin' strangers who are just too hyped to be in a celebrity's house."

"Whhaat? Like that?" Pam asked.

"Yes, girl. Then don't even get me started on the hoochies. It's sad, actually. You see these girls willing to prostitute themselves for these guys, and it's like, 'I roll with the cousin of the next door neighbor of the cat who knows the bodyguard for MC Murderous'!"

"Girl, no!" Pam squealed.

"Yeah, it's like six degrees of separation like a mofo. I'm telling you the shit gets pretty sad after a while. My favorite is when one of the DJs picks up some chick in a club. He starts flossin' by inviting her back to Murderous's house. Well, after he gets the ass and has no need to call her again, she'll show up looking for him!" Vicki shook her head for effect. "What the fuck am I supposed ta do? Or even say. You know Murderous don't even use the same damn DJ all the time."

"Oh, that's some foul shit," Pam said.

"Yeah, but they keep coming. Every week it's a different one showing up talking about 'DJ Spin told me I could visit him here any time I want.' I'm like DJ Spin don't even live here!"

"What do they say then?"

"Most of 'em just jump back in the bucket they rode up in and leave. But there was this one chick who was like, 'Who are you and whatchu still doin' here?'"

"What was she talking about?"

"There had been one of those impromptu parties I was telling you about. Well, it didn't end till nine in the morning. She was there kicking it with one of the DJs, I don't remember who. So about a week later, she comes bangin' on the door. When I told her whoever she was looking for didn't live there, she was like, 'Why you still here?' I said, 'Because I live here.' She looked around like she didn't believe me and wouldn't let me close the door."

"Girl, what did you do?"

"Shit, I started to call security, but I actually felt sorry for her. So I tried to break it down like, 'Look, sweetie, you got played. You ain't gonna hear from that clown again.' But she broke down crying, talking about how she was pregnant, and I had to stop covering for him and so on and so on."

"Dang, girl, it sounds like every day is nothing but a big ole soap opera over there," Pam said.

"It can be. It really can be." Vicki glanced around the living room. It was like she never even moved out. Pam, of course, kept the place nice and neat.

"So what you been up to?" Vicki asked.

"Girl, not a damn thing. Or at least nothing half as exciting as what you been up to."

Full, and a little tipsy, Vicki leaned back on the sofa. Pam got a little more comfortable herself.

"I do miss the quietness sometimes. Don't get me

wrong, I'm glad to have Murderous, but shit, sometimes I just want us to have some alone time. Not possible, though. So many people it seems rely on him for
everything. It's so amazing. He's under a lot of pressure too."

"I'm sure he is." Pam had started wondering at the
real reason for Vicki's sudden visit. But after they'd
talked for a few hours, she began to let her guard down,
resigning herself to the fact that maybe she was being
honest about missing their friendship.

"I'm real happy, Pam. I really am."

"Vicki, I'm glad to hear that. You deserve it. After
all you've been through, I'm glad you finally got what
you wanted."

"Yeah, but . . ." Vicki reached for the bottle and re-
filled her glass.

*Here it comes,* Pam thought. *What the fuck now?
Why can't she stay away?*

"Well, I don't know quite how to say this, but I told
you how much stress Murderous is under. If it's not the
record label execs, it's producers. If it's not them, it's
the bodyguards. Trust me, I don't see how he stays
sober," Vicki said.

"Okay . . . ?" Pam waited. She took a huge gulp
from her glass.

"Well . . . um . . . I was, uh . . . wondering if you know
where I could score some Viagra."

Pam seemed so shocked, she nearly sprayed Vicki
with the Hypnotic she had in her mouth.

# FRANKIE & ERICA

Frankie reminded herself to choose her words carefully. She didn't want to piss LadyRae off, but she didn't want to come across as scared either. When LadyRae finished reading her, Frankie took a deep breath and said, "Look, I wasn't trying to play you. It's just that I'm extremely busy, and I'm tired. I didn't sleep good last night. Here, why don't we go to the back so we can talk?"

LadyRae took her time following Frankie back into her office. "I thought I told you we needed to think about getting rid of that bitch Joy. I can't stand her."

"LadyRae, Joy ain't going nowhere. This is still my business, and I decide who stays and who goes."

"Okay, you got a point there. Besides, I'm sure there'll be some people I'll want to bring in, and you won't agree. So I'll let you keep her. You can even keep that little sweet thing Tracie up front. But I can find something else for her to do. I told you I have someone in mind who would really draw in the numbers. She's too plain, but you know I could fix her right on up."

Frankie exhaled. She didn't know what to say to get through to the woman, especially since she had already made up her mind. "Okay, LadyRae, what's going on? What can I do for you today?" she asked.

"You know, Frankie, you act like I'm botherin' you. The thing is, I'm actually here to do something for you today, and you act like I'm fuckin' with your plans. Again, you got me feeling like I ain't important around here. You think any more about our partnership?"

Frankie's cell phone rang. She didn't hesitate to answer it. "Just a minute, LadyRae, I'll be right back." She got up from the desk and dashed out of the office. She was back before LadyRae could throw a fit.

"Okay, now where were we?" Frankie asked.

"You kiddin' me, right?" LadyRae asked.

"No, I'm not kiddin' you, LadyRae. I'm also a very busy woman with a business to run around here. So if you could go on with what is so important, that would be good, 'cause I got some people I need to see."

LadyRae chuckled. "See, that's why I like you. Straight to the business. I knew you and me would make a damn good team, and I tried to get you to reconsider. You remember, Frankie? It was nearly a year ago, at the nail shop. I asked you and Erica about joining my team. You know I had to leave cocaine alone, especially when I saw what was possible with heroin. It was a real easy transition, and I'm a richer woman for it. But like I told your sister, the streets are getting hotter and hotter, so I need to expand and start cleaning my shit up before the Feds try to knock a sistah down. That's where you come in, Frankie." She smiled. "Your business idea is so damn sweet, I don't see why I didn't think of it myself. I mean, I actually used to lose sleep over why I didn't think of this myself. This is before you became all big-time like you are now. I heard you've spread your wings—San Quentin and Soledad.

I'll bet you are cleaning up. See, that's why I figured it's time for me to step in. I know what you thinking, all the hard work is over. But that's not true. I see where you going, and I think I can add something to the business."

LadyRae slammed her fist on the desk and Frankie jumped. "Am I boring you?"

"Nah, I'm listening, I am, but I got shit I need to get to."

"Well, what I'm saying is, I can have some papers drawn up to split The Hook-Up fifty-fifty. I know you the president, but I was thinking I could be the chairperson or some shit like that."

"Again, LadyRae, it's like I told you before. I already have a partner, my cousin Bobbi. And I can't split anything with you. But I'm glad you've offered. I just can't do it."

"You know, that's the same thing you said the last time I approached you about this. I'm surprised your position never changed. I really thought it would have, but, Frankie, I kind of knew it wouldn't." LadyRae stood. "I think you need more time to think it over," she said, heading for the door.

"My answer is gonna stay the same. I'm not going into business with you. I'm doin' just fine. You need to find someone or something else to help you make that transition."

"I think you'll reconsider," LadyRae said.

"Nah, I'm pretty sure I won't. There's nothing more to think about. I'm straight. And I don't need another partner."

"Well, consider this," LadyRae said. "I may not be able to change your mind, but knowing that I have your sister might."

Frankie's heart stopped.

"Oh, now don't go getting all excited on me. Erica's

fine; she really is. Those papers I was talking 'bout—they'll be delivered by the end of business today. You sign them, and send them back to the address on the envelope. I'll have a copy sent to you, and we'll do what we need to at the county clerk's office; then I'll see to it that you get your sister back. All in one neat little piece."

LadyRae turned and left.

# YVETTE

Yvette sat stunned at what Nyeree had just told her. She didn't know what to think, much less do. She was livid. All this time she had been afraid of Roshawn and his crew, but danger had been right next to her every day and night.

"Don't look at me like that," Nyeree said.

"Like what?" She still didn't want to believe he was a member of the infamous Grape Street Crips. She didn't even hang out in Watts. How the hell did she wind up fucking around with rival gang members and not even know it? This was all Frankie's fault. How could Frankie not have told her she was being hooked up with some gangbanger?

Yeah, Nyeree claimed he was no longer active, but what the fuck did that mean? How are you no longer active in a gang? What'd he do, retire? And like Wayne A. Day, the guy who founded Grape Street, would say, "Okay, Nyeree, thanks for your service. Here, let's set up your retirement paperwork and send you on down to processing."

Yvette regretted not smoking 'cause she could've used a blunt at that very moment. She was baffled.

"So lemme get this straight. You and the rest of your Crips from Grape Street think I got the connection to some jewelry that the Bounty Hunters stole before the raid went down in Nickerson Gardens, right?"

"Yvette, that's what I'm trying to tell you. It was all a mistake. I believe you have the connection, but you don't know you have it. Remember when you was telling me about the reward money you got for turning in Bug? I thought you were saying you had the jewels."

"If I was rolling like that, why would I have been living in that small cramped apartment? And you talking about close to one million in diamonds? Hell, no, I don't know nothing about no fuckin' jewels!" She looked at him, the fear returning to her eyes.

"You've got to think, Yvette. Where did your boy go after you guys left your mom's? You gotta try and think; this is important," Nyeree said.

"I've told you everything I know." She couldn't believe she had been worried about whether they would still have a future and here he was hiding a secret of his own. If she wasn't so scared, she'd be hot. But the truth of the matter was, if the Grape Street Crips were able to find her, it wouldn't take long for the Bounty Hunters to find her too.

Yvette was no fool, and she knew what this meant. She knew for a fact that her days were as good as numbered. She could see her mom, Peaches, crying on TV now, talking about how good her daughter had been and how she was never in any trouble, how she was just an innocent bystander caught up in a gang feud.

"So what are you guys gonna do to me?" she asked, no longer trying to hold back the tears.

"Do to you? Baby, I'm trying to protect you. That's why I need you to try and concentrate. Think back to the night you and Roshawn were going out. What did he do? Where did he stop?"

He wanted her to concentrate, and all she could do was think about all the ways she could die. And they'd definitely get away with it too. Once LAPD found out a killing was linked to rival gangs, it was like they automatically stopped working to bring the killers to justice.

Yvette knew her desire for bad boys, stars, or gangsters would be the end of her, but honestly she figured an unwanted pregnancy would be the worst she'd wind up with. But at that moment, the thought of being pregnant by some wangster who'd go down for some serious time, leaving her and a baby to struggle alone, didn't seem bad after all. She didn't want to get caught up in anyone's cross fire. She should've hung in there with Trevor's sorry ass. At least he wasn't into that gang shit. She jumped when Nyeree touched her.

"Ah, baby, whassup with that? You ain't never had a problem with me touchin' you before."

"I didn't know you were some gangster who was only hooking up with me to find some jewelry either." She had become scared and antsy.

"Damn, like that?" Nyeree drew back. "I thought we meant something to each other."

"I thought we did too."

"Didn't you hear anything I told you? I don't roll like that anymore. And when this is all over, I want us to get away from these streets, baby. Together. I don't want anything to happen to you."

"You still want to be with me?" she asked, unable to hide the hope in her voice.

"Yvette, you not hearing me. This ain't even 'bout you. You just happened to get caught up, but, baby, I want to make sure we both make it out alive and a little bit richer. I need you to *think*."

"Okay, let's see. We met, talked on the phone a few

times, but he never came to my house. Actually, the night of the raid, he picked me up at my mom's boyfriend's house. I was over there, and it happened to be close to some spot he said he had to go."

"Where was that?" Nyeree asked.

"My mom's man lives off Crenshaw and Imperial, so it was easier for him to scoop me from there."

"Okay, then what?"

"Well, we went to the motel next to the casino. I told you that's where Bug was hiding out. We were inside for maybe ten minutes; then we went over to the Gardens, and we were there for nearly thirty minutes before the raid went down," she said.

"Try to think, what did Roshawn say to his boy at the motel?"

"They talked about a passport he was waiting on. Roshawn did give him a whole lot of money."

"A lot like a few grand? Or a lot like in a suitcase?" Nyeree pressed.

"You know what? Now that I think about it, he pulled something out of the armrest in his car. Well, not the armrest, but—"

"A secret panel. So the car is outfitted with custom panels. That's got to be it: They trashed your place thinking you had found it and had it in your apartment, but you didn't even know you had it. Where is his car now? It's still in the shop, right?"

Yvette didn't know whether she should believe Nyeree. Then something crossed her mind. For the entire time they had been together, *she* had been lying to him. What if he was telling the truth? What if he really was no longer active, and he really wanted to settle down? That was the kind of stuff he had said in the letters they'd sent back and forth. Yvette wanted desperately to trust him. She decided at that moment she'd put both her faith and her life in his hands.

They jumped into the Escalade and sped toward her mother's house. When they arrived on Denker and Vernon her mother was in the kitchen cooking. Yvette didn't want to alarm her mother, so she told Nyeree to let her handle things.

"Mom, I want you to meet Nyeree. Nyeree, this is my mother. We call her Peaches." They stood in the kitchen.

"Oh, chile, why didn't you call and tell me you were bringing company? I look like a hot mess," she said, trying to pat her hair and fix her near perfect clothes.

"You look straight," Nyeree said. He peeped where Yvette got her good looks because her moms was tight. She didn't look nearly old enough to have a grown daughter. She was thick, wearing a pair of Apple Bottoms Jeans and a matching fitted top. Her shoulder-length hair, the color of a copper penny, was in soft twists that hung in layers.

After the introductions, he took a seat in the living room.

"We here to pick up that car, Ma," Yvette said.

"Okay, baby, let me give you the keys to the garage. I'm glad you finally came to get that thing. I got a ticket parking on the street the other day."

"I'll pay for it. Here, let me go pull it out." Yvette grabbed the keys and looked back at Nyeree sitting on the couch.

"Baby, you wanna help me with this?" She smiled.

He jumped up. "Oh, yeah, of course." He walked behind her to the side door, then to the garage. "I thought you said it was in the shop," he said.

"Yeah, that's what I said, but I put it in here after the place was trashed. Hell, I didn't know what was going on."

Yvette fumbled with the keys to the padlock for a few minutes, then became frustrated.

"Here, let me take a look at it," Nyeree said.

Yvette was glad to step back; she was sure it was just her nerves getting the best of her.

When he finally got the rusted padlock open and pulled the door up, the garage was empty except for an old lawn mower and a few bikes.

"OHMIGOD! What the fuck? I'm dead, I'm dead!" Yvette went ballistic.

# CARMEN

It had been five days, eleven hours, and thirty-nine minutes since Chip had walked out on Carmen, and she was still hurting over it; she missed him madly. Still, she did what any heartbroken person would've done: She called Gina up, and Gina told her the best thing to do was go out amd get her mind off the fact that her jailbird boyfriend had left her.

Carmen had been reluctant at first since it was going out with Gina that had gotten her into trouble in the first place. But the more she thought about it, the more she figured Gina had been right.

Besides, she thought, if they just went to the little hole-in-the-wall on Western, there was very little chance of her getting in trouble. Quite surely there wouldn't be another woman in there as fine as her. There she'd be able to drink herself into a stupor and forget about her misery. She had convinced herself being alone was the very last thing she needed.

Later that night, she could barely sit up straight by

the time she decided she had had enough. Gina was on the dance floor being felt up by a man old enough to be her father. Carmen wasn't judging 'cause she knew that for Gina it was all about the paper, and Gina didn't care where her paper came from as long as it kept flowing.

Carmen stumbled out to the dance floor. "Uh, I'm about to go," she said to Gina.

"Girl, you drunk. Go sit your ass down." Gina dismissed her and stepped closer to her dance partner, wiggling her hips. When Carmen left the dance floor, Gina was still shaking her ass. At the bar, Carmen looked at the bartender. "Can you call a cab for me?"

Nearly thirty minutes later, the bartender announced her cab had arrived. Carmen stumbled out to the waiting car and sank into the backseat. "Where to?" the cabdriver asked.

"Ah, I wanna go to Jefferson and Van Buren Place," Carmen slurred.

It took a while for the cab to make the left turn onto Van Buren Place, but Carmen enjoyed the time she had to think about what she'd say. It was 1:15 in the morning, and she hoped Chip would be at home. The last thing she wanted was to bump into Mrs. Davis again.

She never felt that Chip's mother had ever really forgiven her for the last stunt. But her mind told her she needed to go to Chip. She needed to tell him she couldn't go on without him.

In the backseat of the cab, she had sobered up as much as possible. She knew she was taking a huge chance, but she had to try. She had been miserable without him, and when she and Gina went out, she was losing her zest for the hunt. Carmen knew Gina had noticed a difference, but probably didn't want to say anything and run the risk of losing her again. Carmen had a feeling Gina only hoped she'd be able to find herself someone to settle down with before Carmen abandoned her for good.

Carmen had tried to offer Frankie's services to Gina. She even offered to pay for Gina, but Gina told Carmen she needed a well-established man. She wasn't in the position to help a brotha get back on his feet. Carmen respected her position, but she knew she couldn't keep club hopping and running into the serial relationships.

She called them relationships, but they were nothing close. Most of the time she'd let someone hit it once, but hardly twice. Carmen knew none of the men they ran through could do any more for her than she could do for herself. Unlike Gina, she didn't mind helping her man get back on his feet. And she wanted that brotha to be Chip, if he would still take her.

Looking up at the apartment now, she was having second thoughts. After all, she told herself, it was nearly two in the morning, and most of the lights were out on the block. When the driver pulled up in front of the fourplex apartment building Carmen took a deep breath.

"Okay, this is it," she said.

"Is this fine?" the driver asked, pulling into the driveway.

"Are you able to wait?" she asked.

"Yeah, but I gotta keep the meter running."

"That's not a problem, but I may be here for a while," she said, sliding out of the cab.

"As long as you willing to pay, I can sit and wait."

Carmen gave him a fifty-dollar bill and said, "Wait and I'll give you another whether I stay or have you take me someplace else. I may need to go out to Beverly Hills."

His eyes lit up. "Sure, lady. You take your time; I'll be right here."

Carmen looked up at the dark building. There was a little light on, but it looked like everyone had been asleep for hours. Still, she wasn't about to turn around, not after having come all that way.

She walked up to the porch and rang a doorbell. Carmen hoped she had rung the right one, but only time would tell, she thought. First a hallway light went on. She hadn't realized the iron-screen door didn't lead to the living room, but instead to a row of stairs.

"Who's there?" Mrs. Davis's voice screamed. And she sounded like she had a serious attitude going. Carmen knew there was no turning away, but she soon regretted being there in the wee hours of the morning.

"Carmen," she said so softly she could barely hear herself.

For a while, it was quiet. Carmen didn't hear Mrs. Davis's voice, and she wasn't sure if the woman had gone back to bed. Then, with little warning, the voice was right at her ear. "Chile, you know what time it is? What's wrong with you?"

"Ah, I was looking for Chip. Is he here?"

"Girl, what's wrong with you? You all right?" Mrs. Davis hit a switch, and the porch light came on. "You'd better bring your tail up in here. Are you . . . Lawd, have mercy, chile, you drunk as a skunk!" Mrs. Davis opened the iron door and nearly dragged Carmen inside.

"You know what could happen to you out in the streets drunk at all hours of the morning?"

"Gotta pay the cab. The taxi."

"What, chile?" Mrs. Davis asked, bolting the iron-screen door behind them.

"Where's Chip? I gotta pay the taxi."

Before she helped Carmen up the stairs, Mrs. Davis looked out of the screen door again. "Oh, is that taxi waiting for you?"

Carmen grabbed her purse. "Gotta pay." She pulled a fifty-dollar bill from her wallet and gave it to Mrs. Davis.

Later, Mrs. Davis gave Carmen a pillow and a blanket. "You need to sleep this off, chile."

Carmen was fast asleep and snoring before her head could make a dent in the pillow.

The next morning, the smell of bacon was so strong in the air Carmen thought she was dreaming. She knew she wasn't when she heard the voices. None of them were familiar.

"What the fuck?" She opened her eyes and looked around the room. "Where the hell am I?"

"Oh, I see you finally woke." Mrs. Davis came walking in with a plate full of eggs, bacon, grits, potatoes, and biscuits. "I know you got to be hungry, as sloppy drunk as you was last night when you came stumbling up here."

"I'm so sorry. I didn't mean to—" Carmen grabbed her forehead. "I'd better get out of here before Chip gets home."

"No use, chile. He done already been here," Mrs. Davis said.

"He saw me like this?" Carmen was horrified. She immediately began looking for a mirror. Her make-up, shit, her hair, she knew she was nothing less than a mess.

"Yeah, well, you was sleeping when he came in, but he saw you. He in the shower now." Mrs. Davis turned and went through a narrow hallway. When she came back, she had another plate in her hand. "This one's for you. I didn't know how much you wanted, but I figured this should be enough to sop up some of that liquor."

"Oh, no, that's quite all right. I need to be getting on my way. I'm sorry for showing up here like that last night. Now, I'd just like to bounce before Chip gets out of the shower."

Carmen started feeling around on the floor for her shoes, purse, and anything else she might have dropped. When she picked up all of her things and turned to leave, Chip was standing there.

"You not gonna eat none of the food my mama slaved over for us?" he asked.

Carmen looked at him, then at the plates of food on the table. "You don't have to eat, but I'm just saying she already don't think too highly of you. Leaving without eating"—Chip pulled a chair out for Carmen, then sat in one next to hers—"that might really put things over the edge," he said.

She looked at the door, then looked at the food on the table again. Damn, it smelled good, and she was very hungry. She had to wait for a cab anyway, she thought.

"Maybe I'll just taste a little," Carmen said.

She and Chip ate in complete silence, and when they were done, both plates were clean. "Damn, your moms can throw down," she said.

"You don't know the half of it. That was just breakfast," Chip said. He smirked and looked at Carmen. "You know how to cook like that?"

"Yep, sure do. I pick up the phone and cook up just about anything I want." She and Chip laughed at that.

"That's okay; woman fine as you, you ain't got to know how to cook. I'd get full just staring at you all damn day."

Carmen smiled.

"Especially when you flash that pretty-ass smile of yours."

"You say the nicest things to me."

"I mean them too."

"How come you ain't asked me why I'm here?" she asked.

"'Cause I already know. What I need to ask you for?"

"You don't know a thing." Carmen blushed.

"Bet. You here because you realized you ain't gonna find anything better than me out in them streets. I meant it when I told you I was ready for something different. You must be tired of the games. You know I stopped playin' a long time ago. And you also know I ain't going nowhere. I'm here to stay. And, besides, I gots to clear my name, 'cause I was damn sure wrongly convicted. I'ma sit right here and wait till you get all that damn playin' outta you."

Carmen walked to his side of the table. "How could you still want me after what I did?"

"Girl, your ass paid to be hooked up with me after what they *said* I did. Now, don't get shit twisted. I ain't no sucka or nothing, but, Carmen, I know it's rough out there in those streets, and I already found what I was looking for." He took her arms. "Do your thang, baby, but be careful—don't let the thang do you."

"Chip, I've been sick without you."

"Me too." Chip tried to kiss Carmen, but she pulled beyond his reach.

"Nah-ah, I ain't kissing you with this breakfast-covered morning breath. You all fresh and clean and shit and I'm all stank. How about we take this back to my place and we can really make up? The way make-up was designed to be made up."

"Wait, slow your roll, baby girl." Chip pulled her arm. "I got mad feelings for you and shit, but I'm still trying to deal with what went down. I think I'ma need some time," he said.

Carmen looked horrified. *He's got to be kidding.*

How could she have read him so wrong? "But I thought . . ." she said.

"I'm just saying, boo, I'm gonna need some time to get my head on straight. I miss you, too, but every time I close my eyes, a nigga can't stop seeing you in the alley getting busy with some fool who don't give a fuck about you." Chip shook his head. "Shit like that don't just vanish with a few sweet words. You feel me, right?"

Carmen was stunned.

# VICKI

For the past few weeks, Vicki had been feeling as lovely as she'd been living. That had been some of the benefits of having Murderous on Viagra. The tricky part was getting time alone to put the erections to good use.

The funny thing was, he didn't even mention anything about the change in his sexual performance. He had to realize that she had noticed the difference. Now she saw their lives in two stages: before the little blue pill, and after the little blue pill.

Before the little blue pill, he could barely get it up, much less fuck her for a good steady fifteen minutes. But after the little blue pill, he was getting his, and she was finally getting hers.

Their relationship was finally perfect. Soon she was no longer bothered by the fact that he didn't have a whole lot of time to spend with her. When they did have some alone time, Vicki made sure they were getting their freak on.

She couldn't thank Pam enough. Pam had taken her to this little spot in Compton to buy the pills. So far it had been all for the good.

One night Vicki decided to stay home instead of going out with Murderous to a party at the Roxbury in Hollywood. She had hoped that her decision to stay home meant the after-party would be held someplace else.

After Murderous and his entourage left, she had sent a car over to pick Pam up. She had the chef prepare an exotic meal and they chilled. Pam walked around Murderous's house like she was in a fancy museum. Vicki took pride in showing her around.

"Girl, you came up, no doubt," Pam said, walking around with her third glass of Hypnotic.

"But trust, it ain't no walk in the park. These bitches be jockin'. It's like they all want to be a rap star's girl. If only they knew the truth, that everything that shines ain't glitter."

"Huh, seriously," Pam said.

"They are sick with it. They just want a piece of a brotha with a microphone," Vicki said.

"Shit, after peepin' this place, I don't blame 'em." Pam laughed.

"Okay, let's go to the theater so we can see what bootleg movies he got."

"Girl, I could get used to this. You straight living lavish," Pam squealed. As they sat in Murderous's home theater watching movie previews, Pam leaned over and asked, "How are the you-know-whats-working for you guys?"

"Like a mothafuckin' charm. Can't you tell? A bitch been floating around this mug." They slapped high fives and started chuckling.

"I can't believe you got him to take Viagra. When I see him in his music videos talking about layin' pipe and how he can stroke for hours on end, I laugh to my-self, 'cause I'm thinking, yeah, who can't with that lit-tle blue pill?"

Vicki looked around the theater. "Girl, do you think he knows he's takin' Viagra? Hell fuckin' no!"

"What?" Pam's eyes bugged. She chuckled. "How the hell do you get him to take them without know-ing?"

"Girl, I put that shit in his food, his drink; I've even tried grinding them up and putting 'em in his tooth-paste."

"Bitch, no, you didn't."

"Girl, I was on a mission for real. Think about it. How am I gonna be on his arm looking all happy and satisfied when I ain't getting fucked proper? It wasn't jumping off like that, so I had to do what I had to do." She smiled. "I took matters into my own hands."

"I ain't mad atcha," Pam said. But she was really thinking, *Is it really that serious?* Vicki knew those pills could've been made out of anything. After all, it wasn't like they got a prescription. They paid some punk named Boo-Boo, and he produced the pills. They didn't know where those pills came from.

"Do you ever worry about the pills?"

"Worry? What you mean? When he's fuckin' me, or when I'm enjoying my fourth orgasm of the day?" Vicki shook her head. "I don't give a rat's ass what's in those pills as long as they keep Murderous doin' what he's doin'."

# FRANKIE & ERICA

Erica had been under duress. She couldn't fathom how LadyRae knew exactly where they had moved. She went over it again and again in her mind. Maybe she should've done things differently, she thought. Lots of good those thoughts had done her. One minute she was waiting for food to be delivered, then, lo and behold, she opened the door to find two of LadyRae's females standing there.

"You ordered Chinese?" the girl asked, holding the brown paper bag.

"Ah, yeah," Erica said. Her stomach suddenly became nauseated.

"Well, here it is. But you might want to put on some shoes. LadyRae wants to talk with you."

It wasn't like they were asking her to go. The minute she looked like she was hesitating, the other one shut her down with a look that said, Don't make LadyRae come and get you.

"I should call Frankie," Erica tried to reason.

"Now that would be just plain stupid," the girl with

the bag said. The more Erica thought about it, the more
she knew the girl was right. What exactly was she
going to call Frankie and say?

They walked her down the stairs to the waiting
Hummer. Erica had never seen it before, and for an in-
stant she forgot she was basically being kidnapped. Or
as LadyRae put it, taken for a ride.

"Say, baby girl, you look so worried," LadyRae said
when Erica climbed into the backseat of the tight-ass
truck. She looked around. The inside was outfitted with
two LCD screens in the headrests. LadyRae had been
watching a movie.

"Nah, I'm straight," Erica mumbled. "Whassup,
LadyRae? I love this truck; you done took it to a whole
'nother level, huh?"

"Yeah, just a lil' sumptin' sumptin'. So, I figured you
hadn't gotten a chance to talk to your sister yet. Am I
right?"

Erica looked toward the floor. She thought about
trying to explain, but deep down inside she knew there
were no words that could please LadyRae at this point.

She watched as LadyRae shook her head. "Don't
even worry about it. I'm callin' the shots now."

Erica wasn't sure what that meant, but she was positive it wasn't good. At that moment she wanted to kick
herself for not at least trying to warn Frankie about
what was coming. The driver slowly pulled out into the
street, and Erica became even more nervous.

"I can call her now, LadyRae. I know just what to
tell her too."

"Go on with that bullshit, E." She shook her head
again. "Now don't make my mood sour. I done already
told you I'm handlin' this now. I usually have my girls
handle shit for me, but this is special. See, when you
going legit, you gotta make sure you doin' it right. You
done showed me that sometimes it takes a real woman

to get shit done right. You had months to work this shit out. Obviously you couldn't, so you can just chill at this point. We 'bout to go eat some seafood at Harold's, have a few drinks, and relax for a while."

"But I got Chinese," Erica said.

"What?" LadyRae frowned.

"You said we were gonna eat seafood. I just ordered Chinese," Erica offered.

"Oh, don't trip. You'll be all right."

LadyRae's female driver had to stop at a red light at the bottom of the hill on Crenshaw and Stockton. A man ran up and started spraying the windshield before anyone could protest. He did the right side, then ran across and did the left with quick precision. When he finished, the driver rolled down the window, gave him a few bills, and the brown paper bag full of Chinese food.

"See? Feel better now?" LadyRae asked Erica as the light changed to green.

When the driver pulled up at Harold's Restaurant off Jefferson, Erica didn't feel any better. The food was always popping there, but she had other things on her mind. She couldn't see a clear way out of the mess she had fallen into. How could she have allowed LadyRae to think Frankie would even think about going into business with her?

"Whoa!" LadyRae said. "I know you know Harold's is the shit. Most people would jump to take your place right now. You need to act like you 'preciate when somebody trying to do something nice for you. What's the problem, E?"

"Nothing, LadyRae. Just thinking, that's all."

"Well, you best start thinking about eatin' some good ole Cajun seafood. Besides, you act like I'm tor-turin' you or something. Shit, we going out to eat. I'ma need you to step up and act right. I know you hungry.

That looked like a lot of Chinese food we gave that crack head."

When the driver opened LadyRae's door, LadyRae looked at her and said, "Why don't ya'll go in and get us on the list for a table? You know I want something nice. We'll be in in a minute."

"You gonna be all right?" LadyRae turned her attention back to Erica. "Now, we ain't about to be up in here actin' the fool, right? I mean, you can handle this, can't you, E?"

Erica sat quietly, too choked up to speak. She couldn't care less about the food at Harold's. Her mind kept thinking about how the shit was sure to hit the fan once LadyRae finally told Frankie the truth.

# YVETTE

Yvette didn't want to alarm her mother, but she was sure they were running out of time. She and Nyeree had to find that car before the Hunters came looking for her. No sooner had she closed the door behind her than the phone rang.

"Hold on, baby," her mother said, picking up the receiver that hung on the kitchen wall. "Hello?" she said.

"What?" Peaches's knees wobbled a bit before she collapsed to the floor.

Nyeree looked at Yvette, and she looked at him. She rushed to her mother's side.

"Ma, what's going on? What's the matter? Say something!" Yvette cried.

"Bruce, Bruce," Peaches mumbled.

Yvette grabbed the phone. "Hello?"

"Yes, what happened? OHMIGOD! Okay, thanks! We'll be right there."

She looked at Nyeree. "Someone just shot up Bruce's house. He wasn't home at the time."

"Okay, check this out. Your moms needs to go chill at the hotel till we find out what's going on."

"Why? They don't know—"

"If they were there, it won't take long for them to come here."

"What are y'all talking about? What's going on?" Peaches hollered as she struggled to pull herself together.

Yvette turned to her mother. "We need to find that car. I can't get into everything right now, but you need to pack some things. We gotta go!"

"I ain't going nowhere till somebody tells me what the hell is going on."

"Ma, where is the car?"

"Mickey must've took it. He came in here yesterday asking me about it after he mowed the lawn."

"What?" Yvette shrieked. "Why didn't you tell me that in the first place?"

"Girl, I know you better lower your voice when you talking to me. Now what kind of shit you done got mixed up in? Mickey probably at the car wash trying to show off that damn car. I told him to leave it alone."

Nyeree looked like he was about to lose his mind. "Okay, Peaches, you really need to go grab some shit. 'Vette, who the hell is Mickey?"

"He's my little brother. He's eighteen. Shit!"

"Okay, chill. Once your moms gets her stuff, we gotta go find him and that car. It's just that simple." Nyeree looked around. "He live here too?"

Yvette nodded.

A few minutes later, Peaches came dragging down the stairs with an oversized duffel bag. "Somebody needs to tell me what the hell is going on," she said through clenched teeth.

Outside, a purple Blazer pulled up just as they were

closing the doors on the Escalade. Yvette noticed it right away. "Who are they?" she asked Nyeree.

"Oh, hold up. Those are my boys. Lemme holla at them for a minute and we out."

Yvette sat nervously trying to block out her mother's ranting and raving in the backseat. She had told Peaches it was imperative that they find the Beamer because Mickey could be headed for trouble.

Peaches wanted to know what kind of trouble. She was pissed when Yvette couldn't come up with answers fast enough. She reminded Yvette about the lie she told when she went to hide the car in Peaches's garage in the first damn place. Yvette left out the details about the gang rival she had thrown herself right damn smack in the middle of. But she knew Peaches would never forgive her if something happened to Mickey.

"You know I'm not letting you live this one down, right?" she asked.

"I know, Ma, I know."

Yvette knew what Nyeree must've been thinking. She knew it was just a matter of time before somebody on Bruce's block told who he kicked it with, and that would lead to Peaches's house. If the Crips had figured it out, she knew the Hunters were on their way.

Nyeree stood next to the Blazer talking to the driver when he suddenly looked to his right. "'Vette?" he shouted. "Is that the Beamer?"

Nyeree ran and jumped behind the wheel of the Escalade. He pulled off toward Central Avenue where the Beamer was slowly cruising down the street, bumping the sounds with the top down. They were rolling four deep, seriously flossing.

Before the car could hit Compton Avenue, the Escalade and the Blazer were in tow. Nyeree pulled up on the Beamer's left-side, and Yvette rolled her window down. At the sight of his sister's face, Mickey stepped on the brakes, bringing the car to a halting stop. Nyeree pulled over to the right and stopped with the Blazer right on his tail.

Mickey fumbled with the radio and looked at his sister. "Um, um, I was just about to take it back to the house."

Yvette jumped out of the truck before Nyeree could park. He quickly jumped out and went toward the Blazer.

"Boy, pull it over right now and get your little hoodlum friends out!" The moment he stopped, his friends jumped out of the car and bolted. When Mickey saw the rage on his sister's face, he took off in the same direction, leaving the keys in the ignition. She ran over to the BMW, relieved that it was still intact.

As this was going on in the middle of Central Avenue, a red Impala heading east slowed and busted a quick U-turn. It was unable to make it to the far right-hand lane, but the passenger recognized both Yvette and his missing ride. Before the car could stop, he jumped out and made a beeline straight for Yvette.

# CARMEN

Carmen was tired of fluctuating between anger and loneliness. One minute she was mad at herself for fucking off the best thing she'd had in a long time; the next minute she was fighting the urge to go do her thang to get back at him. Deep down, though, she knew that would only get her in deeper shit. But, damn, what was a girl to do when her coochie needed attention?

She and Chip had talked on the phone since she woke up with a fierce hangover on his mama's couch, but he refused to meet with her. She wanted him to get over it so they could move on, but it was as if he insisted on making her pay.

He had said he didn't know if he could trust her again. She had wanted to say he could still fuck her while he figured it out, but she knew she couldn't. What got to her the most were the late-night phone calls. At first Carmen felt like he was just checking up on her, so she made sure she kept her ass at home. Chip would call, and they'd fall asleep on the phone. Some nights she'd beg him to come over, but he'd find a way to get her to agree it was best if he didn't. He kept talking about needing more time. She was getting more pissed and hornier by the minute.

After days of late-night phone sex, he came to her one night instead of calling.

They had been going at it nonstop since they reconciled. And this wasn't quite the old Chip either. While he still liked to lick her clitoris, he had learned that Carmen needed and preferred the dick. And he was very happy to incorporate an equal amount of both in their lovemaking. He wanted nothing more than to keep her happy. Chip decided he wanted to show her how good it could be when a man knew exactly what to do to please his woman.

Carmen had decided she was through running the streets. If she could get good dick at home at the drop of a hat, what was the point in going out there and taking risks? The more she thought about it, the more she realized she wasn't missing out on a damn thing up in the clubs and out in the streets. Still, she couldn't face Gina, who simply didn't understand why Carmen was "on his dick" like that—that's what Gina had said when she called to go out and Carmen said she and Chip were staying in.

"So you don't want to go out and catch some fresh bait? Girl, I heard about this new spot out in Century City. I heard it be loaded with ballers. None of those street-level nuccas either."

"I'm straight," was all Carmen could manage. Chip had been sucking her toes, and she was barely able to contain her excitement. She didn't feel bad about not going out with Gina. Carmen wanted Gina to get a man to settle down with too. But her girl let it be known that she wasn't having no part of settling down until Mr. Handsome, Rich, and Generous came along. And since he didn't have her address, or phone number, she had to go searching for him.

"We'll do something Monday," Carmen said, using her eyes to plead with Chip to stop. He kept slopping away, one toe at a time.

"Yeah, if you say so. Peace!" Gina hung up.

"I'm so glad we worked it out," she said a couple of hours later. Carmen stood at the kitchen table with two paper plates laid out. She was lifting slices of pepperoni pizza out of the box. She slapped the slices onto some plates for herself and Chip.

He had already cracked open two bottles of beer and was waiting for her in front of the TV. They had rented movies, ordered pizza, and planned on a quiet evening at home.

Before the movie started, Chip looked at Carmen. "You know I could get you hired at my job, right?"

Carmen didn't quite know how to react or what to say. She reached for the remote control, then hit the PLAY button. He couldn't be serious. She quickly dismissed the thought.

# VICKI

Vicki had barely finished crushing up the pill and mixing it in with Murderous's herb and garlic mashed potatoes when he came strolling into the dining room.

"Damn, baby girl, what's the occasion?" he asked.

"It's been a long time since we spent a quiet evening at the house; you know, just me and you," she said. "I even fixed dinner for us."

Before he could respond, Murderous's DJ and a bodyguard rounded the corner. They stopped suddenly when they noticed the candles and heard soft music flowing through the formal dining room.

"Oh, snap!" the DJ exclaimed.

"We interruptin' something?" The bodyguard looked at Murderous. He chose to ignore the daggers Vicki shot toward him with her eyes.

Murderous didn't want them to leave. They still had some samples to listen to, but he had a feeling Vicki was getting fed up. He didn't want to lose his girl, so he looked at her, then at the bodyguard.

"Ah, yeah, man, my girl surprised me when I walked in."

"That's cool. You want us to wait?" the DJ asked.

Again, Murderous looked at Vicki before answering. "Wait?" he repeated, like he hadn't thought of that option. When Vicki's eyebrow inched upward Murderous shook his head.

"Nah, that's all right. Why don't y'all just bounce, and we'll hook back up tomorrow?"

"Is somebody pussy-whipped or what?" the DJ joked. They started laughing until he caught the look on Vicki's face.

"Y'all trippin'. I'll holla," Murderous said.

The minute they left, he dug into his food like he hadn't eaten in days. Vicki was glad he knew what was best for him, because she was waiting for him to tell those fools to hang around. She was getting tired of coming in second to Murderous's entourage, and she had started to let her feelings be known.

Murderous didn't want her to make good on her threat to leave, so he figured he'd start juggling a few things around. He was planning to take her to Lake Tahoe for Christmas, but unfortunately they wouldn't be going alone. He had to figure out a way to get her to be okay with the plans.

Lately, Vicki had been opting to stay at home when they went out clubbing. He had told her it was all a part of promoting. What kind of rapper stayed home every night? He needed to be out in the streets kicking up some headlines.

"Sounds to me like you talking about looking for trouble," she had said.

As they sat across from each other now, Vicki watched as he ate up his Viagra-laced food. She was tickled, knowing they'd soon be getting busy.

"I thought after this we could go sip wine in the Jacuzzi." She smiled.

"I'm down," he said.

Once Vicki realized Murderous's plate was clean, she didn't want to waste any more time on small talk. She rose from the table and walked to his end.

"I'm gonna slip into some freaky shit so we can move this out to the deck," she whispered.

"I'm right behind you," he said.

"Don't worry about the dishes; just get another bottle of wine out of the fridge and bring the ice bucket out too."

Murderous could do even better. He went to the control panel for his house and dimmed the lights on the deck. He turned on soft music out there and turned the timer on in the hot tub. His mind started thinking about the work they needed to finish, but he quickly pushed those thoughts aside.

He dashed upstairs and stood at the door watching Vicki. She had already changed into her bikini and was examining something in her hand. Since her back was facing him, he had no idea what she was studying so hard.

When he walked up on her, she jumped and dropped the small velvet box. "Damn! You scared the shit out of me!" she sobbed.

"What was you . . . ?" His eyes followed her stare down to the floor.

She reached down and picked up the box. "What the hell is this?" She looked at the box as her stomach turned queasy. Her heart started racing at the same time.

"I didn't want you to find out this way," Murderous said.

"Ah . . . um . . . I wasn't snooping. I saw the Tiffany's bag and thought it was some jewelry. Well . . . ah . . . I mean, it is jewelry, but you know what I mean. I thought it was a necklace or a bracelet or something like that." Vicki's eyes started watering.

Murderous looked at her. "Can you stop running your mouth for a second?" He smiled nervously.

Her eyes darted around the room. She was trying to control the flood of tears she felt rushing forward. When she looked back at Murderous, he fell to one knee and took the box from her trembling hands.

"Vicki, boo, I want you to be down with me for the rest of my life. I guess what I'm trying to say . . . um . . . as is, ah . . . well . . . will you be my wifey?"

"Whoa! Hold up!" she said, still fighting the butterflies in the pit of her belly.

Murderous had a tight grip on her hand. He flicked the box open to reveal a five-carat canary yellow diamond ring.

"Damn!" Vicki said, her voice shaky.

He removed the ring and slipped it onto her finger. "So, whassup? You got a brotha down on one knee—how long you gonna make me wait?"

Her entire face broke into a wide grin. "Fool, what you think? Of course I'll marry your ass. I'll marry you right this minute if you want!" she yelled.

Vicki could hardly believe it. She was about to become Mrs. Steven West! She wanted to call Pam and scream it at the top of her lungs. But she and her future husband had a romantic evening to finish.

The moment she stepped out of his embrace, the phone rang. Vicki was too caught up in her new ring to pay attention to what was going on with his conversation. By the time he walked back to her, the mood had changed drastically.

"Boo, whassup?"

"Vicki, DJ Spin just got killed," he said somberly.

"What?" Vicki shook her head, as if her denial would make it untrue.

"Baby, I need to run."

"No, Murderous! No. Why do you have to go? I don't want you to get caught up in this shit!" she cried.

"You know I gotta go be with his family, see what's going on. I promise. I'll make this all up to you tomorrow, baby. Just bear with me." He kissed her and bolted out of the room.

# FRANKIE & ERICA

It had been two long frustrating days, and Frankie was nearly out of her mind with worry. What the hell was Erica doing with LadyRae? How had she even found her? Frankie had so many questions and absolutely no answers. She sat at her desk with her face planted in her palms.

"I'm telling you what we should do," Joy said. "We've gotta get your sister back, but we can't do it alone. I don't trust that butch-looking woman one bit. Lemme call my friend. You already got the upper hand."

For the first time in a long time, Frankie was scared. She knew Joy was right. If she let LadyRae get away with this, she'd never leave them alone. Hell, she was talking about being partners!

The bell indicating someone's entrance into the office rang. Joy and Frankie heard the receptionist say she'd sign for the package. A few minutes later, the girl brought a large manila envelope back for Frankie.

Nearly an hour later, Joy and Frankie were still astonished by the language in the papers. LadyRae wanted to allocate 60 percent of the profits to herself as the chairperson of The Hook-Up. The documents also indicated that although she was not required to spend specific hours in the office, she would have final say on which inmates would be eligible for the business. She also wanted to have final say about advertising. If LadyRae had her way, Joy, Frankie, Bobbi, and Erica would all basically be working *for* LadyRae.

Frankie sat at her desk, more livid than she had been before they began reading the documents. How could she fight LadyRae? How could she wind up exactly where she and Erica had worked so hard to avoid?

Joy had had enough. She left Frankie and went to her office. Dylan Logan had been one of Joy's clients for nearly five years. He had always told her to call him anytime and for anything. In all of the years she had been doing his taxes, she had never had a problem that needed his attention.

She fingered his business card and thought about what she was going to do. Joy was convinced there was no other way. She had gotten used to working with Frankie, and she didn't want to go back to the way things or the office had been before. She dialed his office number.

The receptionist said Logan was not available and transferred Joy's call to voice mail. She left a message but flipped the card over and dialed his cell number.

"Logan here."

"Captain Logan, this is Joy Hampton. Do you have a minute?"

"For you, Joy, I have five."


Frankie thought of all the reasons she had no choice but to sign the documents. Everything started and ended at her sister. She could hardly think straight. Frankie already had Tracie holding all of her calls unless it was LadyRae. She had yet to receive that phone call. Just as she was thinking about taking to the streets to find Erica on her own, Tracie ran to the back and announced that LadyRae was on hold. Joy jumped up from her desk.

"Wait two minutes before you transfer her back here. Frankie, you ready?" Joy sprang into action. She went and grabbed the things she needed, then ran back to Frankie's office. "Okay, Tracie!" Joy hollered.

"This is Frankie," she said, trying to steady her voice.

"Frankie, what's going on?" LadyRae yelled like she was making a social call.

"Nothing much, just waiting on your call."

"Cool, that's what I like to hear. You know, our last meeting left a bad taste in my mouth, but I'm glad you finally came around. That makes this a whole lot easier. I'm hyped about our partnership too."

Frankie sat listening. She looked up at Joy, who was waving her arms.

"So, are the papers ready? I could send somebody by to scoop them up."

"I thought you said fifty-fifty," Frankie said.

"Yeah, well, that was what I was offerin' in the beginning when Erica was supposed ta set this shit up. But since that fell through and I had to handle it, I figured I'd give myself an extra ten percent. I know y'all ain't trippin' on that, right?"

"Okay, so I'm supposed to turn over sixty percent of the profits from my business to you and do the majority of the work, while you sit back and collect money, just like that. What do I get out of this little arrangement?"

Joy gave her a thumbs-up.

"You get your smoked-out sister back—alive," LadyRae said. "Now enough of this shit. Are the papers signed?"

"Where's Erica?"

"She right here," LadyRae said.

"Can I talk to her?" Frankie didn't realize she was holding her breath until she heard her sister's voice come through the phone.

"Frankie?"

"Erica, how are you?" Frankie asked.

"I'm good. Frankie, I'm sorry. I just want to come home. I promise I'll listen to you from now on. I promise," Erica cried. "Why won't LadyRae let me come home, Frankie?"

"You coming real soon. And don't worry about it. LadyRae told me everything."

"Everything?" Erica asked, her voice trailing off.

"She told me about the money you borrowed from her, the drugs, everything, but I don't want to think about that right now. I just want to get you back here safely."

"Frankie, LadyRae says I have to go now. But I'll see you soon?" her sister asked.

"Frankie, you sign the papers, call me, and I'll send someone to pick them up. When I get the papers and make sure you didn't use invisible ink, I'll drop Erica off at the house. No harm, no foul?" LadyRae said.

Things moved quickly after the phone call. Joy told Frankie to stall as much as she could. Captain Logan said he was trying to get over to the office as fast as possible. He was at a crime scene when she had called.

Joy and Frankie were standing over the phone when Tracie interrupted. "Ah, Mr. Logan is here for you, Joy."

"Great, show him back," Joy said.

Nearly three hours after the call, Joy, Frankie, and Captain Logan sat listening to the tapes they had made of Frankie's conversations with LadyRae. Joy was a bit more anxious. Frankie was antsy, and Captain Logan was trying to contain his excitement. They had been trying to get LadyRae for years.

"So, do we have enough to stop her?" Joy asked.

"Oh, yeah. You ladies have done a great job. Here, I need to make a phone call. I'll be back shortly."

When Captain Logan returned, he walked straight into Frankie's office and looked at her and Joy. "Frankie, I have something to ask you. But first I need to let you know an FBI agent is on his way over. I'd like him to listen to what we have here. If he agrees, which I think he will, I need to know if we can count on you to help us out."

Frankie shrugged. "Of course. What do you need me to do?"

"If Agent Samson agrees, we might need you to get her over here."

Frankie's head was spinning by the time the officers arrived. The two officers reviewed the tapes again. Frankie was getting a bit nervous; she hoped LadyRae wouldn't start getting suspicious. She knew LadyRae had no reason to grow suspicious, but she was still nervous.

"We want you to call LadyRae and tell her you want to sign the papers but that you want to meet with her in person. Tell her you and your cousin Bobbi want to hold a conference call with all the parties involved. We want to get her over here. We've got enough to arrest her." Agent Samson shook one of the tapes. "But this is what we've been looking for for years. This will put her away for a nice little stretch."

Frankie swallowed hard.

# YVETTE

"Yo, Yvette!" Yvette snapped her head in the direction of the voice. Nyeree noticed the sheer horror cross her face. "I need to holla at you, Ma!" Roshawn hollered. He had already jumped out of the car before his homey could complete the U-turn and park. Roshawn had made a b-line straight for Yvette.

Nyeree was standing next to the passenger side of the Blazer. He was telling his homies what he had discovered about Yvette and the jewels and was telling them his theory about the secret panels. By the time the red Impala pulled up, Roshawn already had his hands clasped tightly around Yvette's neck.

The driver of the Blazer noticed it first. "Yo, dawg, whassup over there?"

Nyeree backed up from the passenger side, where he and his homies were talking about what to do with the Beamer. As he tried to rush to Yvette's side, guns came out and bullets started flying.

Peaches ducked to the floor of the Escalade and used her cell phone to dial 911. When the smoke cleared, a couple of bodies were strewn all over the street. Yvette could hear the sirens. She could feel her clothes drenched in warm blood, but she didn't feel any pain.

"OHMIGOD!!! I've been shot!" she sobbed. Nearby residents began pouring out of their houses. "Nyeree!" she yelled. When she moved, Roshawn's body tumbled to the ground. "Heeellp! Somebody call the po-lice!" Yvette cried. She quickly got up and tried to make her way to Nyeree.

The red Impala took off down the street. Roshawn's body lay in the middle of the street along with one of the passengers from the Blazer.

Yvette took Nyeree's limp body into her arms. "Just hold on, baby. Help is coming," she cried, searching Nyeree's eyes to see if he understood what she was saying.

"Go," he whispered. "You need to bounce before the law comes."

"No, I'm not leaving you. I'm not leaving you like this." Tears soaked her face.

Within seconds, several police and emergency vehicles surrounded her and Nyeree. They made way for the ambulance.

"Baby, you going to make it. You just gotta hang in there. Stay wit' me, boo, stay wit' me!" Yvette tried to sound brave. But she saw something scary in her man's eyes. He wasn't fighting.

"You hear me, Ny? You hear me?"

"Yeah, babe, I hear you." His eyes fluttered. "You know you my heart, right?" He smiled.

"Ma'am, we need you to move," a firefighter said.

Yvette allowed them to get to Nyeree, but she refused to go behind the yellow tape the officers had started putting up.

"I'm his wife," she cried, still clinging to his hand as they placed him onto a stretcher and began to load his body into an ambulance. Yvette hopped into the ambulance. When she saw Peaches standing near the yellow tape, she yelled to her mother, "I'm ridin' with him. They taking him to Killa-King."

The police were at the emergency room inside Martin Luther King Hospital, where Nyeree was undergoing surgery. They were there to question Yvette and her mother. Others who survived the bloodshed got away.

Hours later, on the news, Yvette learned that police had in fact found nearly one million dollars' worth of diamonds stashed in the side panels of the BMW.

Peaches was through after Yvette told her the entire story from the very beginning. She didn't leave out a thing.

"I don't have to tell you how stupid you was, right? You should've gave that boy back his damn car."

"I know, Mama, I know now. I still can't believe Nyeree is gone. And it's all because of me."

# CARMEN

"Ssssssslow it down a little. Just a little bit. Yeah, right there. Right there!" Carmen cried.

"Like that, baby?" Chip asked, all too eager to oblige.

"Yes, right there." Chip had been beating up Carmen's pussy for the last hour and fifteen minutes. And she was enjoying every minute of it. He showed no signs of letting up and she was happy.

"Girl, I can't get enough of this sweet pussy of yours," he said as he adjusted her legs on top of his shoulders.

"You don't have to. It's all yours, baby."

"And only mine? That's what I want to hear. Only mine?" he asked, slamming into her with force as he picked up momentum.

"Yes, baby. Yes. I know you 'bout to come, right?"

"Nah, I'm waiting on you, girl. Do your thang. I just need to know if this is where you want it."

"Yeeees," she breathed, struggling to keep her legs elevated. It was her favorite position, and it never failed. That's why it was usually the one Chip ended with; he knew she'd come quickly that way.

"Right there, right?" he asked. "Is that your spot, boo?"

"Yeeess, baby. Yesss! You know it is!" She climaxed so hard she thought she'd burst a vital vein. A few minutes later, Chip collapsed, huffing and puffing just as hard and loud as Carmen.

"Dang, baby, that was the bomb!" she squealed.

"Whew! You sure know how to lay it on a brotha," he said.

"Me?" she quizzed. "That was all you."

"Maybe for the last thirty minutes," he said. "But that first hour, baby, you had me going for real."

Hours after the romp of a lifetime, there was already trouble in paradise. Chip wanted to turn over a new leaf, but Carmen didn't think she had to completely change who she was in order for him to do that.

"I am not looking for no job," she told Chip for the umpteenth time. She was starting to sound like a broken record, and even *she* was growing tired of hearing herself speak on the issue.

"So what are you gonna do, just hang out all day?" Chip pressed.

"I'm cool. I keep busy. Why do I need a job?"

"I'm just saying, you plan to live off your pops forever?" he asked.

"You asking for trouble," she warned.

"What's that supposed to mean? What? Now I can't talk to my woman about how she spends her days or what she's up to when I'm not around? If I didn't care, Carmen, I wouldn't say shit."

"I don't want to talk about this right now." Carmen got up from the bed and walked out of the bedroom. She was sick and tired of going back and forth with

Chip about this. She walked to the bathroom and turned the shower on steaming hot.

As she stripped down and rubbed cold cream on her face, Chip walked into the bathroom.

"I don't wanna fight," he said. "'Sides, I love you, girl."

Carmen stopped what she was doing and turned to face him. "Did you just say what I think you said?"

Chip shrugged. "What?"

"You said you love me."

"Carmen. I love you, girl. I do, but—"

"I know, Chip. You love me, but you don't trust me. So you figure if I have a job, you ain't got to worry about me fuckin' around on you. But what you're not thinking about is, I could meet somebody at work. What would you do then? I could get boned right there in the office. That's where a gang of females come up on fuckin' buddies. You ain't gotta worry about me or us. We gonna make it, boo. I just can't have you sweatin' me over getting no nine to five."

"Whoa! Whoa! I ain't trying to get you all heated. I just don't like the idea of you being here all by yourself when I'm gone, that's all. I'm not worried about you giving my pussy away. My name is all over that." Chip chuckled.

"Well, if your name is all over this, come handle your business," Carmen said.

"Oh, I'm 'bout to." He climbed into the shower right behind her.

# VICKI

Murderous had made it clear—they were going to hop on a plane, go some place exotic for the weekend, and get married. He wasn't having none of the hoopla and frills of some Cinderella-type shit. That's what he told Vicki, and that's what he meant. No, she couldn't bring Pam. No they couldn't honeymoon for a week. No, he wasn't flying what little family she had in to be there. It would be just him, her, a bodyguard, someone from the label, and the publicist who would make sure information was leaked to all of the rags.

Vicki wasn't tripping about it at all. He had given her a week to get it all together. She had been thinking about the Bahamas or Jamaica, until Murderous came in one day, saw some brochures, and told her they needed to go to Mexico because he couldn't be away too long with a new CD dropping on Christmas Eve. His current CD was still climbing the charts.

The day after they buried DJ Spin, Vicki got the ball rolling. She picked up all of the necessary paperwork for the marriage license and the other things she would need for their destination wedding. And even though Murderous said Pam couldn't come, once Vicki decided she was getting married in Cancun, she booked a plane ticket and a hotel room for Pam at the resort where their wedding was being held.

What could he say if Pam just showed up? The day they left for Mexico was one of mixed feelings for Vicki. She was excited because she was about to marry her dream man. But she was pissed when she looked around and found herself surrounded by his normal entourage.

"You never said you were bringing the crew," she whispered as they stood in the international line to have their passports checked. Vicki knew that was why Murderous insisted they meet at the airport. He had said he would be working in Hollywood and had to meet her at LAX.

"Vicki, don't start tripping. We 'bout to go get hitched. It's all good," he said.

And what could she say, really? Before they boarded the plane, a herd of photographers were on hand to snap pictures. Vicki glanced over at Lydia, but since the two hadn't been speaking much lately, she didn't say a word.

Vicki was livid when Murderous left his first-class seat to go into coach to holla at his crew. But her mood quickly changed when she caught a glimpse of the crystal-clear waters below. As the plane prepared to make its descent, she saw the sugar-white beach that stretched along the resort they were staying in and suddenly didn't care about anything but a safe landing.

The Secrets Excellence Riviera wasn't exactly in Cancun but was on the Mexican Riviera. When they landed at the small airport, she and Murderous hopped into an old limo and went to the resort. He told her his assistant and the crew would handle the bags and everything else. He wanted to unwind and relax before meeting everyone for drinks later.

Within minutes of them checking into their ocean-front honeymoon suite, their private concierge was knocking on the door. The little Mexican man whose English was polished dropped off their luggage and told them to call if they needed anything. Vicki loved the room because everything was so modern.

They found a honeymooners' basket lying on the bed, next to his and hers robes and matching slippers. They had a king-sized four-poster bed and a full marble bathroom that had a whirlpool bathtub and a separate shower. The room was tastefully decorated in peach and blue. The private patio was fully furnished with a hammock and speakers outside.

It didn't take long for Murderous to fall asleep in the hammock on the patio, and Vicki couldn't blame him. Although it was close to eighty degrees in December, their patio had a nice breeze. The sound of the waves crashing onto the shore only a few feet away was better than any relaxation recording they could buy. They were gonna be married the very next day. While Murderous slept, Vicki called Pam's room to see if she had arrived.

"Girl, I'm diggin' this spot for real," Pam squealed. "This is tight—my room, the flight, it's all good!"

"Okay, peep this. We're in the honeymoon suite, but Murderous has already conked out. You wanna meet in the lobby so we can get a quick tour, then go to the bar for a quick drink before he wakes up?"

"The main bar or the bar near the pool?" Pam asked.

"Let's go to the one near the pool. I want him to be able to see me from the room in case he wakes up."

\* \* \*

Vicki and Murderous got married on the beach the next day at sunset. She wore a white Vera Wang halter dress, and he was decked out in an Armani linen-shirt and matching pants. They were barefoot and wore no jewelry except the new wedding rings. Everyone in his entourage and Pam partied that night until the wee hours of the morning. They had one more day until they were due to fly back to LA. Or at least Vicki was flying back. She was vexed when she learned that Murderous had to take a charter plane to another Caribbean location for a video shoot. But she was resigned to the fact that she could do nothing about it.

Back at home, she couldn't stop looking at her left hand. Was she really Mrs. Steven West?

"Well, girl, what does it feel like to be married?" Pam asked as they sat on the phone. It had been three days since the nuptials in Mexico.

"Girl, I was more than happy to trade in my playa card. I'm lovin' it in ways I can't even begin to explain. As a matter of fact, Murderous and me are going out for the first time as man and wife when he gets back." Vicki was happy, but she couldn't believe the things the papers had printed about them. They of course had pictures thanks to Lydia and the reps from Murderous's label. But in some of the stories, anonymous sources said things like MC Murderous was just another successful brotha who felt the need to marry a white girl.

She was fuming when she saw a timeline of his career in one of the trash papers. In the timeline, they showed several old pictures of Murderous and the sistah he was linked to at the time. Then of course now that his current CD had gone triple platinum, they showed a wedding picture of Vicki and murderous on the beach.

Murderous had walked in while she was looking

through the paper, and he stood in front of her. "Why do you read those things?" he asked.

"Everybody else reads them."

"So, you get yourself all worked up, though," he said.

"Yeah, how come you don't?" she asked, barely able to tear her eyes away from the story that told how they met while he was in jail. They even had the nerve to cast her off as a jailbird junky. They had done an interview with tired-ass Raymond, who used the opportunity to invite other lonely women out there to write him.

"Aeeey, let me tell you something. In the rap game, any kind of publicity is good publicity. Especially when you got a new CD dropping in days. Besides, Lydia feeds them most of that shit anyway," he said nonchalantly.

"What?"

"Oh, my fault, baby. I thought you knew," he said. "C'mon, let's go get ready."

Vicki thought about what Murderous had said all night long. She couldn't get it off her mind. She even thought about it as she crushed up his Viagra pills later that night. These pills were from the new batch she and Pam picked up when they were in Mexico. Of course she never got a chance to use them, because Murderous never left her side on their wedding night. She had to settle for his old performance, but she wasn't tripping.

She knew she'd get the normal roller-coaster ride soon. Well, soon hadn't come fast enough. So as he showered, she spiked his Crown and Coke with the pills and hoped for the best.

About thirty minutes after he swallowed the last of the drink, Vicki stripped down to her expensive sexy lingerie. She started swaying her hips to the instrumentals from one of his newest tracks.

"That shit turns me the fuck on when you do that," he slurred.

Vicki knew it and knew she was in for a real treat. The pill she crushed looked like it was bigger than the ones she normally used. But she didn't care; maybe he'd stay hard for hours, and she could ride him until she went raw.

"Damn, I'm feelin' you. Keep poppin' that ass, baby," Murderous cried.

Vicki did her best to imitate the video hos and gyrate to the music. The beat was tight, and she had a feeling this would be yet another hit for MC Murderous. When she turned to shake her ass for the last time, it looked like he was dozing off. Not wanting to miss out on the royal fuck she was sure she'd get, she stopped the show and went in for the kill.

Murderous had stripped down to his boxers, and his dick was so rock hard it stood at attention. Vicki was so excited she jumped on him and started gyrating her hips like she was still dancing. It felt so nice to have a nice, stiff dick all up in her. When Murderous reached up and started squeezing her nipples, it nearly drove her insane with pleasure.

"You like that, huh, baby?"

Vicki nodded, struggling not to break her stride.

"Ride this dick, then, ride it, girl. You like it, huh?"

"Oh, yes, baby, yes. I feel it, and it feels so good. This is just what I needed, baby. Don't you dare stop." Vicki was getting wetter.

Suddenly Murderous flipped her onto her back, spread her legs as wide as they'd go, then started humping her like a wild man.

"Oh, yes," Vicki cooed.

She heard Murderous exhale and grunt; then he suddenly rolled off her body and collapsed.

"What the fuck!" Vicki shrieked.

# FRANKIE & ERICA

Frankie's hands shook as she reached for the phone. Captain Logan touched her and signaled to the other agents that he needed a moment. Captain Logan was a nice, big, and tall chocolate man. His features were chiseled, and his shoulders were wide. Oh, how Frankie wished they were meeting under different circumstances.

"Can we get a moment?" he asked. He stood back and watched as Joy and the other agents filed out of Frankie's office. When the last person closed the door, he turned to Frankie and spoke calmly. "You gonna be just fine. Would you like some water or a soda?" he asked.

"No, I'm straight. I'm just a little nervous. I just want my baby sister to be okay."

"I understand. But you know you're doing a good thing here, right? This is extortion, what she's trying to do. It's illegal. While I may not completely agree with the type of business you run here, what you're doing is perfectly legal, and you have every right to be protected against people like her." He wiped his forehead. "We've been after her for years, but she usually doesn't do the dirty work herself. She usually has one of her workers take the fall. And we haven't been able to get anyone to testify against her. Every time we get close, it falls apart."

"So what does this mean to me and my sister if I testify? I mean, what if she gets out? What are we supposed to do? You guys will be long gone," Frankie said.

Captain Logan pulled a card from his jacket pocket. He scribbled a number on the back. "Frankie, you can call me at this number day or night. I won't let anything happen to you. We can always give you guys protection."

Frankie took the card. After examining it for a few minutes, she said, "Your wife won't be mad about me callin' at any time?"

Captain Logan smiled and shook his head. "No, Frankie. There's no wife to worry about. Now, are you ready to do this?" he asked.

"Yeah, I'm cool," she said, all the while laughing at herself on the inside for the old tired line she had just used.

Captain Logan went to the door and called everyone back in. "Okay, this is how we're gonna handle this. We'll be next door in Joy's office. Since LadyRae usually parks in the front when she comes, the van will stay in the back. The bug is testing—one, two, three, how's that?"

A little white man gave a thumbs-up.

"Okay, cool," Captain Logan said. "Now, Frankie is about to make the call, and we'll take it from there. Everyone, take your places."

Frankie dialed LadyRae's number. After a few rings she answered. "Talk to me!"

"LadyRae, it's Frankie," she said.

"Whassup, Frankie? I've been waiting on your call. So you got good news or what?"

"Well, I, ah . . . I was wondering if you would come over to the office. You see, my cousin Bobbi is on her way too. And since we're all gonna be doin' business together, I thought she should be here." Frankie shrugged toward Captain Logan. He nodded, hoping to encourage her.

"Well, shit, I didn't think about that. But you right. It would be best if we all met and knocked this thing out. But why don't I send one of the girls over to scoop you guys? That way we can grab a bite to eat."

"Yeah, that sounds cool, but here's the deal. I didn't want to go into details or anything, but it's Joy. Well, how do I put this?"

"Just spit it out!" LadyRae demanded.

"She don't like you. Says you give her the creeps. So I was thinking if we were all here, you could, I don't know, kind of lay down the law. You know, so she'll understand that things are going to change around here."

"Oh, I feel you. You need some help to keep that ass in check. I knew that square bitch didn't like me. Shit, she better hope I keep her ass on. You know what, I am gonna roll through. I got a few choice words for that hatin' ho. She betta recognize I'm callin' the shots, and her ass can be replaced. Yeah, I'll be there within the hour. Oh, and, Frankie, I'll bring Erica, but understand that she'll stay in the car until we sort things out. After the business, we can go break bread; you know, celebrate."

"Oh, yeah, that's cool, LadyRae. Is she, is Erica okay?"

"Yeah, she straight. I'm sure she's ready for this shit to be over too."

By the time LadyRae arrived at the office, Frankie was a complete mess. Here she was about to cross one of the city's most feared hustlers. She knew she was taking a huge risk by trusting Five-O, but she also knew she couldn't turn over everything she had to LadyRae either.

When LadyRae came strolling in like she already owned the place, she didn't even bother saying hello to Tracie, who quickly picked up the phone when she saw LadyRae's Hummer.

"Frankie, where the hell is your cousin?" LadyRae asked.

Remembering her lie, Frankie got up from her desk and walked to the door. "Joy, can you call Bobbi and let her know LadyRae is here?"

"I think she walked down to one of those beauty supply stores. She'll be right back."

LadyRae sat down. "Hmm, I've been thinking about that bitch Joy. You know damn well I'ma fire her ass, right?"

"We can't just fire her; she'll sue us. It don't work like that, LadyRae."

"Maybe that's not how you do things, but trust me, I'ma fire her ass. And sue? Shiiit. By the time I'm through with her ass, she better hope she can still take a breath. You know, doin' dirt comes second nature for me. I ain't worryin' about being sued. I'll smoke that bitch." LadyRae patted her Louis Vuitton bag for good measure.

"LadyRae, do you think it's fair for you to take sixty percent of the company? I mean, why can't we go back to fifty-fifty?" Frankie asked.

"Frankie, I know you didn't bring me up in here to squabble over minor shit. We done already agreed on how this is going down, right? I mean, I took you at your word; now what you trying to do?"

"I'm just trying to figure this all out."

"All you got to figure out is this. You sign over sixty percent of the company to me, and in exchange you get your sister back alive."

"But what if I change my mind?"

LadyRae pulled her bag open. Frankie saw the gun's handle as she lifted it to take her phone out. "Then I call my girl and tell her to take Erica back to the house until you and me and your cousin Bobbi can work this shit out. And you know what, I want to fire that bitch Joy now. See, I didn't come in here to negotiate. Call Joy and find your cousin, 'cause I ain't got all damn day."

"You brought a gun in here?" Frankie said for the officers' sake.

"Bitch, I don't go nowhere without being strapped."

"Joy!" Frankie screamed.

Suddenly her door swung open, and Agent Swanson, and Captain Logan rushed in with their guns drawn.

LadyRae reached for her bag. She didn't know what to do. "What the fuck? I know you didn't!" she shouted at Frankie.

"LadyRae Marie Jones, you are under arrest for extortion." Agent Swanson began reading LadyRae her rights.

"Do you know what I will do to you?" she said to Frankie.

As an officer started to handcuff her, Captain Logan pulled open her purse. "A gun!" he yelled. "A felon in possession of a firearm? LadyRae, this has got to be what, three, four strikes? Baby, we finally gotcha!" he sang.

"Fuck you, Logan. This shit won't stick."

"Did you hear me? The firearm is your third strike alone. If that don't hold up, I'm sure the extortion charge will. Either way, you're headed to Silver Brand. I'm sure you're familiar with the women's prison up north, right?"

Frankie breathed a huge sigh of relief.

"Your sister is waiting up front. We got her after

LadyRae came inside. She and her girls are going away for a nice little stretch."

"The girls too?"

"Yeah, we can get them on kidnapping charges. I need to warn you, though. Your sister is fine, but she don't look good at all. We're calling a bus to come and take her to the hospital."

Frankie dashed up front to see Erica.

The minute she laid eyes on Frankie, Erica started crying hysterically. "I'm so sorry. Frankie, can you ever forgive me? I'm so sorry."

"Don't worry about it. We'll work it out. Let's see about getting you cleaned up."

# YVETTE

Yvette decided to pass on the apartment off Wilton Place. She hadn't decided what to do with herself, but she knew she didn't want to be alone. Every time she closed her eyes, she saw the image of Nyeree taking his last breath.

She felt better knowing Roshawn was gone and Bug had been recaptured. She had no desire to get caught up in any more gang shit ever again.

One day she rolled out of bed around noon. Her mother, Peaches, was gone, and Mickey hadn't been around in days.

Yvette picked up the phone, which seemed to be constantly ringing.

"Yvette Madison, please," a cheerful voice said.

"This is Yvette. Who's callin'?"

"You don't know me, but my name is Sandra Haruf of Haruf's Family Jewels. We're a five-generation business specializing in antique heirlooms, precious stones, and gems."

"Ah, I'm not interested," Yvette said, preparing to hang up.

"No, ma'am, this is not a sales call. I'm calling you before I give the paper your information. The reason I'm calling is because we understand you helped to recover our jewelry stolen in a recent heist."

"Oh," Yvette said, still not sure where the woman was going with this.

"Well, authorities have finally closed the case and returned all of the stolen jewelry. I'm glad to say all of the pieces have been recovered. Anyway, as a token of our appreciation, we wanted to present you with a small reward. We have one of our diamond bracelets and a pair of diamond stud earrings for you." She lowered her voice. "We're also presenting you with a check for one thousand dollars. We believe it is caring members of the community who help us and law enforcement curb crime. Now we can ship this to you, as we use a bonded courier service, or you can pick it up at one of our locations. If you decide to pick it up, the paper would like to take your picture and run a short story."

Yvette smiled inwardly. She wasn't about to talk to no damn reporters, but she had a good idea just what she would do with that thousand dollars.

"Mrs. Haruf? I'd like you to send it to me. I would really rather not be in the paper. I hope you understand."

"Oh, dear, we do. Okay, let me get your address, and we will have someone drop the package off in the next two hours."

Later that day, when Peaches walked into the house, Yvette came downstairs.

"You feeling any better?" Peaches asked.

"I would if you'd spend Christmas with me in the Bahamas." She smiled.

"What are you talking about, chile?"

Yvette told her mother all about the reward. And to show just how sorry she was for dragging Peaches through that mess, she used the money to pay for a seven-day cruise to the Bahamas.

"You sure you want to spend up all of your money on a cruise?"

"Mama, the boat leaves Thursday. That's in two days. Now, I don't know about you, but when it pulls out into the Pacific Ocean, I plan to be on it with a nice drink in my hand." She looked at Peaches. "The only question left to ask is, am I going alone?"

# CARMEN

Carmen had decided it was time to stop dogging her girl. She and Gina might have taken different paths, but Gina was still her girl. And when Carmen thought about it, Gina was the first real friend she had had in years, a female who didn't turn out to be jealous of her. They agreed to meet for happy hour at El Torito in Hawthorne. Gina had said that's where her newest baller had a place.

It was fifteen minutes past the time they had agreed to meet. Carmen was about to order her second margarita when Gina came whisking through the doors.

"I was about to give up on you and have another drink," Carmen said.

"Sorry, girl. I got caught up, but I'm here now, so let's get this thing started."

"You look great," Carmen said, referring to the fierce little pageboy bob Gina was sporting. It had streaks of red in it, and Gina was working it. Carmen fingered her own hair as Gina sat.

"I just wanted to do something different. I plan to

bring in the new year in Vegas with my new man, so I wanted to go all out."

"Ooooh-wee, a new man? Do tell, girl. Who is he, and where did you pick him up?"

"Girl, he plays for the Raiders, but his moms is from here. So you know how that is. A bitch will be racking up the frequent-flyer miles."

"Whhaat? That's tight."

"Yeah, we met a few weeks ago at this spot in Century City. They had a bi last week—you know, a week with no game—and he was down here visiting his family. You should've seen us in the club. I've already been to Oakland twice," Gina said. "I think this one is a keeper too, girl. I finally got what I wanted—a nice-looking baller with a phat-ass bank account. What more can a sistah ask for?"

"So does that mean you'll be moving to Oakland?" she asked Gina.

"No, girl, he owns a house in Santa Monica. And his moms lives here. He's just there during the season. I can't wait for you to meet him. Maybe the four of us can go out to dinner. We can go to BB King's restaurant in Century City," Gina said.

"Oh, yeah, just let us know. I mean, we'd have to check with Chip's schedule, but I'm sure we can work something out."

When their margaritas arrived, Gina lifted her glass to the air. "Here, let's toast," she said.

"Okay." Carmen raised her glass to meet Gina's.

"To two bad-ass bitches who got exactly what they wanted. Big dicks, good money, and a reason to stay outta them clubs!"

Carmen clinked her glass against Gina's. "What about love?" she asked.

"What about it?" Gina asked, sipping her drink.

Carmen laughed. Her girl Gina wasn't about to

change no matter what. She was just happy the girl finally found somebody, even if it was just for a minute.

They both had what they wanted, and there wasn't anything wrong with two girls wanting different things when it came to men. Carmen was just glad her list included love, and that was exactly what she had with Chip.

"Now, tell me all about your big baller, what's his name? And don't you dare leave out a single word," she said to Gina.

Gina was cheesing.

# VICKI

Vicki spent Christmas in the hospital at her husband's bedside. He was in a coma, and she was riddled with guilt. Pam had just left the room, dropping off a change of clothes.

She had always dreamed of the day Murderous would lose his entourage, but she didn't want it to happen like this. The only person who showed up at the hospital was Lydia, and she had only come the first week. Vicki hadn't heard from anyone since.

That didn't bother her too much. What got her was the gossip rags that were already writing Murderous off. She stopped reading the trash long ago. Somehow it had leaked out that he had traces of a sexual enhancement in his blood, and everybody ran with that part of the story.

While she was nervous about losing Murderous, she was also nervous about them finding out how those drugs got into his system. Pam was the only other living person who knew that Vicki had been drugging her husband. The doctors, though they didn't say it, figured he had taken the pills himself. But Vicki felt like others might have thought he took the pills to keep her happy. The way Vicki saw it, she was doomed whether he lived or died.

If he lived, she'd have hell to pay over why she was drugging him once he found out. If he died and Pam ever got mad and told another person her secret, she'd really be screwed. With each ticking moment, she prayed he'd pull through. She really did love him and wanted them to spend the rest of their married days together. Vicki wasn't ready for it to be over. She'd rather deal with his questions over the pills than the scrutiny she'd face if her secret was ever leaked.

But deep down, a part of her knew what was going to happen. After the last doctor's visit, he had pretty much said if Steven didn't show any signs of improvement, there wasn't much they could do. He also said the longer he stayed in the coma, the worse it would be once he finally did wake up.

Vicki was sick with worry. She had finally found herself a true thug, and now she faced losing him over her own greed and selfishness. She would never forgive herself. As she was beating up on herself, she looked toward the head of the bed and swore she saw his eyelids move.

She rose from the chair. Her heart began to race, and before she could reach for the button to call the nurses, it happened again! Murderous's eyes moved. It looked like they rolled up toward the back of his head. Vicki nervously pressed the button.

Two nurses came running into the room.

"Mrs. West, we need you to step outside for a moment."

"Why? He's waking up. I saw his eyes move. He's waking up finally," she cheered.

One of the nurses began to usher her out of the

room. Vicki was confused. She thought they would want her there for the moment he opened his eyes. Wouldn't they want him to see someone familiar? On her way out, the doctor came rushing in.

Nearly thirty minutes later, she didn't need anyone to tell her that her husband had "expired," as the doctor said. It was like she felt it when he left. They allowed her back in the room with him, but she felt like it was too late then. Maybe she could've encouraged him to hang in there.

Vicki stood at the foot of his bed with her eyes glassed over in tears. How could she be a widow at the age of twenty-nine? She couldn't fathom the idea. MC Murderous was dead! And she was alone.

On her way out of his room, she nearly bumped into a petite older woman. Her chocolate-colored face seemed to be permanently frozen with a frown. She was walking with two younger women, one on each side. Their eyes were red and swollen; the three stopped and stared Vicki down in the hall.

"Is this the bitch?" the older woman hissed.

Vicki looked around. She wasn't so depressed that she was about to let anybody jump raw on her. Before she could control it, she started twisting her neck.

"Who y'all callin' a bitch?" Vicki shrieked.

"You bet' not get comfortable in that house, 'cause that shit ain't going down like that."

"My fuckin' man just died, and you hos are talking about his house? I don't know who the fuck you think you talking to, but you betta ask somebody!" Vicki shook as she spoke.

"Bitch, I'm his mama, and if you think you 'bout to be on easy street with all he worked hard for, we here to let you know you ain't getting a dime. Not one fuckin' cent!"

The woman was all up in Vicki's face. For once in

her life she was at a loss for words. Murderous never, ever said anything about his family, much less his mama. How could he leave her with all this shit to deal with?

One of the younger women pulled the older one back. "Bitch, you better enjoy your time in that mansion," she said.

Vicki didn't know what to think, much less say. Where the fuck were they when he was in a coma? Where were they when they got married?

She had never been so happy to see Pam in her life. Pam rushed to Vicki's side.

"Let's go. You don't have to listen to this shit!" Pam took Vicki by the arm.

That seemed to piss the woman off even more. "You fuckin' sellout!" she lashed out at Pam.

Vicki was emotionally drained. By the time she and Pam made it to the elevator, three security officers had come rushing around the corner. Murderous's so-called family was long gone. Vicki and Pam quietly got on the elevator to leave the hospital.

"Damn! Those bitches made me forget to pick up Murderous's stuff at the nurse's station," Vicki said.

Pam looked at her. "Why don't you go to the car? I'll run back up there and meet you at the car. I'm on the second level right next to the elevator."

"You wouldn't mind?" she asked Pam.

"Girl, no. 'Sides, I don't want you to bump back into Ooga Booga and their mama."

Vicki smiled a bit. "Thanks, girl. I'll meet you at the car."

When Vicki walked off the elevator and into the parking structure, she looked around and spotted Pam's car right away. Unfortunately, Murderous's mother and sisters were parked a few rows down.

"I see that bitch ain't running her mouth now that she alone!" one sister said.

Vicki looked around as if she wasn't sure who they were talking to. She rolled her eyes in their direction. At Pam's car, she flipped them the middle finger and started fumbling for the keys.

Before she could get the door open, one of Murderous's sisters was on her back.

"Now what, bitch? Now what?" she screamed as she started pummeling Vicki's midsection with her fists. Murderous's other sister sat in their car and kept it running. Before Vicki could get her bearings, and start fighting back, she felt something tighten around her neck. She used her fingers to grab at the thin cord that was cutting off her air. When Vicki started falling to the ground, she looked up and saw it was Murderous's mama holding what looked like a phone cord around her neck.

"You gon' die today, bitch. You not 'bout to live off all my son worked for!" the woman screamed as her daughter continued beating Vicki about her face and upper body. The other woman stood by, nervously looking in both directions.

"What you got to say now, bitch?" Those were the last words Vicki heard before everything went black.

Four days later, Pam was at the house with Vicki. Since she had finally recovered a bit, Pam was urging her to make the arrangements to bury her husband. Vicki couldn't fathom all she had gone through— Murderous' death, the ass whupping she took from his mama and sisters, and now his relatives laying claim to whatever they could. Some were blaming her for killing him, others wanted to know if there was a will. She read a story that said something about her signing a prenuptial agreement. Vicki knew she wouldn't have survived the attack had Pam not found her in the garage.

"You've got to bounce back, girl," Pam said.

"Pam, you won't leave me, will you? You know what happened. You won't leave, will you?"

Vicki had been asking the same question for the past two days. Pam didn't know what to do, but she did know that Vicki was in for the fight of her life. Even if Vicki didn't want Murderous's belongings, his distant relatives were saying she planned this to collect on insurance policies.

She didn't care what they said. All she knew was the man she loved was gone. She thought of the carriage ride they shared after becoming man and wife on the beach in Mexico. That's when they talked about starting a family.

"Snap out of it, Vicki," Pam said.

One week later, BET, VH1, and MTV provided live coverage of MC Murderous's funeral. It had turned into a who's who of the rap and entertainment world. Vicki was proud of the way she had sent her husband out. She was even more grateful to Pam for all of her help in getting things done.

There had been so much fighting between Murderous's relatives and the record label, then between the relatives and Vicki, then the bodyguards, DJs, and his assistants. Vicki thought for sure she might follow him to his grave.

Even though she was entitled to everything he had since California was a community-property state, she had lawsuits coming from every direction. One of the rags reported that her and Murderous's marriage wasn't legal because it wasn't done in the States.

Pam had just closed the door on yet another courier, who had dropped off papers from the record label. Vicki wasn't surprised when she read that they were laying claim to the rights to several unreleased CDs and some of Murderous's property.

Vicki sat back thinking that when she asked for a thug, she didn't ask for all this bullshit.

"Hmmm, next time I guess I'll have to be a bit more specific," she said.

Pam looked up from the paperwork. "What'd you say?"

"Oh, nothing, girl, not a thing. I'm just sitting over here chilling. You know me. You know how I do it."

# FRANKIE & ERICA

Frankie had just walked out of her sister's room at the Tarzana Drug Rehabilitation Center and was on her way to the office. LadyRae had done a number on Erica. From the moment Frankie looked into her eyes on their way to the hospital, she knew the deal. She had seen their mother fight her demons far too long to not recognize the look.

Erica was finally at the point where she could receive visitors. And Frankie made the trek to the center a part of her daily routine. She told doctors she wanted her sister there for as long as it took.

Business was, of course, booming. It was funny. After all the stations ran stories about how MC Murderous and Vicki met through The Hook-Up, the phones wouldn't stop ringing. She even had people contact her about branching out.

Joy was trying to figure out how they could include some of the women's prisons as well. She told Frankie that by February of 2005, she'd be ready to unveil their new expansion plans. Her cousin Bobbi had even quit her job but still had an office at CSP; again the warden didn't have a problem with their business. Riots, crime, and inmate assaults had been down 30 percent since the program started. The same trend was being reported at San Quentin and Soledad prisons.

Frankie had to stop attending wedding services; they were just too time-consuming. Although she was no longer attending, she did always send a gift. She told herself she had to be careful because she never knew when she might get a repeat customer.

When Frankie walked into the office, she saw a lovely floral arrangement on Tracie's desk. She reached for her messages and glanced at the vase. Tracie was on the phone giving out their usual "here's what we do" speech.

Frankie walked to the back and heard Joy talking to someone in her office. As she flipped through her messages, one in particular caught her eye. It was from Captain Logan. She made a mental note to call him back.

Agent Samson told Frankie that she and Erica might not have to testify because they were going to try and get LadyRae to plead out. Frankie was hoping that would be the case; the last thing she wanted to do was give her sister a reason to relapse.

The intercom on Frankie's phone buzzed. "Frankie," Tracie said, "these flowers, they're for you."

"What?"

"Yeah, let me bring them back."

Frankie thought maybe one of her clients had sent flowers; they often did. After all, most women were appreciative when they found their Mr. Right. For a split second there was a trace of some other feeling. Frankie hadn't thought about getting hooked up herself; she was far too busy.

It wasn't from a lack of inmates trying, either. They

stayed on her, but Frankie told herself it wasn't good to mix business with pleasure, especially the business she was in.

When Tracie brought the floral arrangement back to Frankie's office, Frankie started giggling. Joy appeared at the door. "Oooh, I saw those when I walked in. Is there something you want to tell us, Frankie?"

"Girl, puh-lease. You know this is probably some woman thanking me for getting it right again." Frankie pulled the small envelope from the flowers and opened it. Her eyes nearly fell from their sockets. She frowned, looked up at Joy and Tracie, then back at the card.

"Well, don't keep us waiting," Joy said.

Frankie shook her head, giggled, then read the card again; she wanted to be sure she wasn't mistaken.

"It's from Captain Logan," she said.

"What!" Joy said. "I've been doin' his taxes for five doggone years, and I ain't never got a rose, much less a whole dozen! Well, I'll say," she teased.

"Oh, yeah, he called for you too," Tracie threw in for good measure.

"What should I do?" Frankie asked nervously. "I ain't had no man sendin' me anything, especially not roses. That's deep," she said.

"Yeah, it is. Now I know damn well we ain't gotta school you on how to hook something up," Joy joked.

"For real, boss. You're only the queen of hookups," Tracie chimed in.

"Yeah, but that's different; that's me working."

"Well, it looks like Captain Logan wants you to do some work for him too." Joy laughed.

"I don't even know what to do," Frankie said again; this time her stomach felt queasy.

"You ain't gotta *do* a thing. Just pick up the phone and call the man back. It's just that simple. Girl, it's all about the hookup, but before you can get hooked up, you got to pick up the dang phone!" Joy ran in and grabbed the receiver. "Here, where are those messages?" She flipped through the stack Frankie had placed on her desk and found the one Captain Logan had left earlier.

"Here it is." Joy quickly dialed his direct line and gave Frankie the phone. She and Tracie sat back laughing as Frankie spoke. Frankie rolled her eyes and used her finger to play with the phone cord.

"Um, yeah, this is Frankie. You called?"